PRAISE FOR CARRIE BEDFORD

"Kate Benedict is a female protagonist to cheer for--a talented architect, a seer of auras, and a young woman who does whatever it takes to keep her friends alive. Charming Amsterdam is the setting for a suspenseful story centering on a majestic old building harboring lethal secrets."
— *Susan Garzon, Ph.D, author of "Reading the Knots"*

"Kate Benedict could be BFFs with Mary O'Reilly. Kate's desire to help, especially when she notices an aura looming over someone's head, spurs her into action that carries with it both mystery and danger. I thoroughly enjoyed the fast-paced action and exotic locales of *The Florentine Cypher*. It is an edge-of-your-seat page turner."
– *Terri Reid, author of the Mary O'Reilly Paranormal Mystery Series*

"An intense edge of your seat mystery with just the right amount of paranormal twist I look for."
– *M.P. McDonald, author of the Mark Taylor Mystery Series*

ASSIGNMENT IN AMSTERDAM

A KATE BENEDICT PARANORMAL MYSTERY

By
Carrie Bedford

Assignment in Amsterdam

Copyright 2019 by Carrie Bedford

ISBN 978-1-7092588-0-0

Also available as an eBook
First eBook publication 2019 by booksBnimble Publishing
New Orleans, La.
www.booksnimble.com

For James, Madeleine and Charlotte
With Love

1

The Underground was packed with miserable, rain-soaked commuters. The smell of damp wool reminded me of a sheep corral I had come across while on a recent visit to Scotland. The poor scared creatures had only been penned up to be shorn, but they didn't know that. It could have been the end of the world for all they knew. We, on the other hand, were taking the Tube by choice.

As the train sped through the dark tunnels under London's streets, I gripped a handrail and looked at the Italian language app on my mobile. Every few weeks, I took a break from reading the news in an attempt to retain my sanity. It worked, but only until I sneaked a peek at the headlines and my hard-won peace of mind popped like a soap bubble.

A scream and a sudden burst of voices caught my attention and I looked up to find out what was happening. Halfway down the carriage, a man in a suit had collapsed and fallen to the floor. Unseen to all but me, the air over his head swirled in dizzying, fast-moving circles. My stomach flipped.

"Let me through," a woman demanded, elbowing people aside. "I'm a doctor."

But even as she crouched down beside the stricken passenger, I saw the rippling air slow and then stop. It was over. I knew the man was dead.

The doctor did her best for the next few minutes, swiftly clearing a space around him before doing chest compressions. Finally, she took off her coat and laid it gently over the man's face and body.

I turned away. The sight of that moving air, even over the head of a total stranger, always unnerved me. To me, it was a sign of imminent death. I called it an aura, for want of a better word. The faster the aura moved, the sooner death would come.

"Bloody hell." The man standing next to me gazed at the lifeless form on the floor. "I hope this doesn't cause any delays. I'm already late for work."

He was to be disappointed. We soon pulled into Blackfriars station but were kept on the train until an ambulance crew had removed the body. Tensions were high by the time the doors opened and we, like well-dressed sheep, surged onto the platform. After following the herd of commuters up the escalators, I hurried through the streets under gusty winds and pouring rain to my office near Paternoster Square.

Nestled among modern, glass-fronted office towers, our building was dated and unattractive, but the inside made up for the shabby façade. With soaring glass ceilings and light wood floors, it was home to a competent and successful architectural firm.

As I stepped across the threshold, the dulcet tones of my boss, Alan, rang across the lobby.

"Kate! Wondered where you were. I've been looking for you." He bore down on me like a freight train at full speed.

A glance at the clock over the reception desk confirmed that it was eight a.m., still early. Even the receptionist hadn't come in yet. But with Alan, nothing was stable in the time continuum. Someone else's early was Alan's late. Tomorrow meant yesterday, and an hour of overtime often stretched past midnight.

"I've got a new project for you, in Holland," he said. "Interested? Come with me, and I'll give you the details."

Peeling my wet scarf from around my neck, I followed, my boots tapping on the light oak wood flooring.

"So," he said, when we were seated on opposite sides of his massive desk, he in his fancy leather ergonomic chair, while I was stuck on a rigid, upright one. For much of the year, he had a strangely orange cast to his skin, probably from using a sunbed. Although we'd all warned him it wasn't safe, for Alan, vanity trumped all, even health. But he had shed a few pounds recently, so that his starched blue shirt didn't strain quite so much over his stomach. Late middle age wasn't being very kind to him, but at least he was fighting back.

As usual, he didn't waste any time. "Amsterdam. Could be a good one for us," he said. "A breakthrough into a new market."

A loud ping on his phone caught his attention. It took him a minute to tap out a text before tearing his eyes away from his screen.

"The client is a multinational financial company. They're currently based in London, but they want to move their headquarters to Amsterdam. Brexit, you know."

I waited a beat and was duly rewarded. "And don't get me started," he continued, going on to deliver an expletive-laden rant against politicians of all parties and the public in general. It wasn't the first time I'd heard it and would certainly not be the last.

"Anyway," he continued. "They're planning to renovate a historic building. The basics have been done. Building permits in process, inspection reports completed. Next step is a feasibility review, and that's where we come in. The client has to be sure we can make the building work for them. Access, space, all the usual stuff."

Alan's phone pinged, and he glanced at his screen again. He had the attention span of a toddler.

"You'll leave for Amsterdam on Monday. Short notice, I know, but that's how it goes sometimes. And expect to be there for about eight days. Give it your very best, Kate. If we do well there, we'll win more European business."

"I appreciate you trusting me with this." I smiled, genuinely pleased that he had chosen me for the job.

We had something of a rocky relationship, due in most part to my occasional but unavoidable absences. After I'd started seeing those strange death-forecasting auras over people several years ago, I'd been drawn into the lives of potential victims as I tried to save them from whatever threatened them. And if that meant taking a few hours or a few days away from work, I did it. I had no choice.

I had told Alan all about the auras a couple of years ago, in the aftermath of a murder investigation that directly affected the firm. He now thought I was insane, but I knew he appreciated the quality of my designs. So, we bumped along, never talking again about my bizarre gift.

"Yeah, well, I was going to send Michael," Alan said. "But someone specifically asked for you, apparently. Someone on the TBA team."

Before I could ask who, he'd picked up his phone. "Off you go then," he said. "Book your flights. Use one of the low-cost carriers. Budgets, you know. Keep me up to date on progress, won't you?"

"I will. Thank you, Alan." I gathered my coat and bag and headed to the door.

"Oh, and Kate?"

Turning, I saw him clenching and unclenching his hands, a habit of his when he was nervous, which was hardly ever, or impatient, which was frequent. "There are some rumors about the building. You'll hear them, no doubt, when you get there."

"What sort of rumors?" I asked.

He waved a hand in the air as though sweeping aside his own words. "Silly stuff. Just ignore them, okay? We need this project to succeed."

I opened my mouth to ask again, but he was typing on his phone again. Knowing I wouldn't get anything more out of him, I strode off towards my office, calling a cheery good morning to a couple of colleagues who were coming in through the front door.

First on my to-do list was to ring my boyfriend Josh to let him know I'd be leaving for a while. Not that it made much difference, as he was already away, managing a development in Bristol that would go on for several weeks. My call rang through to his voicemail and I left a message. At least he was coming home this weekend, so we would have some time together before going our separate ways again on Monday.

I'd just switched on my computer when my mobile rang. It was a number I recognized but couldn't immediately place.

"Kate Benedict," I answered, leafing through a pile of papers on my desk.

"It's Sam Holden."

"Sam!"

We'd been in the same classes at university in London and had stayed in touch since graduating, meeting up as often as possible for drinks or dinner. Sam and Josh got along well too. But when I thought back, I realized it must have been nearly six months since we last saw him. Funny how time runs away with us, with our jobs and relationships and all those other bad excuses for letting friends go.

"Have you spoken with Alan yet?" Sam asked. "About Amsterdam?"

I was confused.

"I'm working with TBA Capital Management as a consultant," he went on. "My job is to manage the transition from their current location in London to the new place in Amsterdam. When I found out TBA had already selected your company for the architectural services, I thought of you and suggested they call Alan to ask if he could get you assigned to the project. It will be fun to work together, don't you think?"

It would be fun to work with Sam. I liked him immensely. He was very smart but didn't take himself too seriously. And he didn't let the traumas of his personal life affect his generally sunny attitude.

"I'm flying in tomorrow, just to get my bearings before we all start work. I'll come pick you up at Schiphol airport on Monday morning," he said. "Send me your flight details when you have them. See you soon."

2

On Monday morning, the flight arrived in Amsterdam on time, and I was soon walking through Arrivals, looking out for Sam. I passed a row of black-suited drivers holding signs for the passengers they were meeting, names from all over the world scrawled on white cards.

Then I saw my own name written on one, held by a grinning Sam, never one to pass up a chance for a joke.

"May I take your case, ma'am?" he asked, folding the card and chucking it into a nearby bin.

I couldn't answer. I just stood there gripping the handle of my rolling suitcase as people rushed past me, like streams of water around a rock.

"Kate?" he waved a hand in front of my face. "You okay?"

"No," I screamed. "No, no, no."

Then I realized, to my relief, that I wasn't screaming out loud. The words were ricocheting around in my head, and Sam was looking at me with an expression of confusion.

Over his head, the air moved in gentle circles, like ripples on a pond. Why? What could possibly be the danger to him?

I pulled my eyes away and looked into his, turned my lips up into a smile and then gave him a hug. "It's lovely to see you, Sam. How are you doing?"

"Great," he said. "Really good, thanks."

He was looking good. As usual, his mop of light brown hair flopped down over his hazel eyes. Even when he'd just had it cut, it managed to look unruly. His clothes, however, were tailored and pressed, his trouser creases sharp.

"I'm super excited we get to work together," I said, working hard to keep my voice from shaking.

"Me too." But I noticed that his grin had faded. "It should be an interesting assignment."

Interesting. That was a fairly understated word, coming from him. I was dying to know more, but our conversation was limited as we pushed our way through the noisy, crowded terminal.

Once we were on the train to Amsterdam Central Station, I settled into the upholstered seat, finally feeling my heartbeat slow down. I needed time to come to terms with Sam's aura so, for now, I'd do my best to act as though nothing was wrong.

"So, you're enjoying this consulting job?" I asked.

Sam had worked for a property development company for his first few years after graduating, but now he worked for himself, assisting companies with moves like the one TBA was planning. It was stressful, being self-employed, but Sam seemed to thrive on it. And he made good money.

As the train left the station, watery sunlight fell through the windows, highlighting the moving air over Sam's head. I shivered, looking at it, but kept a smile plastered on my face.

"Everything okay?" I asked. "Any news apart from the job? What about that doctor you were dating?"

He shook his head. "Didn't work out. We're both so busy."

"I hope you're not working too hard. It's not worth risking your health for a job, you know."

"I know. Work was an issue but... well, maybe we weren't a good match."

"Did you break up with her or what?"

"I did. About a month ago. She was a bit upset."

I'd seen *Fatal Attraction*. The ex-girlfriend could be the threat to Sam. I didn't know when his aura had appeared. It could have been when they split up.

He gave me a quizzical look, but I kept going, delving for any information that might explain that aura. "What about your family? How's Sarah?"

Sam and his disabled sister, Sarah, lived with his grandmother in Surrey. For the last fifteen years, after losing her daughter and son-in-law, she'd cared for Sam and Sarah as her own. Although she was eighty now, she was a force of nature. Nothing seemed to stop her. But Sam's income was vital to the family's well-being. Gran's pension and Sarah's disability allowance didn't go far. If he ever felt the stress of it all, he never let it show.

"Everything is good," Sam said. "Sarah's doing well, and Gran is too. We all are. What's with all the weird questions, Kate?"

I was saved from answering when the train came to a stop. Sam grabbed my suitcase and we headed through the impressive Neo-Renaissance station building to the taxi rank where tourists mingled with businesspeople in a long queue. I didn't mind the wait, enjoying the experience of being in a new city, hearing foreign languages, seeing different architecture. I gazed around, happy to be distracted from the sight of Sam's aura.

When we were in the taxi, I gave up on the personal questions and asked about the project, the reason I was here. "Tell me more about this big old house we're going to be working on."

"It's a magnificent building, dating back to 1650, the height of the Golden Age in Holland. The most recent owners are a Dutch couple, Tomas and Eline Janssen. After Mr. Janssen died recently, his wife decided to sell. My client, TBA Capital, wants to convert it into their world headquarters."

"I was wondering about that. Isn't it a historic building? Change of use is usually tricky with those."

"It is listed, but we've already obtained the permits from the city of Amsterdam. It turned out that wasn't too hard because the house was used for offices for a while—I'll tell you more about that later. And a few of the neighboring buildings have been converted into commercial use properties."

"No issues there then. That part sounds straightforward enough."

"I hope so. The price has been agreed, and the sale is contingent only on us confirming that the renovation is feasible. Once that's done, the real work starts. You complete the designs and construction begins. TBA Capital wants to move in by the end of the year."

"That's tight."

Sam nodded. "We can make it work. Although it's going more slowly than it should."

"Any particular reason?"

"Not really. Just delays getting some of the paperwork we need. I'm sure it'll work out okay."

"Well, I can't wait to see the place."

"We'll go straight there then. You can check in at the hotel later. I'm looking forward to seeing your reaction to the house. And there's something I want to show you. I did some digging around over the weekend and came across something unusual. I'm hoping you'll be able to explain it."

I raised an eyebrow. "What kind of unusual?"

"You'll see."

"Has it got anything to do with some rumors Alan mentioned? Have you heard about them?"

For a second, Sam's expression changed. A crease formed between his brows. But then he smiled. "Nothing to worry about," he said. "A place with that much history is bound to be a topic of gossip and speculation."

I tilted my head and raised an eyebrow. "What kind of gossip?"

"Oh, the usual stuff. People who died under mysterious circumstances, lights in the windows at night. But all historical. Nothing recent. As I said, it's what you'd expect for an old building. A maid trips over a cat in the dark. The next thing you know, there's a wild beast roaming the hallways. A visiting dignitary falls down the stairs after a night of drinking and breaks his neck. But someone claims he was pushed. The tale is embellished as it passes from one person to another, so that it eventually bears no resemblance to the original incident."

My feeling was that he was protesting too much. It was almost as though he needed to convince himself that the stories weren't true. But he was a down-to-earth, practical Londoner, unlikely to be upset by a few silly folk tales. Given his aura, however, I would take them seriously too.

"How's Josh doing?" he asked, not too subtly changing the subject.

"He's away, overseeing a project in Bristol. A new medical center."

"I like Bristol, but Amsterdam is amazing. I'm sure you'll like it."

The taxi pulled up outside a massive four-story house built of cream-colored stone. It stood apart from its neighbors on a corner, overlooking a canal that gleamed under the winter sun.

"This is it," he said. He grabbed my suitcase, carried it up a short flight of steps to a tiled landing and pulled a bunch of keys from his pocket. Was it my imagination or did he hesitate before unlocking the glossy black door?

I stepped into a lobby with a high ceiling of white plaster and gold-painted beams supporting a massive crystal chandelier. On each side of the hall, a door of polished oak was set in the walls, and a wide staircase rose upwards in the middle. It had a nice old-world charm to it, but I was a little disappointed. With all of the talk of rumors, I'd been expecting a creepy old place hung with cobwebs.

Sam walked over to a door off to one side and pressed a button. "We'll take the lift. Even though we're only going up one floor, to the apartment level. Not sure I see the point of that."

"Just wait until you're seventy with bad knees." I grinned at him. "You'd be glad of it then."

It was impossible to imagine Sam as old and infirm. He rarely sat still and, when he did, he simmered with pent-up energy. But something was wrong. Something threatened him. Could it be a health issue? It seemed unlikely. I followed him into the mirror-lined cubicle. Weirdly, I never saw auras reflected in mirrors, or glass or water.

For a moment, I gazed at Sam's reflection, free of the swirling air, and wished that was the reality.

The lift rose at a measured pace and delivered us to a large landing at the top of the staircase. We walked through an arched opening into a massive sitting room lavishly decorated in the style of the early eighteenth century. Pale green walls were inset with large gilt-edged panels that held an array of oil paintings and mirrors in gold frames. Sconces threw a glimmering light over Persian rugs, red velvet couches and upright chairs upholstered in gold satin. The effect was almost overpowering, an onslaught of color and texture.

"It's like a museum," I said. "Did the Janssens do the decorating?"

"Yes. They renovated this entire floor about eight years ago. Apparently, it was uninhabitable when they bought it."

"Interesting choice of style. I mean, it's luxurious, but not very practical. Sort of like living in Buckingham Palace, I imagine. Is the whole house like this?"

Sam shook his head. "Hardly. They did a complete renovation of this floor, and a partial re-do downstairs. Just enough to create the entry lobby. The two upper floors haven't been touched."

I stopped to look up at a towering chandelier that hung over a decorative marble table, but Sam kept going, so I hurried to catch up with him. We peeked into a formal dining room dominated by a mahogany dining table the size of the bedroom in my London apartment.

And the Janssens' kitchen was bigger than my entire flat. Lit by a line of windows that overlooked the canal, it was chock-full of commercial grade stainless steel appliances and gleaming zinc countertops.

"I'll make some tea if you want some," Sam offered.

"Sounds good." I'd had a very early start that morning and the tea on the plane had been awful. "The owner doesn't mind if we use the kitchen?"

"Not at all. As we will practically be living here for the next week, Mrs. Janssen said we're welcome to use the facilities. She even had the maid bring in a few supplies for us."

I sat down at a vast glass-topped table while Sam put the kettle on. Under the bright LED lights, his aura rippled.

"Let me help you with that."

Startled, I turned and saw a middle-aged woman coming into the kitchen. She wore a knee-length brown wool skirt and a pale pink twinset. Her greying hair was pulled back into a severe bun. A bun over which the air rotated rapidly.

"Tessa De Vries," she said. "I'm Eline Janssen's personal assistant. Call me Tessa."

The sight of that aura made me forget my manners. I ignored the hand that she held out to shake mine, my eyes fixed on the swirling air over her head, but Sam jumped in. "I'm Sam Holden. This is Kate Benedict."

"Very nice to meet you both. I understand you're going to buy the house?" She spoke good but strongly accented English.

"Well, we're here to clear contingencies and prepare a feasibility study," Sam said. "But, yes, in principle, my client is planning to buy the property."

"Good, good. That will make Mrs. Janssen very happy." Tessa bustled over to the fridge and took out a bottle of milk. "English tea, I assume?"

"Er, yes, please. Thanks." Sam looked a bit flustered, probably at the idea of having someone waiting on him. I was flustered, too, although for a different reason. Two auras. What the heck was going on in this crazy house?

I leaned my arms on the table to steady myself while I tried to make sense of what I was seeing.

Sam gave me a puzzled look. "What's wrong?" he mouthed.

I shook my head and mustered a smile, sitting up straight. I had to work this out quickly. Were Sam and Tessa facing the same danger? It seemed unlikely. They didn't know each other and they had no connection that I was aware of.

Tessa handed me a porcelain mug of tea and conjured up a plate of ginger biscuits from somewhere.

"Please join us." I pointed to a chair.

"Well, thank you," she said, quickly preparing a third mug of tea. She sat down opposite me, next to Sam, which was a bit disconcerting, as I could see both of their auras swirling. Tessa's, I noticed, was moving faster than Sam's. In my experience, rapid movement was a signal that death was close.

As I'd done with Sam earlier, I shot a series of questions at Tessa, and she seemed happy to answer them all. She'd been working for Eline for about eight years, mostly assisting with her busy calendar.

"She's very involved with a couple of charities in the city and organizes several fundraisers each year," Tessa explained. "So, I help with her schedule and handle her correspondence, make travel arrangements—that sort of thing."

Her brows drew together. "Of course, it's all different now, since Tomas died. I try to keep her busy, to keep her distracted, but the poor dear is bereft. She moved out of the apartment a few weeks ago, which was a very good idea in my opinion."

"Why?" I asked.

Tessa glanced around as if to make sure no one was listening. "The house is... she didn't feel comfortable... Well, it's just too big for one person, isn't it?" She stood up abruptly and rinsed her mug out in the sink. "Do let me know if there's anything at all I can do to help you. I live just ten minutes away. Here's my phone number. Please, really, don't hesitate. The sale will be good for Eline, give her an opportunity to move on. Me too. When I'm sure she's settled, I'll move back home. My mother lives in The Hague. I want to go back and look after her. She's in her eighties now."

Tessa smoothed down her skirt and then straightened up. "Good luck." She sighed deeply and then tilted her head, looking at Sam. "You seem like a very nice young man. I wish that... I hope nothing goes wrong. Look after yourself."

With that, she walked out.

"That was odd," I said, shaken by her words. Was she warning Sam about something? Something to do with the house? Something to do with his aura?

"Funny old bird," Sam said, apparently undisturbed. "Shall we get on? We have lots to do."

"Give me a minute."

I ran out of the room and down the stairs. "Tessa!"

The woman stopped on the bottom stair.

"I wondered... what did you mean when you said you hope nothing goes wrong?"

As I walked down the stairs to join her, Tessa eyed the front door as though considering a hasty retreat. Then she turned to look at me and attempted a smile. "I have a nephew about the same age as Sam. I'm always telling him to look after himself too."

"It seemed like it was more than that." I knew there was more to it. Sam and Tessa were both in danger, and I was sure Tessa knew something that might help me save Sam—and her too, if I could.

"I'm sorry," she said. "I really have to go. I'm late for a meeting. I'll see you again soon, I'm sure."

She reached out and patted my arm before turning away and letting herself out of the front door. I stood for several seconds, trying to decide whether to chase after her.

"You coming?" Sam called from the top of the stairs.

I went up to join him. In the kitchen, I picked up the card Tessa had left with her number on it. I'd call her later, see if I could set a time to see her. I had a lot of questions.

3

"Do you want to look at the plans and paperwork?" Sam asked, dragging my thoughts away from Tessa and her strange words.

"I'd rather see the rest of the house first and whatever it is you found over the weekend."

"Okay. Follow me." Sam paused to pick up two rechargeable torches and handed one to me. While I was wondering why we needed them, he led the way out of the kitchen along a hallway decorated with gilded fleur-de-lis wallpaper and lined with doors.

"Bedrooms." Sam pointed to the row of doors on our left. "Five of them, with en-suite bathrooms and a room that was probably once an office. We'll look at those later."

At the end of the hall, we came to what appeared to be a solid wall but, when Sam pushed on it, I heard a click. The wall turned out to be a door that opened away from us into a dark space. He switched on his torch to reveal a narrow staircase, its wood treads scratched and hazy with dust.

"These were the service stairs," he said. "They're now the only way to access the upper floors because the Janssens removed the main staircase from the apartment up."

"That's odd. Didn't they intend to renovate the rest of the building then?" I asked as we began to climb.

"I don't think so. Strange, considering there are two huge floors up here, each about the same size as the refurbished apartment, and then there's the ground floor with the lobby and dozens of unused rooms."

Sam stopped when we reached a small landing. "I call this the blue floor. You'll see why."

Tall windows along the front wall illuminated a massive salon with eggshell-blue paneled walls. Black-spotted mirrors hung on the walls and white sheets covered sofas and tables.

"The house stood empty for about fifty years before the Janssens bought it," Sam said. "It seems as though they just left these upper floors as they found them. The electricity isn't working up here or on the top floor."

"No, but these front windows are magnificent," I said.

We walked the length of the building, peering into old bedrooms and antique bathrooms with rust-streaked tubs. Each room was decorated in a shade of blue, from aquamarine to cobalt.

Towards the far end of the long hallway, Sam led me into a bathroom. The first thing I noticed was a jagged hole large enough to walk through. It was centered in one of the blue-paneled walls, which were streaked with black mold. The room reeked of mildew.

"I was worried about the evidence of water damage in this room, so I broke through the panel yesterday," Sam explained. "Hoping to find the source of the water and work out how big of a problem it might be."

"Not exactly your job is it? To fix plumbing." I chuckled.

"True, but there was no point in waiting for the building contractor to do it. And I found this."

He turned on his torch and stepped through the opening. I followed suit and found myself in a wide corridor hung with cobwebs. The flooring was bare stone and thick with dust. The air smelled musty. I sneezed violently and pulled up the collar of my jacket to cover my mouth and nose.

"Sorry," Sam said. "It's not a very hygienic environment, but I need you to see what I found. There are the utilities, as I expected." He pointed the torch at the old iron pipes and fraying electrical cables that ran along the brick wall at the back. Then he walked off into the dark shadows, with me close behind, playing the beam of my torch along the brick walls, keeping an eye out for spider webs. I wasn't keen on spiders.

Sam came to a sudden stop. It took me a second to realize that the light from his torch was illuminating a block of concrete.

"It's a pillar," he said. "I worked out that it's about six feet square. See, there's space along the back for all the utilities, and just enough room to squeeze through on this side."

Without hesitation, he turned sideways and edged through the tight space between the wall and the pillar. I swallowed hard. Claustrophobia was right up there with my fear of spiders.

"Are you coming?" Sam's voice echoed around the concrete slab.

Holding my torch firmly in one hand, I pressed myself into the narrow opening and inched my way through. The rough cement scuffed against my favorite jacket. That was good. It gave me something to worry about other than being stuck here forever, unable to move backwards or forwards.

I felt Sam's hand on my elbow and then I emerged into the corridor beyond the pillar. Sam was right. The pillar was about six feet square and rose from floor to ceiling.

"Is it structural?" Sam asked.

"Definitely not," I said, shining the light up and down its grey, rough sides. "We're very close to the back wall of the house, which provides all the required structural support. This didn't show up on any of the plans you sent me."

"That's what I thought. I walked all the way to the end, assuming there would be an access point for the water pipes and the electrical cables, but the corridor just stops at a brick wall. There seems to be no way to get in or out, so how would they have got in here to do repairs?"

"Maybe they didn't do repairs," I said. "That would explain all the water damage."

"So what is this pillar thing?"

"Perhaps someone's buried in it," I joked.

He rolled his eyes. "It's going to be in the way. Can we demolish it?"

"We can think about it, but let's get out of here," I said, anxious to leave the dusty, cramped space. Overcoming my nerves, I worked my way back through the narrow opening with Sam close behind me.

I thought about the pillar as we clattered back down the service stairs. Sam was right that it was going to be in the way of whatever we decided to build up there. We needed to work out what its function was, but nothing immediately came to mind.

"Let's look at the plans again," I suggested. "Maybe they will shed some light on that pillar."

Back in the kitchen, I sat at a vast glass-topped table while Sam pulled out papers from his briefcase and spread them out on the table.

"You have digital copies of these," he said. "The plans, such as they are. We have a complete layout for this level, and our contractor verified its layout and measurements, but only to the paneled wall. He didn't know about the corridor behind it. Or about the pillar of course."

"You have a structural engineer coming?"

"Yep, although there was a delay. He was supposed to arrive last Friday, but they decided to send someone else instead. He'll be here later this morning."

I flipped through the rest of the papers, some of which were in Dutch. "Who built the house originally?"

"A chap called Jacob Hals. He was a co-founder of the Dutch East India Company, or, in Dutch, the Verenigde Oost-Indiche Compagnie. The VOC, as it was commonly known."

"Thank goodness. I couldn't get my tongue around the Very... whatever you called it."

Sam chuckled. "Me neither. Not more than once anyway." He

stood up to fill two glasses with water and brought them back to the table. "The house was built to impress, as you can tell from the size. By the mid-1600s, Hals accumulated incredible wealth and he wanted everyone to know it."

"He made his money with the VOC?"

"He and many of his peers. At its height, the VOC was worth more than the combined value of Amazon, Apple and Google today, which is hard to imagine. They created it to develop and protect trading routes with the East Indies for spices, tea, silk, all that. They issued stock, letting the public buy shares, which was a whole new way of operating. And, get this, they established an army and built their own warships to protect their interests. They were very successful colonists."

"Sounds like the British Empire," I said.

"Yes, but this was just a company."

The doorbell interrupted him, so I started to make some tea while he went to answer it. A couple of minutes later, he came back with another man, tall, with cropped grey hair and wide shoulders. Although he wore a suit and tie, he would have been at home in a military uniform, with his rigid posture and unsmiling face.

"This is Kate Benedict, our architect," Sam made the introduction.

"Ah. I'm William Moresby." The man had a plummy London accent. "I am the Senior Controller for TBA Capital and will be handling the upcoming purchase of the property. I will also be overseeing the renovation work when it starts." He glanced at the kettle in my hand. "And ensuring that everyone on the team adheres to the highest levels of professional conduct."

"We have permission to use the kitchen, Mr. Moresby," Sam said. "Maybe you'd like a cup of tea?"

I waited for our visitor to tell Sam to call him by his first name, but he didn't. Mr. Moresby it was, then. After an uncomfortable pause, Moresby pulled out a kitchen chair and sat. "I'd rather get on with things."

Sam, always the one to find the positive in any situation, started talking about the building permit, his tone warm and open, as if

Moresby had become his new best friend. I wasn't so sure, although I'd do my best to get along with the pompous ass.

"Any news from Pieter Janssen yet?" Moresby asked.

"Who's Pieter?" I looked at Sam.

"Tomas Janssen's nephew. He and Eline, Tomas's wife, are the co-inheritors of the property. The nephew works in Geneva, apparently, and has been slow in signing the sale paperwork. But it's all in hand. He…"

A sudden explosion of noise in the living room set my heart racing. I didn't think anyone else was in the house.

Moresby leapt up and headed for the living room. Sam and I followed. A large gilt frame lay face down on the floor. On its descent, it had hit a wall table and taken a Chinese vase with it. Shards of flowered porcelain lay scattered over the rug.

The painting, like the others in the room, had hung by golden chains from a picture rail about ten feet up.

Sam picked up a length of chain that lay coiled among the broken china. "One of the links came undone," he said after examining it. "The frame must have been too heavy for it."

Sam helped Moresby to balance the heavy frame on the table and lean it against the wall. The picture, appropriately enough, was of Adam and Eve's fall from grace. Naked, watched by a smirking serpent, they trudged with heads bowed out of the Garden of Eden.

"Can one of you clean up the mess?" Moresby said, pointing at the china shards.

Sam bent to gather a fragment, but I told him to stop. I didn't want him handling knife-edged slivers of china with his bare hands, so I hurried to the kitchen to find a broom, came back and swept up the remains of the vase, which had shattered into a thousand pieces when the frame hit it. Why would a painting suddenly throw itself off a wall? When Moresby wasn't watching, I picked up the broken chain and slid it under my bag on the chair. I wanted to look at it more closely, to see if the link showed any signs of tampering.

"I'll get someone in to hang it again," Sam said.

I turned to look at him and noticed that the air over his head was rotating more quickly. That was not good. It could be a matter of days. I clutched at the edge of the table, steadying myself. The undulating air was mesmerizing, driving away conscious thought and making me feel dizzy.

"Kate? Are you okay?" Sam asked. I realized I was staring at him. Moresby was watching me.

"Sorry, just a bit startled by the noise." I let go of the table and straightened up.

"Right," Moresby said. "Shall we resume?"

Resume? How could I? It was impossible to imagine something terrible happening to Sam, but I'd never been wrong about the significance of that moving air before. Unless I identified the source of the danger, and soon, Sam would die. Still, I turned my mouth up in a smile and walked on shaky legs to the kitchen where we took our seats again. Sam started talking about permits and plans and schedules, and I tuned out.

These wretched auras had first appeared to me about three years ago, not long after my mother died. Most, I'd soon realized, represented a death sentence, but I'd managed to change the fate of the victim if I had enough time. Not like that poor chap on the train last week. I'd seen his aura too late to be of help. On other occasions, however, I'd been able to intervene by persuading someone to change their plans for a trip, or by calling for an ambulance before anyone else knew it would be needed. And I had prevented a couple of murders from taking place. I straightened up, remembering those I'd managed to rescue. I could save Sam. I had to. I didn't know what to make of Tessa's aura, but I'd do my best for her too.

At that point, Moresby closed his notebook and stood up, saying we could reach him at his hotel if we needed him. "I'll expect your progress report this evening," he said brusquely.

With a nod in my direction, he stalked off. When we heard the ping of the lift button, Sam sighed and leaned against the counter.

"I was warned that Moresby might be difficult to work with." Sam looked at me. "But don't let him stress you out. I'll deal with him. It'll be fine."

Nothing would be fine. Not until Sam was safe. I wouldn't tell him yet about the aura, not until I came closer to understanding where the risk lay. Besides, if I blurted out the news right now, he'd think I was crazy and probably ignore me. It wouldn't be the first time my warnings had gone unheeded, or worse, been laughed at. I needed to think about how and when to tell him.

"Vincent!" Sam called out suddenly, making me jump. A loud meow gave me a clue as to who Vincent was and I looked down to see a large grey and black cat with intensely green eyes gazing up at Sam. The kitty wound around his legs, purring.

"He makes an appearance every so often," Sam said as he opened a cupboard under the sink. "There's a cat flap in the door that leads from the lobby to the garden so he may belong to the Janssens. Or he may be a stray. I've been feeding him."

"That's why he's so nice to you," I said. "But how do you know he's called Vincent?"

"I don't. That's just what I call him."

I watched as Sam poured cat food into a dish and set it on the floor. Vincent devoured every last scrap before curling up at Sam's feet. A minute later, the ping of the lift arriving sent the cat darting for cover.

"Are we expecting anyone else?" I asked. The kitchen felt like a bus station with all the comings and goings.

We both walked to the living room to find out who our latest visitor was. I guessed at once that this must be Eline Janssen. Attractive, in her early fifties perhaps, she was elegantly dressed in black wool trousers and an expensive black and white designer jacket with large gold buttons. As she walked into the room, she pushed aside a wayward blonde curl that had escaped from her chignon.

An aura coiled in the air over her head.

"Oh!" I exclaimed, and then bit my lip.

After shooting a questioning glance at me, the woman smiled. "I'm Eline Janssen," she said.

Sam and I introduced ourselves and invited her to sit down, which seemed awkward, considering it was her apartment.

"Would you like tea, Mrs. Janssen?" I asked.

"Please call me Eline, and yes I'd love some, but don't go to any trouble." Her softly-accented English was excellent. "Shall we sit in the kitchen? It's more comfortable."

Under the kitchen lights, she looked tired, with dark circles under her eyes, a reminder that she was mourning her husband.

"Oh, it's no trouble." I set out three mugs and put teabags in a china pot. The activity was soothing and gave me time to recover from my shock at seeing Eline's aura. Three auras in one place. That was a first. And it scared me.

"How is the project going?" she asked once she was seated at the glass-topped table. She picked at a piece of lint on her jacket while she crossed and uncrossed her legs. She seemed really anxious.

"Very well," I said. "We're making progress, aren't we, Sam?"

Eline's features relaxed a bit. "That's good to hear. I was very excited when TBA Capital approached me about the purchase. I might buy something else in Amsterdam later. It will be a relief to not be responsible for this big old house. After Tomas died, I was anxious to sell up as quickly as possible. For now, I'm staying with my friend Karen because I don't want to live here alone."

"I can understand that," I said. "Even though it is a beautiful place."

Eline nodded in agreement. "Tomas was passionate about this renovation, even though we never got any further than this apartment." She gazed around the kitchen as though she were looking for someone. "That was fine with me though. I couldn't see the point of remodeling all those rooms upstairs, and even Tomas seemed to lose interest in that idea by the time we'd finished in here."

I set the mugs of tea on the table and sat down next to Sam. Eline took a sip of her tea. I noticed her hand tremble as she lifted the mug to her lips.

"How long did the renovation take?" I asked after a long silence.

"A couple of years," Eline answered. "It was a lot of work. We wanted to honor the history of the house by preserving as much as possible, like the floors and the wood paneling. We had to redo the walls, but we used a specially prepared lime plaster that matched the original, and we even refurbished a lot of the fittings, like the lighting and the mirrors." For a moment, Eline's dark brown eyes shone. "Tomas oversaw every detail. He only had one craftsman working at a time so that he could watch over him. He said he didn't want crews of workers running around unsupervised."

That seemed a little over the top to me, but Eline was clearly proud of her husband's achievement.

"The history of the house is fascinating," Sam leaned forward towards her. "It was built by a VOC founder, I read."

Eline nodded. "That's right. Jacob Hals. I'm sure it was spectacular when it was first built. Tomas found a few old documents recording some of the original purchases for wood and tile. The sums of money were astounding, but then Hals was a billionaire by today's standards."

"Do you know what happened to the house over the last few decades?" I asked. "It seems as though it stood empty for quite some time."

Eline blinked a few times. "Does it matter? Tomas bought the place legally, you know. All the purchase documents are legitimate."

"Oh, I never meant to imply that anything was wrong," I said, a little taken aback by her response. "I love history and old buildings, so I'm always interested in the backstory. I just wondered who'd owned it and why it was abandoned. It's sad to think of such a splendid house being left empty."

Eline nodded. "I agree. But Tomas handled the purchase and he probably knew more of the house's history than I do. I'm sure Arte could tell you more. He's our lawyer. He dealt with Tomas's will and he's managing all the paperwork for the sale."

"Arte Bleeker?" Sam asked. "We're hoping to meet him soon."

"Yes. He's been a rock for me since Tomas died. I'm not sure I would have got through all this without his help."

"Do you know when we might hear from your nephew?" Sam asked. "He's been a little difficult to reach."

"I don't know, sorry. Mr. Bleeker will know more than I do." She set the cup down, her hand trembling slightly. "Oh, I meant to ask. Whatever happened to the painting and the vase?"

"The painting just fell off the wall. Scared us to death." Sam smiled to show he was joking. But it was no joke. Here I was, staring at two people with auras. Two people who could die any day now. And there was Tessa too. The danger had to have something to do with the house.

"That's very odd," Eline said. "Tomas was very fastidious about things like that."

"We met Tessa earlier," I said, my mind on auras. "She seemed nice."

"She's wonderful." Eline smiled. "I don't know what I'd do without her. If you need anything at all, just ask her. She'll be happy to help. Anyway, I'd better get on."

"Oh, do you have a cat?" Sam asked. "We appear to have one. He comes in through the cat door at the back of the lobby downstairs."

Eline looked surprised and then she nodded. "Ah, that's right. Tomas wanted a cat and he had the cat flap installed but he hadn't realized that I'm very allergic. The one you're seeing must be a stray. I hope it's not bothering you. I can have the door sealed up the door if you like."

"Oh no, don't do that. I love that cat."

Eline looked dubious. "Well, if it's all right with you." She finished her tea. The mug clinked on the table as she set it down too fast. "I'll be coming in to pick up more of my things, if you don't mind. I'm not far away and can drop in each day. If there's anything at all I can do to help you, I will."

It was Eline who needed help, I thought. "Please do," I urged her.

Perhaps I could do something to avert disaster if I got to know her better.

I suppressed a sigh. Three auras and three people who seemed to have no obvious connection—other than the house. Eline seemed desperate to sell it. Sam's client was anxious to buy it, and Tessa worked for the woman who owned it. Yet, Moresby didn't appear to be in any danger. For myself, there was no way of telling. Because I couldn't see auras in mirrors or photos, I'd never know if I had one, which, right now, was a very sobering thought.

Eline stood up, sliding the kitchen chair noisily across the expensively tiled floor. "I'll be in our—my—room, packing a few things. Just personal stuff. They advised me to leave the apartment furnished and decorated until the sale is completed, just in case it falls through and we have to continue looking for a buyer. But I certainly hope that doesn't happen." Her hands were clenched so tight that her knuckles were white. "I'll let you know when I'm leaving. Oh, and can I give you my mobile number? Just in case you need me for anything?"

We all exchanged numbers and, when she'd gone to her room, Sam collected our cups and put them in the sink. "That poor woman really wants this sale to go through," he said.

"There's no reason why it won't," I said, catching the tea towel he chucked at me. I stood up to dry the mugs he was rinsing out. "Is there?"

"I hope not. TBA Capital has paid a hefty deposit which they'll lose if they back out now. We just have to clear the final contingencies and it should all go through. Fingers crossed. This is a big project for me, and I'll get a bonus if I meet their timetable. Everyone wants this project to be successful."

"I hope so too," I said. "Selfishly, I need a big design hit to help convince my boss I deserve a raise and a promotion. I'm not sure he takes me very seriously."

"Really?" Sam turned and leaned against the sink. "But you're the superstar. Top of our class and all that. It seems to me that your boss is lucky to have you."

I blushed. "You're exaggerating. And Alan is hard to please."

I couldn't explain that my employment had teetered on the brink several times when I'd got caught up in trying to save someone with an aura and taken days of unauthorized leave from the office. For now, I couldn't mention auras at all.

"Onward, then," Sam said. "Shall we go over the plans one more time?"

"Okay. I just need to make a call first."

I went down in the lift to the lobby and called Josh. I knew he'd be working too, but I was missing him. After one ring, he picked up. "Hello, sweetheart, how are you doing?"

The sound of his voice made my skin tingle, and I swallowed a lump in my throat. The pause was just long enough for him to worry.

"What's wrong? Are you all right?"

"I'm fine," I said. "But Sam has an aura. And so does the lady who owns the house we're working on." I stopped. There was no point in mentioning Tessa. That would just make Josh worry even more.

"Do you think they're connected?"

"I don't know yet. I only just met Eline. I'm keeping an eye on Sam while I try to figure out what's going on." My throat clogged up again. "I can't bear to think of anything happening to him."

"God, no. He's a good guy." Josh went quiet for a few moments. "Can you send him home? Get him out of there?"

"I'll try. If there's any chance that the danger is linked to the house, then that's the best thing to do. I don't think I can do anything about Eline, though."

"Are you in any danger yourself?"

"No," I said firmly. "I'm just terrified for Sam." Just then I heard the lift descending.

"Sorry, I want to talk but I have to go," I said, ringing off as Eline stepped into the lobby, pulling a Louis Vuitton suitcase behind her.

She smiled when she saw me there. "I'm glad to have met you and Sam," she said. "You seem like good people."

"Thank you," I said. "We're excited to be working on this project."

Something struck me. It may have been indelicate, but I asked anyway. "Eline, I'm sorry about your husband. Did he... er, was his death unexpected?"

Eline nodded. "A heart attack. His family had a history of heart disease and he was older than me by ten years... but still. He was too young to go like that. The doctors did what they could, but he didn't make it."

"I'm sorry," I said again. It seemed, from what she'd told me, that

Tomas's death was a natural one and quite probably unrelated to whatever it was that threatened her.

And Tessa and Sam.

Eline let go of her suitcase and, to my surprise, held out her hands to grasp mine. A huge diamond ring glittered on her finger. I stared at it, dazzled by its size and brilliance. I'd never seen anything like it.

"I'm trusting you and your team to make sure this sale goes through," she said.

I looked up to see her eyes glistening with unshed tears. "Of course," I assured her. "We're all giving it our very best, I promise."

Eline let go of my hands and swiped a finger under her eyes. "I'm sorry. I've been so emotional since deciding to sell. I feel I'm letting Tomas down, abandoning this place. He always said we'd be here forever. But now I'm alone, and the apartment is just too big."

"I'm sure he would want what's best for you," I said tentatively. I had no idea what Tomas would want. But Eline seemed to accept the reassurance.

"Yes, yes, I'm sure he would," she said. She grabbed the suitcase handle and straightened her shoulders. "Thank you."

"Eline, before you go, can I ask you another question? Apparently, there are lots of rumors about odd things happening in the house over the years. And I thought Tessa seemed a little nervous about the house too. Have you heard of anything like that? It won't make a difference to the sale, I promise. I'd just like to know." I waited, hoping she might tell me something that would explain the presence of the auras.

But her expression was blank. "Rumors? No, I've never heard them. And, as far as I know, Tessa loves it here."

I opened my mouth to ask another question but decided against it. She was radiating stress. I could feel tension around her like heat coming from a fire. She had enough on her mind already.

"Never mind," I said. "I'm sure there's nothing to it."

4

I watched Eline close the front door behind her before going back up to find Sam pacing the living room.

"Let's grab some lunch while we talk about the project," he suggested. "And we can get you checked in and dump your suitcase at the hotel."

Happy to get out, I grabbed my jacket and bag while Sam picked up my case. We took a taxi to the hotel, a charming period building in the Museum district.

"I chose this because it's so close to the Van Gogh and the Rijksmuseum," Sam said while we waited to check in. "If things go according to plan, we'll have some free time, and I know you love art and all that stuff. And you're only a couple of blocks from the Vondelpark, so you can go running there in the evenings. It's beautiful and very safe."

"Thank you." I squeezed his arm, grateful for his thoughtfulness.

My room was on the fourth floor, stylish and contemporary with a view of a canal. I unpacked quickly and took the lift down to join Sam in the lounge. I didn't want to leave him alone for long. He'd loosened his tie, undone the top button of his crisp blue shirt and was talking on his mobile. He rolled his eyes when he saw me and pointed to his phone.

The conversation sounded intense, although I tried not to listen in as I sat down opposite him, sinking into the soft cushions of a dark grey sofa.

"Yep, understood, Terry. No problem." Sam rang off and sighed. "Terry is TBA's legal counsel. He's fretting."

"Why is he concerned? Is there a problem?"

"Well, things are just moving more slowly than we hoped. Terry's a worrier. It'll be fine."

I had my doubts. Nothing could be fine with all these auras manifesting themselves. I needed to warn Sam, let him know that something strange and scary was going on. But just the thought of telling him made my head ache.

"Lunch?" I said.

"Righty-o." He got up and put on his jacket. "I know a place about fifteen minutes away, a nice walk."

On the street, we turned right, heading north through crowds of tourists milling around outside the Rijksmuseum. Trams clattered past us. The sun was a hazy white disc in a pewter-colored sky, barely casting shadows and offering no warmth.

"This is the Prinsengracht canal," Sam told me when we crossed a bridge and paused to look down into the water.

Accustomed to the broad reaches of the Thames River, I thought the canal looked narrow and confined between its stone banks, but, on both sides, wide pavements were busy with pedestrians and cyclists. The air rang with the jangle of bicycle bells.

We continued our walk, slowed by my frequent stops to gaze at an architectural detail on the tall, skinny houses built of brick or grey stone with steeply sloped black slate roofs. Many still had the large roof-mounted hooks used to lift goods from canal boats into the attics of the homes.

My hands and toes were cold by the time we arrived at Rembrandtplein and entered the café, which was warm, steamy and smelled of coffee and pastries.

Sam and I found a table in a quiet corner and then he went to the counter to order cappuccinos and sandwiches. Left alone, my mind whirled with thoughts of auras, but I made sure I was smiling when Sam came back with our food and drinks.

"What's bothering you?" I asked after watching his face for a few moments. This was not the cheery Sam I knew.

"Over the weekend, when I was checking everything out... it was strange. Not just the pillar."

"What happened?"

He shook his head slowly. "Nothing specific. It was more of a feeling. As though someone was watching me poke around. In fact, I definitely felt watched. When I was up on the top floor, I heard sounds, like echoes of voices. And footsteps too."

"Mice in the attic?" I suggested.

"Louder than that."

"There has to be a reasonable explanation, Sam. The building is empty. Maybe a cat running across the roof? You've seen my flat, up on the top floor. Well, a couple of years ago, I heard noises at night. It sounded like someone whispering, and it went on for weeks. It was really unnerving. Then I realized there were birds nesting in the eaves. That was what the noise had been."

Sam smiled. "I'm sure you're right. But all that empty space, those floors and rooms that have been abandoned? It's odd, don't you think?"

"Odd, yes, but not scary. I've worked on abandoned buildings before. It's unsettling, but at least there aren't any squatters in the house. I've seen a few places that became squats. Not a pretty sight."

Sam nodded. "I'm sure I'm overreacting." He reached over to squeeze my hand.

I squeezed back, trying to blink away tears that burned my eyes. Did he have some kind of intuition that he was in danger? Instead of dismissing his anxiety, perhaps I should take advantage of it and convince him to leave.

I thought about that. Putting him on the next flight to London might save him. Or it might not. He could get hit by a car on the way to the airport. There could be a terrorist attack, or a plane crash. Maybe that ex-girlfriend of his was an evil stalker. I swallowed hard to keep down the acid rising in my throat. Contemplating the myriad ways in which Sam could die made me feel sick.

"Eline seemed incredibly stressed," Sam said. "Is it because of the house sale? She wants to be out of it, that's for sure. But I suppose I would too, under the circumstances. Just get it over and move on with her life."

I thought about that. Eline was more than stressed. She was in danger. Maybe she knew something about the house that we didn't. Just like Tessa.

I lifted the top piece of bread off my sandwich to inspect the middle. The thick slices of aged gouda looked appetizing, but as soon as I ate the first bite, I felt nauseous. Food and auras didn't go well together.

"What's the deal with Pieter?" I asked. "I hadn't realized there was a co-inheritance situation there. Do you know why Mr. Janssen included his nephew in his will?"

"I looked into it when we first received the sales documents. It seems that the nephew's parents died when he was young..."

Sam paused and closed his eyes for a second. I put my hand over his, silently consoling him for the loss of his own parents.

After a few seconds, he cleared his throat and continued. "Tomas Janssen looked after the boy after that. It seems he treated him like his own son, as he had no kids of his own. He was fifty when he married Eline and that was his first marriage. They don't have any children."

"How old is Pieter?"

"He must be in his forties now and hasn't lived in Holland for over twenty years."

"Is he deliberately delaying the purchase? Does he not want to sell?" Seeing that Sam had already finished his sandwich, I pushed my plate towards him. "Want mine?"

Between bites, Sam answered. "As far as we know, he's happy to sell. After costs and legal fees, he and Mrs. Janssen will be getting about three million euros each. For some reason, he's just dragging his feet. Maybe the fact that he's out of the country is slowing down the paperwork." Sam paused. "Although there's more to it than just that. It took far longer than it should have for anyone to produce the original house deed. And I've had trouble getting basic information, like property boundary reports and utility contracts. But Terry is working on it. I'm sure he'll get it sorted."

I wondered if Sam was worrying unduly. Legal documents were an integral part of the process of developing property. On several occasions in London, projects had stalled for months as the various parties worked their way through mounds of paperwork. But it usually worked out in the end.

"Well, I hope Pieter gets a move on," I said. "The delays are probably what's stressing Eline out too. I wonder if she and Pieter get along? Perhaps there's some friction between them? Maybe she didn't think Tomas should have left his nephew half of her home?"

Sam shrugged. "I don't know. But unfortunately for her, there's no getting around a will."

It struck me then that Pieter might be the source of the danger to Eline. After all, if she died, he'd inherit all the money from the sale of the house. I decided to contact her and see if we could meet again. I could ask her some questions about Pieter. Even a casual conversation might yield some useful information.

Sam looked at his watch. "We should get back. The structural engineer, Alex, texted that he should be there in about half an hour."

"We can get him to look at the concrete pillar then." I stood and picked up my bag. "We need to find out why it's there and if we can take it out. It's going to be a bit of a challenge to work around it."

As we walked back, I tucked my arm through Sam's. If a wayward bike or an accidental fall into a canal were possible dangers, I was ready to protect him. Besides, I appreciated the warmth of his arm against mine. The wind had strengthened, carrying a sharp edge of cold with it.

A young woman with a honey-blonde ponytail was leaning against the front door when we reached the house. Dressed in skinny black trousers with a black turtleneck under a tan jacket, she looked rather like a model. She pushed away from the door when she saw us.

"Hi. I'm Alex. Sorry, I'm a bit early." She stuck out a hand to shake ours.

I'd assumed Alex was a male. Judging from Sam's expression, he had too. Alex smiled, one of those wide smiles that lights up the eyes. "No worries, I get that a lot. Most people don't expect their structural engineer to be female." She shifted a tan leather satchel on her shoulder and gave an exaggerated shiver. "Shall we go in? It's brass monkeys out here."

Inside, we took the lift up to the first floor. Alex wandered around the room, pausing to examine portraits of old men in ruffled collars, a collection of blue and white porcelain artfully arranged on dark shelves, and sets of silver candlesticks holding cream-colored candles. The scent of beeswax lingered in the air and a gilt carriage clock softly chimed the hour.

"Bloody hell," she said. "It's like a museum. Can you imagine vacuuming all those rugs?" She ran a finger along a tabletop as though testing that it had been dusted recently. "Is the whole place like this?" she asked.

"I'll show you." Sam beckoned us to follow him.

Alex left her satchel on the sofa, but first retrieved a tablet and turned it on. I took a notebook and pencil with me, prepared to take more detailed notes.

First, we showed Alex the rest of the apartment, with its contemporary kitchen and multiple bedrooms. She sighed at the sight of an immense clawfoot bathtub in one of the en-suite bathrooms.

"A bubble bath in that would be heavenly," she said. "With a glass of champers and a good book. I could soak for hours."

Sam hurried us out, his face slightly flushed. When I grinned at him, the flush deepened.

"Moving on," he said. "Follow me. Oh, and we'll need these." He picked up the torches and found a third one in a drawer. "There's no working electricity up there," he explained to Alex.

Her eyes widened when he pushed on the hidden door at the end of the hall. "Brilliant," she said. "You'd never guess it was there."

"Apparently, the people that owned the place in the early 1900s used this floor as spillover accommodations for their guests," Sam said as we climbed the stairs. "The house was abandoned in the 1960s and remained empty for about fifty years until the Janssens bought it."

When we reached the salon, we stopped to let Alex look around. This time, I noticed the quality of the flooring and of the paneling that covered the walls in the salon. The wall paint had faded, softening the original blue color, but the wood itself was still in surprisingly good condition. A thin layer of dust muted the chestnut color of the floors but again I was amazed at how intact the oak planks were. Considering the building had been empty for so long, it had survived remarkably well. It was a fighter, obviously, refusing to fall into disrepair. And someone had done a semi-decent job of keeping the place clean. It was perfect for renovation.

It was arctic up here, though. I rubbed my arms to warm them.

Sam noticed. "Yes, we'll need to wear warmer clothes. There's no need to dress up. Jeans and sweaters will do."

"Thank you," I said, rejoicing at the prospect of abandoning my heels, suits and silk shirts.

Alex flicked dust off her fashionable jacket. "I'm enjoying the project more already."

"There's something you need to see," Sam said, heading towards the bathroom where he'd broken through the paneling. I stood back while he led Alex through the jagged hole to inspect the concrete pillar.

When they returned, Alex looked thoughtful. "I don't think it's supporting the upper floor, so I don't know why it's there. I'll have to do some more investigating."

"I was thinking it could be the shaft for a dumb waiter, but the location isn't right for that," I said. "You'd think it would come out in the old kitchen if it was being used to bring up food."

"Old kitchen?"

"I haven't been down there yet, but the plans show kitchens, sculleries and pantries on the ground floor."

"Ah, right. Maybe a laundry chute then?"

"Maybe. Some of those spaces downstairs must have served as washing and drying rooms a couple of hundred years ago. And with a house this size, the servants would have stacks of bed linens to deal with. But I didn't see an opening in the pillar, so..." I turned to Sam. "Is there any sign of it on the third floor?"

"No. But then I haven't broken through the back wall yet. Shall we go up and take a look around?"

Alex frowned. "Fourth floor, surely? Oh wait, sorry. That's in the States. There, the ground floor is the first floor. You'd think I'd be better at remembering the difference between the two, given that buildings are my job." She laughed. "But in my defense, I went to university in the US and their floor numbering is ingrained in my head."

"Where did you study?" I asked.

"MIT. Civil engineering. I loved living in Boston. That's where my dad lives now, so I go back often. Anyway, yes, let's go to the *third* floor."

The layout at the top was odd, consisting of only two ballroom-sized chambers with tall windows at the front that revealed beautiful views of the street and canal below. Although the walls were paneled and painted, this time in green, there was no furniture to give any hints of how the rooms had been used in the past.

"I think this is where the offices used to be." Sam turned in a circle with his torch held high to illuminate the second chamber.

He could be right. These open areas offered plenty of space for desks.

"When?" I asked. "VOC offices?"

"No, the VOC had its own headquarters, the Oost-Indische Huis. It's still standing, a national monument now, I think." He pointed the light into the far corner. "The building department indicated that there were offices up here in the nineteenth century. Import merchants, apparently."

We moved slowly, taking notes as we went. There was no sign of the concrete pillar.

"If it does continue up, it's probably behind the paneled wall, as it is downstairs," I said. "Can we break through up here too?"

Sam looked dubious. "It was a lot of work breaking through that paneling, even though it had rotted out. We don't have much time. I think for the purposes of the feasibility study, we assume there's a utility corridor like the other one."

"It'd go faster with a sledgehammer," I said. "If we can get one."

"Let's not worry about it now," Alex said. "We can get to it later. I've got loads to do already."

It took us nearly an hour to complete the tour, and by that time I was numb with cold and anxious to reach the warmth of the apartment.

If Alex was chilled, she didn't complain. "That was exciting," she said as we piled into the kitchen. "Can we make tea?"

"I'll do it," Sam said.

"Funny, isn't it?" Alex looked around the kitchen. "The apartment is like a stage, all dressed up. The rest is just backstage space that the public never sees." She blushed when Sam looked at her with raised brows. "I act," she explained. "In a small off-off-off West End theater in London. It's my hobby, and I love it. Anyway, that's enough of that. Is it okay if I plug my computer in here?" She'd brought in her leather satchel from the living room and now pulled out a shiny laptop. That satchel was like Mary Poppins' carpet bag. It held a lot more than its size suggested.

Alex and I sat together at the kitchen table while Sam perched on a long stretch of white marble counter. It reminded me of when he was a student. It seemed then as though he never sat down properly. In seminars, he'd turn chairs around and straddle them with his arms across the back or sit on tables or counters as he was now. Sometimes he didn't sit at all, but leaned against a wall or doorframe. As far as I could tell, his professors and lecturers weren't bothered and some even seemed to find it entertaining. When I'd asked Sam about his funny habit, he'd been surprised, as though he hadn't even realized he was doing it. Then on further thought, he'd told me that, after his parents died and Sarah was injured, he'd lived strictly by the rules, in an attempt to ward off another disaster. He was never late, never missed a lecture, and always turned in his assignments early. His unconventional seating preference was, he said, his petty rebellion.

I opened my laptop but found it hard to concentrate. All I could think about was Sam's aura and what it signified. I glanced up at him. He was staring at a piece of paper, but I could tell he wasn't reading it.

Vincent reappeared just then and stood on his back legs to nuzzle Sam's leg. Dutifully, his servant jumped down to fill a dish with food.

"Sweet cat," Alex commented. "Did he come with the house?"

"More or less. We think he's a stray." Sam picked up the paper he'd been staring at.

"What are you working on?" I asked. "It must be something enthralling, judging by your expression."

"Just reading the background paperwork on the property," he answered. "It's interesting because there's a gap in the ownership history back in the fifties."

"Huh. That information should be on record at whatever the Dutch version of County Hall is, shouldn't it?" I asked.

"Yep. But no one has come up with anything yet. Maybe we'll go over there ourselves one day this week to see what we can find out."

I heard a noise in the hallway, a floorboard creaking, and then another. Hardly aware of what I was doing, I moved closer to Sam, positioning myself in front of him.

An elderly man walked in. His grey hair corkscrewed out from under a flat cap and he wore a dark waistcoat under a plaid jacket. I put my hand on Sam's arm. The apparition looked like a domestic servant from a century ago. Only this one had an aura rotating slowly over his head. I looked from him to Sam and back again. Four people under threat of death in the same house? That was very worrying. Actually, it was terrifying. I didn't have much time to dwell on it though because the old man started talking, his voice thick and raspy from decades of smoking.

I didn't understand a word of what he said but, to my surprise, Alex answered him in the same language.

"Who is he?" Sam asked.

"This man is the caretaker. His name is Henk. He comes in every day to look after the place, apparently."

I sat back down, feeling dizzy. Henk was elderly, so perhaps his aura connoted death by natural causes. But still, it would be an unlikely coincidence if it wasn't linked in some way to Sam's. I double-checked Alex, staring a little too long at the space over her head. Definitely no aura.

When Henk pointed to the table, Alex spoke to him, her voice rising in frustration. And then she stalked off.

"Follow me," she said to us. "We'll have to work in the dining room."

The dining room was more like a banquet hall, its table big enough to seat twenty on dark oak Georgian chairs with gold satin upholstery. A crystal chandelier that matched the one in the living room sparkled overhead.

After we'd dumped our papers at one end of the long table, I looked at Alex. "You speak Dutch?" I asked.

"Yes, my mother is Dutch. She lives in London, where I grew up. Mum insisted on speaking Dutch to me when I was little, and we'd sometimes come over here to see my grandparents and cousins. That's why my firm chose to send me to work on this project, because I speak and read the language. And, of course," she laughed, "because I'm so damned good at what I do."

"So, this Henk character?" Sam asked.

"He says he always has his coffee and tea breaks in the kitchen. At the table. So, he suggested we move elsewhere. Funny little man. He's very full of himself. Says he's been working here for sixty years, since he was a kid."

"He doesn't work for the Janssens then?"

Alex tilted her head. "He does. That's what he said, but they've only had the property for ten years, right? They must have inherited him with the house when they bought it."

"He'll know all about the place then," Sam said. "Maybe he can fill in the gaps and tell us who lived here before the Janssens bought it. It would be interesting to know more of the building's history. And maybe he'll know what that pillar is for."

"We'll ask him," Alex said. "But let's give him his tea break first. And we need to crack on. We have a lot to get done today."

Sam said he had a conference call scheduled with Terry and some other TBA people, so Alex and I gathered our things and set off for the top floor. That was where I envisaged placing the conference rooms and executive offices. We hadn't been working for long when Sam came up.

"Just got a call from Moresby. He's going to meet the Janssens' lawyer at his office and thought I should be there. We're hoping to, finally, get some of the paperwork we've been waiting for."

"I'll come with you," I said. There was no way I was letting Sam out of my sight.

"Me too." Alex picked up her tablet and tape measure. "Some fresh air sounds good."

5

It turned out that Bleeker's office was close, a ten-minute walk to an old brick building with a beautiful gable roof, overlooking the Prinsengracht Canal. The front door led to a spacious lobby decorated with black leather chairs and tall green plants in white ceramic pots. Dominating one wall was a six-foot-wide engraved glass plaque assuring us that we'd entered the offices of Bleeker, Smit and Meyer.

Moresby was already there. When I introduced him to Alex, he frowned. "Why are you all here? It's a business meeting, not a school outing."

"Because I was so looking forward to meeting you," Alex responded.

He frowned some more and went off to check with the receptionist. She accompanied us to a conference room and offered us coffee. Minutes later, a man, presumably Bleeker, entered. He was tall, as the Dutch often are, with chestnut hair swept back in a way that added to his height. A hint of silver at the temples gave him a distinguished look.

"Armani," Alex whispered. I wondered how she knew that. To me, his light grey suit just looked nice.

"Arte Bleeker," the man said as he shook hands with Moresby and then each of us in turn. "Shall we sit down?"

When we'd grouped ourselves around the conference table, Bleeker set down a bulky folder. "I made copies of the permits for the work on the apartment as well as certified copies of the purchase document," he said, giving Sam and Moresby each a folder of papers. "And I have the complete plans for the apartment renovation if you'd like them?"

"Excellent, thank you," Moresby said as he leafed through the pages. "This means we can move the project along at full speed." He looked at Alex and me. "I cannot stress enough the need for you to give this your complete attention and effort. We have deadlines, and it's my job to ensure that we meet them. Sam here will give you his fullest support, won't you?"

Sam nodded. "Of course. Although I would like to point out that today is the first day the team has been together." Moresby's brow furrowed. Bleeker looked amused. "But we're ready to get going. You'll see good progress over the next few days, I promise."

"Anyone have any requests?" Bleeker asked. "Mr. Holden?"

"Sam, please."

Bleeker nodded. "Sam, I heard that you sent a list of questions to Mrs. Janssen? It would be best to come to me with that sort of thing. She's rather fragile at the moment, understandably, and we want to support her as much as possible. What can I do to help?"

Sam explained that he had needed a copy of the electrical plan for the renovated apartment. He held up the papers Bleeker had just given him. "But I assume it's all in here?"

Bleeker nodded. "You should find everything you need. Is there anything else?"

"Are there any structural plans for the whole building?" I asked. "We've all got copies of architectural plans for the apartment, of course, but it would save a lot of time if we could get hold of any structural drawings."

"What is the difference?" Moresby asked.

"Architectural plans include scaled and dimensioned floor plans, exterior elevations, window and door placement," I explained. "As well as mechanical drawings to show wiring, heating and cooling ducts, plumbing and waste. It would be useful for Alex to have construction drawings that show load-bearing walls, roof weight, that sort of thing."

I thought about mentioning the mysterious pillar but decided against it.

Moresby nodded. "I see."

Bleeker shook his head. "I'm sorry. Given the age of the house, there are no plans on record with the building department. Does that create a problem?"

"Not particularly," Alex said. "It just means starting from scratch and takes more time, but I've done that before. No worries."

"Mr. Bleeker," Sam said after a short pause. "Have you heard from Pieter Janssen? I understand that we're still waiting for his signatures on certain documents. Which is rather holding things up."

Bleeker shook his head slowly. "I understand. We have messages in to him. I'll let you know as soon as he gets in touch."

Sam pinched the bridge of his nose and looked pained. "TBA Capital is on a tight deadline, as I'm sure you know. We'd like to have an idea of when we can expect the papers to be signed."

Moresby leaned in. "I second that, Mr. Bleeker."

"Please rest assured I will do everything possible to expedite the documents."

Sam and Moresby exchanged looks, and Sam shrugged. It seemed there was nothing more to be done.

"In that case, we will let you get on with your work," Moresby said.

He'd just got to his feet when the conference room door opened. A woman stepped in, looking worried. Whatever she said to Bleeker had him looking worried too. Seconds later, Eline Janssen burst into the room. Her eyes were red, her expression distraught.

As she spoke in Dutch to Bleeker, Alex translated. "I don't know who she is but she's talking about someone called Tessa," she whispered to me. "Apparently, she's dead."

My body reacted before my mind could. My hands began to shake. I took them off the table and clasped them tightly in my lap. Tessa's aura had been moving fast, but I hadn't imagined she would die so soon.

"That's Eline," I told Alex. "Did she say what happened to Tessa?"

"She fell down some stairs, I think. It's a bit muddled."

I could see why Alex was having trouble following the conversation. Eline was almost hysterical, sobbing and clutching at Bleeker's arm. He remained calm and soothing while his assistant kept offering Eline a glass of water. Moresby moved to the window and stared outside. I guessed raw human emotion wasn't something he was comfortable with.

Sam stood up. "We should go," he said to us. "We can't do anything here to help."

Bleeker nodded in acknowledgement, and we gathered our things and left, collecting Moresby as we went.

"Goodness," Alex said, once we were out on the street. "Poor Eline."

I told her about Tessa's visit earlier in the day, leaving out the aura part. I had to work out what to do about Sam. And Eline. Death had struck awfully close to both of them. I didn't have much time.

Moresby said he was going back to his hotel and admonished us to work hard for the rest of the day. Instead, the three of us took a detour on our way back to the Janssen house, pausing to view the Magere Brug, the Skinny Bridge, over the Amstel River. We all needed a moment to get over Eline's unexpected and dramatic appearance. Sam and Alex had expressed their sympathy for Eline, but they had no reason to be unduly concerned about what had happened to Tessa. So, I tagged along after them, glad of some time to think.

When they stopped to buy waffles, I had one too, but I didn't even notice the taste of it. Fingers sticky, a little giddy from the sugar rush, we finally piled into Janssens' kitchen, where Sam laid the folder of papers on the table before going to the sink to wash his hands.

"Can I take a look at the original purchase document?" Alex asked.

"Help yourself."

I looked over her shoulder as she opened the folder and took out a piece of thick creamy paper covered with typed legalese and lots of stamps and seals. It was in Dutch, and I didn't understand a word. I noticed Tomas Janssen's name, though, and another one.

"Martin Eyghels," I read out loud.

"Yes, he was the seller," Sam said. "It's not clear when he bought the place. Sometime in the late 90s. Still, it all looked normal to me."

"Do you think the house is over-valued?" I asked. "It's a lot of money, given that more than half of it is undeveloped."

"Originally, I thought that too, but it is a massive building and has a lot of land for being in a city." He put the paper back in the folder and stood up. "I'm going to call Terry to tell him what we've got here. He'll be happy we're making some sort of progress after weeks of asking. I'll be in the dining room."

"I need the loo," Alex said.

As she wandered off up the hallway, I heard noises in the living room and went to investigate. Henk was up on a ladder, hanging the picture that had fallen.

That reminded me to check the chain that I'd hidden in my bag. My examination made my stomach flip. There were scratches on the metal. Did someone deliberately damage the link? It looked as though it had been forced open just enough to hold the weight of the painting for a while, and I wondered how long it would have taken for gravity to act on it. Was it done recently, like today? A week ago? A year? Or was I imagining it and the scratches had been caused when the link simply broke apart from old age or an inherent weakness?

Hearing Alex's footsteps, I shoved the chain inside my bag. Until I knew more, I didn't want to alarm her or Sam.

"Let's go sit and make our to-do lists?" she suggested.

"Okay." It was hard to muster any enthusiasm when my mind was racing with thoughts of auras and what might be causing them. But, I reflected, getting this project completed might be a good way forward. The sooner we were done, the sooner I could get Sam out of here. I needed to think about Eline too. She'd said Tessa's death was an accident. I couldn't see how that could be connected to what threatened Eline.

"I can't wait to get started," Alex said. "Funny old place but it's got fabulous potential."

By the time we'd finished our planning session, some of my anxiety had faded. I was eager to get on with my job and determined to do my best. Moresby wasn't my favorite client, not by a long way, but I'd make sure that his company ended up with a beautiful building for their headquarters. Although, I thought, it was too bad TBA Capital was yet another financial trading company. London was teeming with them. Manipulating money, my dad called it. Money that only existed in some parallel electronic universe. Money that had made London one of the most expensive cities in the world to live in. My little fourth floor flat was hardly as big as one of the conference rooms I had in mind, a tiny fraction of the size of the Janssens' apartment.

"Shall we go take another look upstairs?" Alex suggested. "You too, Sam?" He'd just come in after his long phone call.

"It's almost five," Sam objected. "I was thinking happy hour."

"Thirty minutes," she said. "We'll start with the top floor as that should be the easiest. Then the drinks are on me."

"I'll go make some more calls then."

After making sure, discreetly, that he was safely ensconced in the dining room, I followed Alex upstairs. The barn-like areas of the top floor were faintly lit by a line of windows along the front of the building, with views down to the canal. In the early evening light, the waterway was a strip of bronze, with ripples from a passing barge carved into its surface. Cyclists and pedestrians crammed the pavements, and lights were already shining in the windows of the houses on the far side of the canal. It was a pleasant and peaceful scene, a striking contrast to the turmoil and pain I felt, thinking about Sam's aura.

"Wake up, Kate," Alex said. "Things to do."

I nodded and took a good look at the green paneling along the back wall. As Sam had said, it was in excellent condition.

"We know there's a corridor behind the paneling on the blue floor and it's about eight feet wide," I said. "Do we assume it's the same here?" I walked over and tapped the wood.

"Makes sense," Alex said. "When they installed gas for lamps and pipes for running water, they'd have run the plumbing along the back. Far easier than digging into stone or brick to cut channels for pipes. Then they probably added the electrical cables in the 1930s."

"But we haven't found an access point yet. They must have been able to get in and out."

"That is odd," she agreed.

"I think we'll have to persuade Sam to take down part of this wall so we can take a look. And at some point, the construction crew will need access to pull out all the old pipes and cabling."

I leaned closer to the wall, remembering what Sam had said.

"What are you doing?" Alex asked.

"Just listening. Sam mentioned he heard noises up here over the weekend. But, honestly, it was probably mice or maybe birds in the eaves."

"Maybe." Alex was distracted, crouching on the floor, with a plan spread out in front of her. I peered over her shoulder.

"Did you add in the concrete pillar?" I asked. "We need to note it on the plans."

"Uh huh."

Realizing I wouldn't get a response while she was concentrating so hard, I straightened up.

"I'll leave you to it." After deciding to do more research on the pillar by myself, I hurried back down the stairs and grabbed a copy of the plans from the kitchen table, calculating measurements in my head. It seemed that the concrete block would be located over the butler's pantry next to the kitchen so I started there and found a built-in cupboard that seemed to be in the right place. I opened the door and examined the construction. As I expected, it was reinforced with a hefty stone lintel over the doorway. The side walls were constructed of solid stone with their footings deep in the flagstone floor. That suggested that there would be more reinforcement down below.

Plans in hand, I hurried down the elegant, blue-carpeted stairs which curved down to the entry hall and opened the oak door set in the wall. Inside was a corridor painted drab green that led into a vast and ancient kitchen with chipped white-tiled counters and a soot-covered fireplace with a spit and several pot-holders. The smell of soot and ash lingered, embedded in the plaster and tiles. I looked up at the beamed ceiling and glanced at the plan I was holding. I was right underneath the apartment kitchen. The difference between old and new was extreme. I couldn't imagine cooking anything down here.

After a quick look around, I walked through a long, winding corridor that gave access to a jumble of sculleries, laundry rooms and storage cupboards. Most of the rooms were the same: empty spaces with stone floors. But finally, I found what I was looking for. In the gloom, the room almost resembled a chapel, with stone columns rising to support a vaulted ceiling. There was no altar, however, and no decoration. It was simply another level of reinforcement, providing support for the concrete block above it. Why, though? What purpose could it serve? It seemed the answer had to lie beyond the paneled wall on the top floor. I climbed the stairs to find Alex still staring at her plans in the near darkness.

"We'll need to organize some portable lights," I said. "We'll have to work late if we're going to meet our deadlines."

We'd just gathered our things and were heading back towards the stairs when there was an almighty crash below, followed by panicked shouting. With my heart in my throat, I took the stairs two at a time and raced towards the sound.

Henk came barreling towards me, waving his arms and yelling. I pushed past him and dashed towards the dining room, almost running into Sam as he came out.

"What the hell happened?" he demanded.

"No idea," I said, as Alex called to me from the living room. "Kate, you'd better come and see this."

She and Henk were standing a few feet away from a pile of broken glass and twisted metal. An electrical wire drooped from the ceiling. The room's massive chandelier had fallen on to the decorative table below. Hundreds of crystal shards glistened like ice on the sofas and the rug. The table, surprisingly, was intact.

"Henk says he was trying to rehang the picture that fell yesterday," Alex said, pointing to a step ladder over by the wall. "He nearly fell off the ladder in shock when the chandelier plummeted down behind him."

I gazed at Henk. For all his shouting, he didn't look particularly shocked. But his aura still circled over his head, so the chandelier crash hadn't been what threatened him. He said something to Alex.

"He says it's an omen." She rolled her eyes. "He says the house doesn't want us here."

"I think it's Henk who doesn't want us here." I said.

"Why on earth would Henk want us gone?" Alex undid the tie that held up her ponytail and ran her hands through her blonde hair. She looked younger with her hair down, I thought. When she tied it back up again, it added a couple of years.

Noticing that I was watching, she smiled. "I sometimes wear glasses just to make myself look older. Otherwise, the guys on the construction sites call me 'pet' or 'darling' and ask me if I shouldn't be at school. Drives me nuts."

I sympathized. I'd had similar problems when I'd started work. Now I was worrying about my first wrinkle.

"Well, Henk will probably lose his job once the sale goes through," I said, thinking out loud. "Maybe he's trying to frighten us off so that TBA cancels the purchase."

I felt a little guilty about criticizing the old man, who was obviously at risk of dying in the coming days. "There can't be that many potential buyers out there for a property like this," I said. "It could take years. That would allow dear Henk to sit and drink coffee in the kitchen for the foreseeable future."

Henk probably didn't know that his future was destined to be short-term. And if he did, then he had even more reason to maintain the status quo. Staying in a familiar job in a house where he'd spent decades would be preferable to the upheaval of leaving.

"Can you tell him to deal with the mess?" I asked.

When Alex asked him, he grimaced and shrugged a lot but finally toddled off to find a broom and a bin. Once we were fairly sure he would actually clean it all up, we escaped to the kitchen. Sam went back to the dining room to continue his phone call.

"There's something weird going on," Alex said. "Pictures and chandeliers don't just fall to the ground for no reason. Not in a newly-renovated apartment with rock-solid construction."

I agreed. From what Eline had said about her husband's perfectionist approach to renovation, it was unlikely that fixtures would have any trouble staying in their place.

"Maybe Henk is right, and we shouldn't be here," she said.

I was surprised. Earlier, she'd seemed so enthusiastic about the project. "I doubt Sam would even consider giving up on the project because of a couple of minor incidents," I said.

"Not that minor. Someone could have been seriously hurt or even killed when that chandelier fell."

I thought about it. This could be the impetus I needed to get Sam away from the house. But I suspected it would take a lot more than that to convince him. I'd have to tell him about his aura. Much as I hated the thought, the time had come to be honest with him.

"We'll talk about it with Sam when he's free," I continued. "It will have to be his decision. Meanwhile, we should keep working. There's a huge amount to get done."

I started to open my laptop but stopped when Alex spoke. "So, you and Sam." She paused. "You look so sad sometimes when he's in the room. Is there something going on there? Do you fancy him?"

I hadn't realized my concern was so obvious. Or maybe Alex was particularly observant. Either way, I wasn't sure how to respond. "No, of course not," I said finally. "We're good friends and have been for years."

Alex raised an eyebrow.

"I am a bit worried about him," I continued. "He's under a lot of pressure with this project. It's one of his first since he began consulting, so it's really important."

"Ah, I see. I'm sorry if I misread things. So, do you have a boyfriend?" She stuck her long legs out in front of her and stretched her arms above her head.

"Yes. His name is Josh and we work for the same firm. We've been together for nearly three years now." I tapped on my phone and showed her a recent picture of him.

"He's cute," Alex cooed. "His eyes are stunning. I've got a shirt that's the same aqua color."

I looked at Josh's photo for another few seconds before putting my phone away. "What about you?" I asked.

"Nope. I had a boyfriend at university in Boston for a year. Felipe. He was gorgeous, but we went our separate ways. He's working in Asia now."

"And you live in London?"

"Yes, my Dad went back to the States when he and my mum divorced about ten years ago. I enjoyed being closer to him while I was at university but by the time I graduated, he had a new girlfriend and Mum was by herself, so I decided to come back to England for work. She's doing fine now, though, so I started applying for jobs back in New York. In fact, I had an interview scheduled for this week but I had to pass on it because of this project."

"Oh, no. That's bad timing."

Alex shrugged. "Yes, but at least this development will look good on my applications going forward." She grinned. "There's always a silver lining, right?"

I smiled at her. She had a positive attitude. "It'll look good if we get it finished," I said.

"Too right. Better get on with it."

But Sam came back just then, insisting it was time to leave for the day. After he'd locked the front door, we strolled in the encroaching darkness along streets full of walkers and cyclists. Alex had suggested we have drinks at the local *bruine kroeg*, a brown cafe, so called for its dark wood and smoke-stained walls. An essential part of Amsterdam life, Alex told us, the brown cafes offered coffee, newspapers, beer, wine and drinks.

Dating back to the 1600s, this one was packed with locals and tourists. Every inch of wood, from the ceiling beams to the plank floor, gleamed in the light of period lanterns. The noise level made it hard to hold a conversation, but I was all right with that. I'd left home at five in the morning to get to the airport and I was tired, not to mention a little fuzzy from the Genever-based cocktail Alex insisted we all try.

Still, I had a strange feeling that someone was watching me. It was almost physical, as though a finger was poking me in the back. I swiveled my barstool and scanned the crowd behind me. Seated around bar tables, groups of young people yelled at each other in Dutch or English. I heard a little German too. No one was paying attention to me, but I remembered what Sam had said about feeling that he was being watched inside the house.

I surveyed the bar again. There was one man sitting alone, perched on a stool near the door, his head bowed over a beer. In a hooded sweatshirt, with a backpack at his feet, he looked like a tourist. And he probably was, traveling solo and stopping for a drink. Perfectly normal.

Alex tried to persuade us to have another round, but we convinced her it was time to go find dinner. By the time we'd put on our coats, the tourist's seat was empty. We paused at the door, bracing for the cold we knew waited on the other side. When I stepped out, I glanced up and down the street and saw a man with a backpack staring into the lit window of a bookshop just a few meters away. Was he the tourist from the bar? Was he lingering there deliberately?

"What's the matter?" Alex asked me. "You look worried."

"It's nothing."

I was being irrational. Dozens of men with backpacks were strolling past or looking in windows. Tessa's death, all the auras, my fears for Sam. It wasn't surprising I was on edge. I knew from experience that I was susceptible to imagining the worst when dealing with an aura—everyone in sight was a possible threat. But I'd also learned that it paid to be alert and vigilant, quick to suspect any stranger, or friend, come to that. Until I knew Sam was safe, that would be how I'd operate.

6

In spite of a luxurious mattress, I didn't sleep well. All night, my mind kept cycling through possible threats to Sam and Eline. After dinner, I had walked Sam to his room, nervous about leaving him alone overnight. But, short of camping on his floor, there wasn't much more I could do. So, I was up early and, at seven, I texted him good morning and was glad to receive an instant response, evidence that he was okay for now at least.

After showering, I opened the wardrobe and happily pushed aside the dressy jackets and trousers I usually wore for work. Instead, I pulled out a pair of jeans, a comfy cream-colored jumper and flat boots. With my aubergine-colored puffy jacket, a scarf and thick socks, I'd be ready to face the freezing wastelands of the Janssen building's upper floors.

I met up with Sam in the hotel's breakfast room. He looked well-rested, but his aura still circled, once again killing my appetite. I sipped coffee while he demolished a cheese omelet.

"Sam, there's something I need to tell you," I began.

He held up his hand as his phone buzzed. "Sorry, I have to take this. Let's head over there."

"You're just showing off," I kidded him. "Walking and talking at the same time."

With him on his mobile, we made it all the way from the hotel to the Janssen house. As he was still listening, I mimed that I was going to take a look around the outside of the property. I hadn't paid it much attention the day before, but the outside appearance of the house would offer TBA Capital's clients an important first impression of the company they were doing business with.

From the street, the building was attractive and well-maintained, obviously another improvement made by Tomas Janssen. Black window frames contrasted nicely with the soft pale stone of the facade, and the design was pleasingly symmetrical. On the ground floor, there were three large windows on both sides of the front door, which was centered under a carved stone pediment. On each of the three floors above were seven tall windows. It was truly impressive.

I walked the length of the building to its end. Located on a corner lot, it appeared to be as deep as it was wide, providing ample space for the multitude of rooms we'd explored inside. Behind the house, black wrought iron fences lined with dense hedges created a barrier between the city pavement and the property. I peeked through a gap in the hedge to see weed-strewn gravel paths winding through over-grown boxwood topiaries. It appeared that the Janssens hadn't had much interest in gardening.

When I heard voices, I retraced my steps to the front door. Alex had arrived, also dressed in jeans and a puffy jacket. She wore sturdy work boots.

"I wear these to construction sites," she said, lifting one foot to show me. "Steel-toed to prevent accidents. I didn't bother to bring my hard hat, though." She grinned. "Although maybe I should have, in case of falling artworks or light fixtures."

She and I laid out our drawings and laptops in the kitchen, while Sam went to his customary spot in the dining room. We hadn't been working long when the doorbell rang.

"Probably Mr. Moresby," I said. "He must have forgotten his keys."

Instead, when I ran down to open the door, a strange man stood on the doorstep. He was in his forties, slender, with dark hair going grey at the temples and wore a smart suit and tie. My first thought was that he was a lawyer, maybe a colleague of Bleeker's.

He held out a hand to shake mine. "I'm Pieter Janssen," he said.

"Ah, the nephew."

He tilted his head and then smiled. "I suppose so. Yes, I'm Tomas Janssen's nephew."

Remembering my manners, I introduced myself and waved him in. He walked into the lobby and waited for me to close the door.

"Come on up," I said, noticing that he seemed hesitant. Considering he was co-inheritor of the house, he didn't seem very proprietorial about it.

As we walked up the stairs, I told him about the others on the team and the plans we were working on. He didn't say much in response other than that he wanted to see the house one more time before it was sold.

When we reached the living room, Henk was there, looking up at the bare wire where the chandelier had hung.

"You must know Henk," I said to Pieter.

He nodded stiffly as Henk glared at him. After a few seconds and without a word, the caretaker stalked out of the room. That was awkward. Ever the polite hostess, I felt the need to apologize for Henk's behavior.

Pieter shook his head. "Don't worry about it. He's always been a little eccentric."

That was an understatement, but I didn't argue. I led the way to the kitchen, where Sam and Alex were chatting. I introduced everyone and offered Pieter tea.

"No, thanks. I won't stay long. Just wanted to say goodbye to the old place. Do you mind if I do a quick walk around?"

"Go ahead," Sam said. "But before you do that, can I just verify that you're planning on signing all the paperwork soon?"

He shifted, looking a little embarrassed at being pushy. But he was right to ask. We needed Pieter to get those documents signed.

"Yes, sorry for the delays. I'm meeting the lawyer later today with Eline."

"Mr. Bleeker? We saw him yesterday. He seems very professional, and nice, too."

"That's good to hear. I haven't met him yet, but Eline seems to like him. So, don't worry about the documents. We'll get everything taken care of."

I wondered if Eline would have calmed down enough to sign paperwork. She'd obviously been distraught over Tessa's death.

Sam beamed. "Great. That's good news, thank you. Enjoy your tour. Don't mind us. Take your time."

Pieter nodded and moved off into the hallway. I watched him go and took a seat at the kitchen table opposite Alex, who was chewing on her bottom lip, her brows drawn together in a frown.

"What's wrong?" I asked.

"Nothing. Just thinking."

"You look worried."

She shrugged. "Do you think we should have asked for some kind of identification? I mean, we just let in a stranger to wander around. Eline didn't mention that Pieter was coming."

"True, but that doesn't mean he shouldn't be here," I said.

"Well, I'll go keep a discreet eye on him." She stood up. "Back in a few minutes."

I looked at Sam. "It was all right to let Pieter in, wasn't it?"

His phone rang just then. "Terry again," he said. "I'll take this in the dining room."

Left alone, I tidied up the kitchen and wandered to the windows for a view of the busy street below. Even from up here, I could hear the ring of bicycle bells. A man on a houseboat was cleaning the deck, while several barges moved slowly along the canal. The houses on the opposite side of the water were beautiful. Tall and narrow, under gabled roofs, they were painted in a rainbow of colors. I remembered reading that, back in the sixteenth century, taxes were based on the width of the house, which led Amsterdam's good citizens to build ever narrower and taller homes. It would be easy to fit four or five of them into the expansive width of the Janssen house. Jacob Hals hadn't let a few tax bills stop him from building this massive house, clearly intended to impress his friends and foes.

As I was about to turn away from the window, I caught sight of a figure in a grey hooded sweatshirt. He was standing at the edge of the canal, hands in his pockets, apparently watching a cautious driver edge into a parking space, the nose of the car hanging out over the water. Could he be the same man I'd seen the previous evening at the bar?

I waited, expecting him to look up at the house, but he never did. Once the parking show was over, he lit a cigarette and ambled away.

Still, unable to shake the feeling that the house was being watched, I set off up the hall to find Alex. The bedrooms were quiet and empty, so I climbed the service stairs to the next floor. When I reached the landing, I heard a faint murmur of voices. We'd noticed earlier that noise seemed to echo through the abandoned rooms, magnified like whispers in a church.

I moved towards the sound, hurrying past the shrouded furniture of the old salon. The voices stopped, and I paused. The sudden silence was oppressive.

"Alex?" I called.

She stepped out of a room about ten yards in front of me. "Is something wrong?" she asked.

I felt silly, embarrassed by my own nervousness. "No, nothing. Just checking you're all right. Where's Pieter?"

"We were just doing a walk around up here," Alex said. "I was asking him if he knew anything about the false wall."

Pieter appeared just then, brushing dust off his jacket. "I don't," he said. "I didn't spend a lot of time here. Just a few visits after Uncle Tomas moved in."

The two of them joined me, and we started walking back towards the stairs.

"I went to boarding school in Geneva and university in

Lausanne," Pieter continued. "And then I got a job and moved back to Geneva. I didn't visit Amsterdam very often. But Uncle Tomas was always good to me. His death hit me very hard. I was shocked when I learned he left the place jointly to me and to Eline."

Pieter's voice rose over the clatter of our footsteps on the wood treads.

Back on the apartment level, we returned to the kitchen. I could hear Sam talking in the dining room beyond, still dealing with TBA's legal counsel.

"Well, I'll be off," Pieter said. "I appreciate your time and apologize for arriving without warning." He shook hands with us and made to leave. Then he turned back. "Oh, just one thing I almost forgot. Eline asked me to pick up some papers from her room. Something we need for the meeting with the lawyer. Do you mind if I go get them? It'll save her a trip over later, she said."

"I'll come with you," Alex said. "I can show you which room it is."

She flicked a glance at me, and I nodded. Pieter might be co-inheritor, but I didn't feel comfortable letting him poke around in Eline's room by himself. Alex would keep an eye on him.

Less than a minute after they left the kitchen, Henk walked in. I wondered where he'd been. He seemed to have an uncanny ability to disappear and materialize at will. Not speaking to me, he took a mug from the cupboard and made himself a coffee, a break from his regular routine. He obviously hadn't been pleased to see Pieter, but I couldn't ask him about it; not knowing a word of his language made communication impossible. When the old man took his mug to the kitchen table and sat down without even glancing at me, I left.

I trailed up the corridor to Eline's room to find Pieter and Alex talking quietly in Dutch as they sifted through a pile of papers on top of a chest of drawers.

"Did you find what you needed?" I asked from the door.

Pieter turned, a sheet of paper in his hand. "I think so. This should be it."

Alex straightened the pile of documents and looked around the room, crowded with cardboard boxes piled against one wall, stacks of books on the bed, and several suitcases. "There's still a lot of stuff here for Eline to move," she said. "We should offer to help her."

I nodded. "Good idea."

"That's very kind." Pieter folded the document he'd found and put it in his pocket. "I'll let her know when I see her later."

A thought struck me as we walked Pieter down to the front door. "Was Eline shocked, too, to learn you were going to inherit half of the proceeds of the house?" I asked.

Pieter's steps slowed. "I don't know. But I don't think so. She knew that Tomas had been like a father to me when my dad died. I assume that they'd talked about it before he drew up the will."

I opened the front door, and we gathered on the pavement at the bottom of the steps. It was good to be out in the fresh air, even though it was chilly.

"And you jointly agreed to sell the house?" I asked.

Alex shot a look at me, eyebrows raised. I knew I was being rude, and that this should be none of my business, but I was trawling for information, anything that might cast light on the threat to Eline and Sam.

Pieter didn't seem fazed by the questions though. "Actually, no. I was surprised when I heard she wanted to put it on the market. But it really was her choice. I could understand that she didn't want to live alone in this." He waved a hand up at the building.

"Did Alex tell you about the strange things that have happened? The falling chandelier, and the painting that crashed to the ground?"

Pieter glanced at his watch.

"We'll walk with you for a while," I said. "If that's okay."

Alex ran back up the steps to pull the door closed. I felt a twinge of anxiety at leaving Sam alone in the house, but I was getting desperate. A few more minutes with Pieter might be helpful.

"I told Pieter about those things," Alex said when she joined us again.

"They sound like pranks," he said. "Although I don't see the point of them. Or who would execute them."

"Henk?" I asked.

"I doubt it. Henk's a fixture in the house. He wouldn't do anything to damage it."

We stopped talking, separated for a few moments by a family of four walking abreast and taking up the pavement. Pieter crossed the street to walk along the side of the canal. When Alex and I caught up with him, we all stopped to admire a pretty painted barge gliding gently past us.

"I always wanted to have a boat," Pieter said. There was a wistful note in his voice.

"Well, you still can, can't you?" I asked, thinking about the money he'd make on the house sale. "If not here, then in Geneva, on the lake?"

"Maybe. One day."

He turned away from the water and started walking again.

"Have you heard the rumors about the house?" I asked, quickening my pace to keep up with him.

"Rumors?"

"You know, stories about past owners who used it for gambling and smuggling. Unexplained deaths, that sort of thing."

"Things that go bump in the night?" He weaved around a clump of parked bicycles and paused to let a small tour group pass. "Yes, I've heard the rumors, but they're just fairy tales. Uncle Tomas never had any problems there."

I sensed my questions were starting to irritate him, but decided to persevere a little longer. "Is Eline doing all right?" I asked. "She seemed a little...fragile." I couldn't exactly come out with the real reason for my concern. "I wondered if she's ill, or something? Of course, Tessa's death was a big shock too."

This time, Pieter stopped and looked at me. "Tessa's dead? I didn't know. I haven't seen Eline yet. We just spoke on the phone. She didn't say anything about being unwell. But she's mourning, you know. Tomas's death was a terrible blow. So unexpected. We had no time to plan."

His cheeks flushed pink and he turned away as I wondered what he meant. Did 'we' mean Eline and him? And plan what?

"We should go back," Alex said to me. "Let Pieter get on with his day."

I nodded. I'd pushed it as far as I could and I hadn't learned anything useful.

7

Alex and I walked back to the Janssen house in near silence. I was running through everything I'd heard from Pieter, trying to dredge up the details to see if he'd said anything that would help me learn what threatened Sam and Eline. There was nothing. Apart from that strange comment about not having time to plan. Alex marched along with her eyes on her feet. I guessed she'd been embarrassed by my probing.

"I was just trying to get to the bottom of the pranks," I offered by way of explanation. "I hoped Pieter might know something."

"I can't see how," she replied. "He hardly ever visited."

"But he cared enough to come by and say goodbye to the house," I pointed out. "Which means he must have spent enough time here to feel some sort of connection to it."

Alex moved away to avoid a woman pushing a baby in a pram. I shivered. We'd gone out without our coats, and the air was growing colder as black clouds thickened over a row of stately houses on the far side of the canal.

"What do you think Pieter meant about not having a plan?" I asked Alex.

She shrugged. "I suppose he meant they didn't have time to talk much about selling the house."

I wasn't so sure. Maybe Pieter and Eline were planning to be together now that Tomas was dead. I almost made the suggestion out loud, but I could tell Alex wasn't interested. She seemed out of sorts.

When we arrived back at the house, we saw Moresby on the doorstep, looking for his keys.

Alex frowned. "The grinch is back," she whispered. But she smiled and used her key to unlock the door, waving Moresby in. Together, the three of us climbed the stairs to the living room where we found Henk vacuuming. There was no sign of the errant chandelier, apart from the bare wire hanging from the ceiling and a large plastic crate on the floor that held a pile of unbroken crystal drops.

Moresby was his usual charming self. "What the hell happened here?" he asked.

I told him about the chandelier falling and was rewarded with a look of utter disbelief.

"I probably shouldn't have been swinging on it like that," Alex said, her expression deadly serious.

It took a moment for Moresby to realize that she was making a joke. His brows drew together in a deep frown. "Very funny."

"But it's actually a serious problem," I said. "No one was hurt, but what if one of us had been standing there when it fell? Or under that picture frame that came off its chains? There's something odd going on."

"You'll be telling me the place is haunted next," Moresby said. "Where's Sam? We need to talk."

Sam must have heard our voices. He came into the living room and motioned to us all to sit. "What can we do for you?"

"We have no time to deal with distractions," Moresby said. "I thought we'd have something to show my Board of Directors by now."

Alex snorted.

Sam shook his head. "We've been here for less than two days, Bill," he said.

I bit my lip to stop myself from laughing. I doubted anyone called William Moresby *Bill*.

If looks could kill, Sam would be dead. That thought sobered me up immediately and I got to my feet. "I'm getting back to work," I said. There was no point in wasting time arguing with Moresby. "I can have some very preliminary drawings ready for you to by tomorrow, if that helps?"

Moresby attempted a smile. With all the effort of a weightlifter raising a dumbbell, the corners of his mouth turned upwards. "Thank you. I appreciate it. Listen, I want us to get along. I'm sorry if I've offended." The smile disappeared. "There's a lot of pressure from Head Office to get the final decision on this property. One or two of the board members think we should be relocating to Luxembourg, not Amsterdam, and every day that goes by gives them an opportunity to press their case. Personally, I like this building and the location. I want this to work. I just need the feasibility study wrapped up so I can present it, and then we'll be ready to sign the purchase documents. I'm totally dependent on Sam here to get me what I need."

Sam stood up. "We're all on the same page then. For now, it's probably best if you don't mention these odd incidents to your directors. That might give them a reason to back out. Let's hope we've seen the last of the weirdnesses anyway."

I doubted that, not with the auras over Sam and Eline. And we weren't even talking about Tessa's accident.

"Assuming that all goes well, we'll aim to get the study finished early." He looked at Alex and me. "Can we get this done by Friday morning?"

Alex looked dubious. "It's a lot of work. But I'll do my best."

For my part, I was thrilled at the idea of being done early. That way I could get Sam back to London and possibly out of danger.

"Definitely," I said.

"Excellent." Moresby beamed.

"However, if anything happens to jeopardize the safety of the team, I will strongly recommend withdrawing the offer to buy the building," Sam continued.

Moresby's habitual frown was back in place, but he stuck his hand out to shake Sam's. "Understood."

When he'd gone, Alex got to her feet, and we followed her to the kitchen. Sam opened a tin and showed it to Vincent who was prowling along the counter.

"Is there any human food?" Alex asked hopefully. Sam opened the fridge to reveal a half-empty bottle of milk and two bottles of white wine.

She picked up her puffy jacket. "I'm going to run out and buy food so we can work through lunch," she said. "Can I take your orders?"

Sam asked for something called a *broodje haring*. "A herring sandwich," he explained.

"Yuck. Gouda for me," I said. "Or Edam, I don't mind which. But definitely no pickled fish."

As soon as the lift doors closed behind Alex, Sam's phone rang and he answered, mouthed, "It's Terry," and wandered off to the dining room.

Left alone, I thought about my earlier conversation with Alex. She thought the incidents were significant, warnings intended to keep us away from the house. I wasn't so sure, but I couldn't shake the feeling that we were being watched by the man in the grey hoodie. It was time to come clean with Sam, tell him about his aura. And Eline's. And the fact that Tessa'd had one and was now dead.

While I waited for his call to finish, I scrubbed the counters and rinsed out Vincent's food bowl, which he'd emptied completely. The physical activity helped to calm me. I was ready to do this. As soon as Sam came back to the kitchen, I threw the cleaning cloth in the sink and turned to face him.

"Sam, there's something I need to tell you," I began, but his damn phone rang again.

"Sorry," he said as he picked it up. "It's my grandmother," he whispered. "What's wrong, Gran?" The color had drained from his cheeks.

She seemed to talk for a long time before Sam's features relaxed. "Okay. Keep me updated. I can come home if you need me."

"Is everything all right?" I asked, anxiety knotting my stomach.

"Sarah had a fall but she's fine. She tries to be stronger than she is and occasionally she pushes it too far. She has a few bruises. The doctor told her to stay in bed for a couple of days."

"I'm glad she's okay." I squeezed Sam's hand for a second. This was the ideal opportunity to convince him to leave. "If you need to go back, you should. Perhaps I can take over some of your work?"

Sam shook his head. "Thank you, but Gran said they were managing. I'll get a flight home on Friday. We'll be finished here by then."

I took a deep breath. Henk was busy, Alex was out. It was now or never.

"I really need to talk to you," I said.

His mobile rang again. "It's Terry. I'll join you in a few minutes."

"No." I put my hand on his arm. "This is important."

Eyebrows raised, Sam declined the call and hoisted himself onto the counter. "Go on then."

My cheeks burned as I explained how I could see auras that predicted death. To Sam's credit, he didn't interrupt or laugh or mock me, all common reactions when I'd told people in the past about this bizarre gift of mine.

"The thing is, Sam," I said. "You have an aura. And so does Eline. Actually, Henk does too." I sighed, knowing how ridiculous this must sound to him. "Tessa did as well."

Ignoring the look of disbelief on Sam's face, I rushed on. "I think you should go back to London. My feeling is that the threat is somehow tied up with the house. If you leave, it's possible that the danger will pass."

Sam lifted his chin and gazed into my eyes. "You're kidding, right?"

"No, I'm not and I wouldn't joke about something like this."

"But everyone dies. Don't we all have these aura thingies all the time?"

"They only appear to me a week or two before...the end. They are a warning of imminent death. That's why you need to fly to London. Right now."

He jumped down from his perch on the counter and paced around the kitchen, before stopping and leaning with his back against the fridge. "Have you always seen them? When we were at university?"

"No, only for the last few years, since Mum died. That's when it started. I had this...I don't know what it was...encounter near Dad's house in Tuscany. After the funeral. Mum appeared and talked to me. And then I met this nun, Sister Chiara, and she told me about my new gift and how I had to use it to help people."

Sam's eyebrows had disappeared under his mop of hair and he was biting his lip.

"I know, it's all mad. You don't have to understand it," I said. "But you do have to believe me. Please. It could save your life."

When he shook his head, I begged him. "Trust me. Please. Call Josh if you like and ask him. He'll tell you about the other times. But I think you'll be safer if you leave."

"All right," he said eventually.

I was amazed. I hadn't expected him to agree so easily. "You'll go home? Today?"

"No. I meant all right, I accept your story about your... gift. But I can't leave yet."

Agh. "Why not? Sam, your life is in danger."

"Look, Kate, if I walk out now, it'll wreck my consulting business. I won't get paid by TBA and word will get around that I abandoned them in mid-project. And I'm not just thinking of myself. My sister and grandmother depend on my salary too. You know that." He held up a hand to stop me from interrupting. "It's my job to see this project through and that's what I intend to do."

"But, Sam, there's something threatening you. You could die."

"I understand that." He picked up a tea towel from the counter and played with the corner of it, rolling the fabric into an ever tighter coil. "But bad things do happen to people. My parents were warm and wonderful, doing everything they could to look after Sarah and me. They played by all the rules to make sure we were secure and protected. They held our hands when we were out walking, put antiseptic on our cuts, and childproofed our rooms. But they couldn't foresee the tree that fell in the storm that night. They died. Sarah nearly did. I didn't even have a bruise. Trying to predict every danger is impossible, Kate. I tried that after my parents died. I was afraid of everybody and everything. I could hardly walk out of the house. But I got over it, little by little. And now I refuse to let fear rule my decisions."

I leaned back in my chair, one hand over my eyes. I knew all too well how Sam felt. That the world was a terrifying place, full of threats and risks. Made all the worse for me by these auras, these shimmering reminders of our mortality.

I rubbed the tears from my eyes and sat upright, angry that I was feeling sorry for myself. I had so much to be happy for. Dwelling on the negatives did no one any good at all.

"I have this ability for a reason, Sam. And right now, that reason is to save you. That is what I intend to do. You can stay, if you insist, and finish up the project. But we need to work fast and wrap it up early. And I'll be at your elbow until it's over. Understood?"

"Okay." He folded the towel and put it on the counter before coming back to sit down again. With his hands clasped on the table in front of him, he bowed his head for a moment. When he looked up, his eyes were clear and untroubled. "You said that Henk and Eline Janssen have auras too?"

I nodded. "More to the point, Tessa had one. And, Sam, she's dead."

Sam's head jerked back.

"Yes," I went on. "Now that was an accident and almost certainly not related to whatever it is that threatens you. But it's a big coincidence that you, Henk and Eline are in danger."

I rubbed my temples with my fingers. A headache was building. "We need to find out what the common thread is between you three. I don't believe much in coincidences, so I'm sure the same danger threatens you all. Or, honestly, maybe just you and Eline. Henk is old. His might be different. Anyway, we need to work out why you and Eline are at risk."

"Without disrupting the project timeline."

"Right. We can keep working and I promise I will do my best, if only to get this damned project over and done with. But my primary goal is to uncover the source of the threat."

"What threat?" I heard Alex's voice and swung around to see her standing in the doorway, a bag in her hand.

Sam gestured her over. "Come and sit down. Kate has something to tell you."

I hadn't intended to tell Alex about the auras, but there was no getting around it now. So, once again, I described my strange ability.

When I stopped talking, Alex leaned back in her chair and looked from Sam to me and back again. "You believe this... stuff about auras?" she asked him.

"I trust Kate." Sam shrugged.

"But it's bonkers," she said, keeping her eyes on him, avoiding looking at me. I shifted on my chair. This was the reaction I was used to seeing when I opened up about my gift. Disbelief and a sudden reassessment of me, from normal working professional to crazy woman. But I needed Alex on my side. If Sam insisted on staying, I could use her help in watching out for him.

"Alex," I said. "I know it sounds like the ravings of a lunatic, but I'm telling the truth. I've had several years of experience with this now. I've seen people die. Tessa had an aura and she's dead. But I've helped save others. There was a child who didn't drown, a boy who survived a medical emergency." I cast around for a convincing example. "Remember the assassination attempt on Simon Scott just before he took office?"

Alex's eyes widened. "You were there for that?" she asked. "You saved him? Our Prime Minister?"

I nodded, aware of the shock on Sam's face.

"Bloody hell," Alex responded. "I'm not sure I understand any of this, but I like you, Kate. Besides, life is so much more interesting when it's weird, so I'll go along with it for now." She stared at the space over Sam's head. "I can't see anything though."

"No, but I promise you it's there. And before you ask, no, you don't have one. Neither does Moresby."

"Ha, can't say it'd bother me if Moresby did." She smirked. "He's such a pain."

Her grin faded as she leaned over and grabbed hold of Sam's hand. "We'll look after you," she said. "Don't worry."

"I don't need looking after," Sam said. "But I appreciate the thought."

Alex sat back in her chair. "So, the house has to be the source of the danger, right?"

"That's what I think," I said.

"These odd incidents, like the painting and the chandelier falling, are more than just accidents then." Alex tapped a well-manicured finger against her cheek. "But if someone is trying to actually hurt or kill Eline and Sam..." She stopped and patted Sam's arm. "Sorry. That sounds so cold. But if that's the intent, why mess about with pranks that have a really small chance of actually causing harm?"

"I think they were intended to frighten us off, to make TBA cancel the purchase," I said.

"That seems a bit far-fetched." Alex looked dubious.

"Maybe. But if it's true, then the question is who? Who's trying to stop the sale from happening, and why?" A deep frown creased Sam's brow. "What would be the motive? Who stands to gain if the house remains unsold?"

The list of suspects had to be short, consisting only of people who had access to the house. Henk, of course, but he had an aura too. I was suspicious of Moresby but that was mostly because he was such a cold fish and I didn't like him. Right now, I couldn't understand the link between the strange stuff happening in the house and the danger to Sam or Eline and Henk. If there even was a link.

"Could it be Pieter?" Sam asked. "Not for the pranks, obviously, but perhaps he doesn't really want to sell the house."

Alex stood up. "I think better when I have a cup of tea in my hand. Anyone else?"

Sam and I both nodded, and she filled the kettle with water

exactly to the three-cup line. I always filled the kettle to the top, even if I was only making tea for one.

"But he's going to inherit a huge chunk of money from the proceeds of the sale," Sam said. "He could buy a luxury apartment anywhere in Amsterdam if he wanted to."

"I think we should ask Eline," I said. "She knows Pieter, for one thing, and she may be aware of other people who have, or have had, an interest in the building. Maybe someone else put in an offer, but TBA offered more."

Sam shook his head. "There were no other bids. But it's worth talking to her." He paused and then looked at me. "Will you tell her about the aura and warn her that she's in danger?"

My stomach did a flip. I hated telling people about auras and I'd just been through the wringer with Sam and Alex. It wasn't easy to announce imminent death to anyone, friend or stranger. But I had a responsibility.

"Yes," I replied. "I'll tell her. She needs to be aware, to take extra precautions about her safety. Next time she comes over, I'll do it."

"You should phone her now," Sam said. "She gave us her mobile number."

8

While Alex finished setting out our sandwiches, I trudged into the living room, reluctant to make the call to Eline. It was something I'd rather put off. The phone rang and rang, but she didn't answer, and finally it clicked to voicemail. Although I didn't understand the Dutch greeting, I left a message anyway, asking her to call me back as soon as possible.

Relieved to have avoided the conversation, at least for now, but also feeling guilty about my relief, I returned to the kitchen where Sam was scrawling notes on a piece of paper. When he'd finished, he pushed it across the table to show Alex and me.

"This is what we have to get done to finish the feasibility review by Friday. I think it's doable, right?"

I quickly reviewed the list. It looked good to me.

"Definitely, let's get on with it," Alex said.

I agreed. Speed was the solution. The sooner we were done, the sooner Sam would be back in London, where I hoped he would be safe. It bothered me that I couldn't know that for sure, but I suspected it was a better bet than staying where he was.

"I see you have a sledgehammer on the list?" I asked. "Does that mean we are going to break into the paneling on the top floor?"

"We have to if we're to complete the project," Sam said. "We need to know what's behind that wall and get it drawn up."

"Can't we just assume it's a utility corridor, the same as on the blue floor?" Alex asked. "I'd take a bet it has the same dimensions and is full of old pipes and cables."

"Maybe, but I'd rather be sure," Sam said. "We don't want any nasty surprises further along. The contractor will bring the hammer over tomorrow morning."

"Great." I flexed a bicep. "I can't wait to see what we find up there."

Fueled by our late lunch, we worked hard for the rest of the afternoon. Alex was doing complicated math on her laptop, Sam was typing furiously, and I used my architecture app to work on my layouts. They would be in good shape by the deadline.

Just after five, Sam lifted his head. "Weird," he said. "The house feels really quiet. It's strange."

Alex raised her eyebrows. "It's always quiet. It's ninety-five percent empty."

I focused on listening for a few moments. It wasn't actually quiet. The huge built-in refrigerator hummed, and our keyboards were clacking. Yet I understood what Sam meant. There was a sense of dead air, the same lack of sound I experienced when I worked late at the office after everyone else had gone. But the three of us had been here alone for hours. There had been no mass exodus of people to account for the hush that had fallen over the house.

"It must be that the streets are emptying out," I said.

"We can't hear any noise from the road." Alex pointed at the triple-paned windows along the kitchen wall. She shrugged and went back to staring at her figure-filled screen.

Sam looked at me for a second and then gave a rueful grin. "This place is getting to me," he said. He pointed at my laptop. "Onward then."

I gave him a mock salute. "Yes, sir."

A couple of minutes later, Vincent padded in and coiled around Sam's ankles. Still typing with one hand, Sam reached with the other to pet the tabby. The cat's loud purr drowned out the warble of the refrigerator. I found Vincent's presence comforting, a little domestic normality in the vast strange house.

Still, by some sort of tacit agreement, when Alex said she had to do more analysis upstairs, Sam and I went with her to the blue floor. We were getting in the habit of sticking together. Sam's contractor had delivered portable lamps earlier, which helped us to work in the fading light. Their brilliance faded the blue of the walls of the bedrooms and bathrooms to dull grey. Alex worked fast, taking the measurements for a beam that would support a wall where we would be cutting a door through to make a large conference room. We were soon back in the welcome glow of the kitchen. Then she remembered something else, and we all trooped back upstairs and down again. Every transition from the ancient part of the building to the modern apartment was a temporal shift, moving from an indistinct past to a concrete present, a jolt that took a few seconds to come to terms with.

We'd just sat down for the third time when my mobile rang. It was Eline.

"You called me?" she asked.

"Yes." I struggled with what to say next. I couldn't do this by phone, I decided. "I wanted to see if you'd like to join us for a drink?"

Once we were there, I'd find a way to grab some time alone with her.

"That would be lovely," she answered. "I'm busy now, so maybe later."

"Do you know a place that's not too loud? Last night we were in a bar where we couldn't hear a word, it was so noisy."

Eline laughed. "There are plenty of those. Where are you staying? We can find somewhere close to your hotel perhaps."

When I told her, she gave me the name of a wine bar close by and we agreed to meet there at eight.

I explained the plan to Alex and Sam. "I'll just need to have a few minutes alone with Eline," I said. "To explain that she's in danger."

"Wouldn't it be better if we stay with you while you talk to her?" Alex asked. "If we tell her we believe you, she's more likely to as well."

"Thank you," I agreed, glad to have their support. I didn't know how Eline would react. I'd often been surprised by people's reaction when I told them I could see their fate.

At eight, the three of us arrived at the wine bar. I liked Eline's choice of venue. Plushly-upholstered benches and chairs were grouped around black coffee tables glowing with tea lights in glass jars. Soft uplights illuminated a vaulted brick ceiling, and jazz played quietly in the background. The other patrons were mostly young people in business clothes. Hardly a tourist in sight.

We decided to wait for Eline before ordering but, by eight fifteen, she hadn't arrived, and I fidgeted nervously next to Alex. The more this dragged out, the harder I was finding it to envisage telling Eline about my strange gift. I hated talking about portents of death, especially with Sam's aura rotating over his head as a stark reminder that he was still in grave danger. Time was passing, and I had no idea what it was that threatened him.

At eight twenty, Sam went to the bar to get our drinks while I phoned Eline's mobile. The call went straight to voicemail. "Hi Eline," I said. "We're here at the wine bar. I want to be sure we're in the right place. See you soon."

Sam had set down our drinks by the time I rang off. After another ten minutes, Alex stood up. "I'll get more peanuts. Dinner's going to be late."

While she was engaged in an animated conversation with the barman, I took a few deep breaths, trying to calm myself down.

Sam grabbed my hand. "Relax. We'll all do this together. And if Eline doesn't believe you, well, then you've done your best."

Alex returned with peanuts and olives and set them down on the table. She and Sam soon finished them off. Every time the door opened, I looked up to see if Eline had arrived. By nine, she still hadn't.

"I'm worried," I said. "Why set a time to meet and then not come? She could have just said no on the phone."

"We could call the lawyer," Alex said. "Maybe Eline and Pieter are still with him. They had a meeting set for early evening, remember?

Pieter told us. Or maybe it's over, but Bleeker might have another contact number for her."

"A bit weird, don't you think?" Sam ran his hand through his hair, leaving tufts standing upright. "Us calling Bleeker out of hours? He's probably not allowed to share personal information about a client anyway."

"That's true," Alex said. "Should we go to the police and tell them Eline is missing?"

Sam and I looked at each other.

"We have to do something," I said.

"The trouble is, we wouldn't be worried if it weren't for the aura," Sam said slowly. "We'd just think she got held up or that we got the time wrong, or that she changed her mind about coming."

"Which is what the police will think too," I said. "If everyone reported a friend who forgot a drinks date or who turned up late, the police stations would be overwhelmed."

I'd had a handful of embarrassing and painful interactions with police officers in the past few years, trying to convince them that someone was about to die without being able to explain how I knew.

"Let's give it another fifteen minutes," Alex said. "And then we should go eat. I'm starving."

We waited mostly in silence. My stomach was in knots. I'd been nervous all evening about telling Eline she had an aura and what that signified. Now, dread had wound a rope around my chest, and I found it hard to breathe. What if it were too late? Was it possible that she was already dead?

"It's okay," Sam said, patting my hand. "There are a dozen good reasons why Eline hasn't shown up."

We were putting on our coats when my phone beeped. I snatched it from my pocket. It was a phone call from Eline.

"I'm so sorry," she said. "Something came up."

"I really want to talk to you," I said. "It's important."

"I'll see you at the house tomorrow morning then. Sorry for standing you up."

With a click, she was gone.

The anxiety I'd been feeling drained away, leaving my skin cold and my knees wobbly. "She's okay," I told the others. "But she's not coming."

"It was a bit rude of her to not let us know earlier," Alex said. "Still, I'm glad you heard from her. And now I'm about to pass out from lack of sustenance. Let's go."

Outside, we paused while Alex checked an address on her mobile. She'd been researching likely restaurants earlier in the evening. "Follow me," she said.

As expected, Alex had chosen a good place to eat. Sam devoured a plate loaded with fresh fish and vegetables while Alex opted for meatballs. I wasn't hungry. I picked my way through a salad and sipped a half glass of white wine, my stomach churning every time I looked at Sam. His aura was clearly visible even in the dim restaurant lighting.

By the time dinner was over, I was feeling exhausted, ready for an early night. We started back towards Sam's hotel and had been walking for a minute or two when I got a strange feeling, a prickling on the back of my neck. I turned and saw a man about twenty meters behind us. He was wearing a dark jacket with the hood pulled up.

I stopped. "Give me a minute," I said to the others. Without pausing to think, I took a few steps towards the man, who continued walking in my direction. "Are you following us?" I called when he was several meters away. He looked around as if verifying it was him I was yelling at and then carried on walking. "You," I said. "Why are you following us?"

I felt a hand on my arm and glanced over to see Sam, his face creased with worry. "What are you doing?" His voice came out in a loud whisper.

The guy with the hoodie hurried past, casting nervous looks at us.

"I thought he was watching us. I've seen him before. At the bar last night and then on the street near the house today." My heart was pounding.

Sam took my hand and nodded at Alex. We started to walk again, me sandwiched in between them.

"Bit of an overreaction there," Alex said, winding her arm through mine and smiling to soften her critique.

"I'm sorry." I felt my heart rate settling back to normal. "I don't usually confront strange men on the streets. I was just...I'm worried about Sam, obviously, and Eline, and the stuff going on in the house."

Alex squeezed my arm tighter. "Look on the bright side. Nothing strange has happened since ten o'clock this morning. We've had twelve hours of peace and quiet. And Eline is fine, so try to stop worrying. Maybe once the feasibility study is complete and we get out of here, the auras will disappear. At the very least, you get to go back to London on Friday, days earlier than we expected. But for now, I say we enjoy ourselves. What's the point of being in Amsterdam if we don't sample the night life?"

"Really?"

"Really. A friend of mine told me about this bar where they do amazing cocktails. And dancing. My treat. You up for it, Sam?"

He grinned. "Why not?"

I let myself be dragged along, channeling Alex's energy. She seemed to bring out the social side of Sam too.

We crossed an arched bridge where we stopped to admire the moon's reflection on the water and the houseboats moored along the canal walls. When I looked up to make sure the others were enjoying the idyllic scene, I noticed that they were touching hands, their fingers entwined. I turned away quickly to hide the smile on my face. I was happy for Sam. And I knew I could rely on Alex to help me protect him.

9

I ate breakfast alone in the hotel dining room on Wednesday morning. At about midnight, I'd decided to leave Sam and Alex to enjoy each other's company and had taken a taxi back to the hotel. Sam had said he would set an alarm for eight thirty. Although I'd planned to sleep in too, I'd woken at dawn after another restless night.

Sipping coffee, I overheard a couple speaking English at the table next to me. The woman looked upset as her partner patted her hand. He caught my eye, and I looked away, embarrassed to be caught watching them. But that didn't seem to have bothered him.

"We had a shock this morning," he told me. "Me and the wife found a body in a canal just around the corner from here. We always walk before breakfast." He patted his ample stomach. "Trying to lose some weight."

"I'm sorry. That must have been distressing."

The mention of a body made my heart gallop. I grabbed my phone and texted Sam, telling him to text me back.

"Do you know who it was?" I asked.

"Nah. It was hard to see much. The police came and took all our details..."

A muffled sob from his wife distracted him. He resumed the hand-patting and then carried on talking to me. "Nice chaps. They told us that they lose a dozen tourists or so every year, usually blokes that've had too much to drink. Often, when they stand on the edge to relieve themselves—"

"Kevin!" His wife's cheeks turned pink. "It's not polite to say that."

Kevin chuckled. "Well, anyway, sometimes they fall in. Most of the time, the police chaps said, they are hauled out before any damage is done, but if it's late at night and they're alone, it's very dangerous."

For some reason, this caused another storm of sobs from Kevin's wife.

I glanced at my mobile where it lay on the table next to my plate. Still no text from Sam, but it was only eight. He probably wasn't awake yet. I sent him another text, though. "Call me."

Kevin pushed his chair back and helped his wife to her feet. "Let's go back to our room, dear. Can't disturb everyone's breakfast." He looked over at me. "I'm so sorry."

They hurried away before I could answer.

It struck me that Kevin hadn't said if the body was a male or a female. And, really, what were the chances that it would be Sam? My attempts to calm myself didn't work very well. When I got to my feet, my legs were as wobbly as if my bones had dissolved. I gripped the edge of the table while I concentrated on regaining my balance and then dashed towards the lift, berating myself the whole time. I shouldn't have left Sam with Alex last night. It was totally negligent on my part. I was the only one who really understood how significant the appearance of an aura was. For others, it was easy enough to disbelieve, to ignore something you couldn't see. I was waiting for the lift when my phone pinged.

It was a text from Sam. "*Good morning!*"

I leaned against the wall, taking a couple of deep breaths to chase away the lump that had formed in my chest. A few moments later, the lift arrived, and Sam stepped out. The relief that he hadn't drowned in a canal made me almost giddy—until I realized that the air over his head was moving rapidly, far more quickly than the day before. That was not good.

"Everything all right?" he asked.

"More or less. Do you want breakfast?"

"Silly question. Of course I do."

We walked back to the dining room, where Sam loaded a plate with scrambled eggs, ham, cheese and olives. He grabbed several bread rolls, and we ordered more coffee. Once we were seated, I told him about the couple who'd found a body. "It was close to the hotel."

"And you thought it was me," he said, spreading butter on a roll.

"I did, for a few minutes."

"I wish you wouldn't worry. I'm going to be fine."

"You don't know that. And the evidence says otherwise." I raised my eyes to look at the aura that swirled wildly over his unkempt brown hair. "You need to take this seriously, Sam. It's not a joke. People with auras have died. I've seen them."

He changed the subject. "We've got a lot to do today."

"I know. I think…" I yawned before I could finish my sentence. That got Sam yawning too. "I can't do late nights anymore," he said. "Although it was good fun at the time."

"Did you stay out dancing all night?" I grinned at him, glad that he and Alex seemed to be hitting it off.

"Not all night. Although I feel as though I did." He finished eating and stood up to put on his coat. "Let's go. We may as well get started."

Outside, it was cold. I slipped my arm through his, and we walked to the Janssen house mostly in silence. There was no sign of the sun today. The sky was ashen, the canal we'd just crossed was the color of slate and, when we reached the house, its stone walls were grey and drab. I felt my energy drain away just looking at it. Still, I squeezed Sam's arm and hurried him up the steps to the front door.

We found Henk in the kitchen sitting at the table, cradling a cup in his hands. In response to my good-morning greeting, he nodded back but didn't say anything. That was fine with me as I wouldn't have understood him anyway. Breathing in the enticing aroma of coffee, I headed for the espresso machine.

I'd just handed a cup to Sam when Alex bounded into the kitchen.

"Sorry I'm late," she said. Unlike me and Sam, Alex looked as though she'd had a solid eight hours. Her skin glowed and her eyes were bright. "But my excuse for being late is that I bumped into an old friend of my mother's. I mean, literally. I was dashing for a bus and ran straight into him. Once he'd caught his breath, we recognized each other and went to grab a cup of coffee. My treat, considering that I'd knocked him over. Anyway, that's why I'm late, sorry."

She grinned but her smile faded when she noticed Henk camped at the kitchen table.

"We'll work in the dining room," Sam said, heading in that direction.

"Does your friend know anything about this place?" I asked Alex.

"Actually, he does." Alex closed the dining room door. "Don't want that strange old coot listening in."

"Henk? He doesn't even speak English."

"No, but he might overhear names. Anyway, Willem, this friend of my mum's, works here in Amsterdam as a financial advisor for one of the big banks. Because of his job, he mixes with the city's more affluent crowd and he met Tomas Janssen fairly often. He says Janssen was a strange guy, very rich, but quite discreet about it. No one really knew where he made his money."

"Does Willem know Eline?" I asked Alex.

She nodded, setting her blond ponytail bouncing. "He's met her quite a few times at galas and fundraisers, that sort of thing. I got the impression he likes her rather more than he liked Tomas. Not that Tomas was a bad person or anything."

"What about the house? Does he know much about it?"

"Well, I told him about the strange things that have been happening here, but he seemed more amused than concerned, to be honest. Anyway, I'm going to have dinner with him tonight and he'll tell me more." She turned to me. "What about Eline? Have you heard from her since last night?"

"No," I said, "but I wasn't expecting to. Remember, she said she's coming over this morning."

"The contractor is coming soon too," Sam said. "With the sledgehammer. He and I can take down a panel on the top floor."

"You'll just find another service corridor like the one on the blue floor," Alex said. "I've already drawn that space up on the plans anyway."

"Well, at least if we look, we can sign off the plans as accurate." I got to my feet. "Oh, and I researched Friday's flights this morning, Sam. We could fly to London together on the 2.10 if you think we'll be all done by then?"

"Sounds good to me," he said.

"What about you, Alex? Will you be heading back to London too?" I asked.

"Not yet. I've been staying with my aunt this week and she wants to take me on a trip to Bruges. I've never been. So, we'll do that over the weekend, and I'll fly back on Sunday. I'm really excited to see the Memling Museum. Well, that and the beer."

Her smile faded when she looked at Sam. "Sorry, I didn't mean to bang on about touristy stuff. I know you have more serious things on your mind."

"No worries," he said. "I want to go to Bruges one day too."

"Then we'll all come back and do that together," I said. "Put it on your calendars for the summer."

I'd just picked up my notebook when I heard a faint ping as the lift came up from the ground floor.

Sam looked up with a smile. "Oh good, that will be the chap with the sledgehammer."

It wasn't. It was Moresby. He threw the dining room door open and burst in, sweat beading his brow, his breath coming in short bursts.

"Did you hear? Eline Janssen is dead."

10

Moresby pulled out a chair and perched on the edge of it. It took him a moment to catch his breath. "I got a phone call from the lawyer, what's his name, Bleeker. He said he'd just heard the news."

"Oh, poor Eline." Alex sat back down with tears brimming in her blue eyes. Her usually rosy cheeks were pallid. My knees were wobbling again, and I lowered myself into my chair. I didn't dare look at Sam yet.

"Do they know what happened?" Alex asked.

I braced, already guessing what Moresby would say.

"She fell into a canal and drowned."

"When?" I asked.

"I don't have any details. Bleeker sounded very upset and said he'd ring me back when he knew more."

"Was it an accident?"

Moresby's eyes widened. "I'd assume so. Why would you think otherwise?"

I shrugged. There was no reason to get into a long discussion with Moresby until we had more information.

When I glanced at Sam, I saw that his face was ashen. Eline's death had probably finally squashed his doubts about the significance of auras.

"My main concern," Moresby went on, straightening that ramrod spine of his. "Is that we waste no time in finalizing the study and getting my Board to sign off on it. The nephew has been willing to sell all along, and I assume he won't change his mind now."

I had briefly entertained the thought that Moresby was distressed because someone had died, but obviously that wasn't the case. He was merely upset at the prospect of a delay with the project.

"It would be naive to think that this won't throw a spanner in the works," Sam said. "God knows how long it will take to iron out all the paperwork." He walked to the window and stared outside.

I knew what I had to do. Get Sam back to London, away from the house. There was no real evidence that Eline's death was in any way linked to the threat to Sam, but I wasn't taking any more chances. If the project was canceled, Alan would have to suck it up, although he'd probably whine about it for months to come.

Moresby's mobile pinged. He read the message and told us that the lawyer was on his way over. "Let's find out more from Bleeker before we panic," he said, tapping his fingers on the table.

"I think we should plan to give up on this project," I said.

Moresby shot to his feet and leaned over me. "And why would we do that?"

"Well, for one thing, because the seller just died."

Moresby turned away and began pacing the length of the room. Sam stayed at the window, staring out at the grey sky. Alex had cradled her head on her arms on the table, the way we used to take naps in nursery school. I doubted she was sleeping though.

When the front doorbell chimed, I scrambled to my feet, just to have something to do. "I'll get it," I said.

In the living room, I lifted the phone that connected to the entry door. A deep voice growled at me. "Sam there? I got the hammer."

"I'll buzz you in."

While I waited for the lift to come up, I stared at the painting of Adam and Eve, which Henk had put back up. Then I turned in a slow circle, looking at the dizzying array of gilt-framed art, the antique furniture, the delicate pieces of china on the ornate tables. Who knew what Eline had planned to do with it all? Would everything now go to Pieter? He was about to inherit the entire building, worth a huge amount of money.

I was contemplating that when the lift doors opened, and the contractor stepped into the room. As promised, he was carrying a massive sledgehammer, its iron head already dinged and dented from a previous wrecking activity.

"We've got a problem, so you'll have to hold off for a while," I told him. "Just leave the hammer in the kitchen."

"I don't have all day. Got another appointment this afternoon," he grumbled. "But call me when you need me then."

I hurried back to the dining room to find Sam, Moresby and Alex all on their phones. I thought about calling Alan, but decided it was too soon. We needed to talk to Bleeker first to get some kind of insight into what would happen next.

Almost thirty minutes passed before he arrived. He was dressed in a navy cashmere suit with a pristine white shirt and maroon tie, but his well-cut hair was sticking up in places and his face was drawn. His cheeks were flushed as though he'd been running. I remembered Eline saying that he had been a source of strength and support for her when Tomas died. It must have been a shock for him to lose two of his clients in such a short space of time.

We all settled in chairs around the big dining table and waited for Bleeker to speak.

"I'm sorry to confirm that Eline Janssen died last night," he said.

"When did it happen?" I asked.

"They say she drowned in the early hours of the morning. Her body was spotted in the water by some tourists, apparently. They alerted a street-sweeping crew who called the police."

Kevin and his wife.

I thought back to my brief phone call with Eline. That had been at nine p.m. Something had happened before that to stop her from coming to meet us as planned. But what? And where had she been after that call?

"How did she end up in a canal?"

"I don't know. Her friend called me, but she was too upset to say much. A terrible accident apparently."

A heavy silence filled the room. I shivered, imagining the weight of all that cold water over my head. Had Eline struggled to reach the surface after she'd fallen in? Or was it suicide? She'd been so upset about Tomas's death that it had to be a possibility. In that case, was it only a coincidence that she and Sam both had auras? Maybe they really were completely unconnected. Or perhaps the danger all along had been that Eline's death would cancel the project and Sam would return home earlier than planned. If the risk to him lay in London, I had no idea what to do.

I didn't realize I'd groaned out loud until Alex put her hand over mine. "Are you all right?" she asked.

Bleeker was looking at me with concern too, his brows drawn together. "I realize this is all very distressing," he said. "But we have to discuss the impact of Eline's death on the estate's business affairs. I'm sure you all realize that we will need to delay the house purchase, perhaps for a very extended period of time."

Sam turned away from the window to look at him. "How long?"

Bleeker shrugged. "I can't say, I'm sorry."

"But the nephew will probably still want to go ahead with the sale?" Moresby asked. "And he'll have the right to do that?"

"Yes, of course, he retains the right to sell the property, which will belong to him in its entirety. That's the way Tomas Janssen wrote up the will. In the event of Eline's death, everything goes to Pieter Janssen. But we don't know for sure that he will want to proceed with the sale now that it is solely his. He may want to live in it. But that's a future issue. For now, I need to work on the inheritance documents, the passing of property from Eline to her nephew."

"Are we talking weeks or months to get this sorted?" Sam asked.

"Months?" Moresby spluttered. "We can't wait months." He took a white handkerchief from his breast pocket and wiped his forehead. "What a bloody disaster."

"Bit of a disaster for poor Eline too," Alex muttered.

Moresby ignored her. "I put my reputation on the line by choosing this city and this building," he said, staring up at the ceiling as though remembering a happier time. He frowned. "They'll never trust my opinion again." He glared at Sam. "And you won't get paid."

"I apologize," Bleeker said.

"But surely someone can get a message to Pieter and find out what he wants to do about the house?" Sam asked. He was rubbing his temple as though he had a headache.

I sympathized. My head was pounding with a toxic drumbeat of anxiety, guilt and frustration. I was terrified for Sam, I had failed to save Eline, and the future of the project was uncertain. I rolled my shoulders, trying to work out the tension in them. They felt like steel coils.

"Of course," Bleeker said. "But in the event that Pieter still wishes to sell, we will need him to sign a number of documents and for that he will have to come to Amsterdam."

"He's already in Amsterdam," I said. "We met him yesterday. He said he and Eline had an appointment with you late yesterday afternoon. You didn't see him?"

Bleeker shook his head. "I didn't. There was no appointment that I know of."

Alex and I exchanged looks. I felt the weight of an iron slab pushing on my shoulders. Had the man who'd visited yesterday been an imposter? It wasn't the nephew? We needed to tell the police.

"But, Mr. Bleeker, the man we met said he was Pieter Janssen and that he and Eline were planning to see you. Are you sure there was no meeting?"

The lawyer shrugged. "As I said. Perhaps they met with one of my associates though. I will check."

"Have you met him before?" I asked. "To be honest, we're not even sure it was Pieter who came here yesterday."

"I haven't," Bleeker said. "All our communications to date have been by phone. Listen, it is probably best if you let your respective companies know that there will be a delay. Perhaps you'd all prefer to return to London until I notify you that we are ready to proceed again?"

"Go back to London?" Moresby slapped his hand on the table. "Impossible. When I go back, it's with the bill of sale in hand, or not at all."

The way things were looking, Moresby might be permanently displaced. I had a picture in my head of him wandering the streets of Amsterdam for years to come.

"Can't we finish the first phase?" Sam asked. "If we're able to spend a few more hours here today, we can wrap up our reports and give Mr. Moresby the document he needs to present to his Board. That will keep things ticking over while you deal with the will. At least we'll minimize the amount of time we lose."

Poor Sam. If this fell apart, he wouldn't get paid by TBA. And I knew this project was important to him for more than just the money. He'd have nothing to show for all the time he'd put in and no references from a happy client.

Bleeker was frowning. "I'm not sure about that. It would be best if you were to put things on hold for now."

"There's a lot at stake here," Sam argued. "We just need a few hours to finish up. Then, if Pieter does decide to proceed as planned, we won't have wasted any time."

"Good plan," Moresby said.

"Very well." Bleeker nodded. "As long as you do nothing that has a material impact on the property, you may stay."

His mobile rang and he stood up and moved towards the door to take the call. After only a minute, he came back to his chair.

"That was Pieter Janssen," he said. "He has asked for a meeting this afternoon and apologized for missing our appointment yesterday."

"The appointment you didn't know you had," I said.

"There must have been an administrative mix-up. I have a new receptionist. Anyway, for now, I don't know what Pieter will do about the house, but I will let you know as soon as I've talked with him."

"We'll stay here until we hear from you," Sam said.

Bleeker nodded. "I'll be in touch."

11

W hen Bleeker had gone, Moresby jumped to his feet. "Let's get on then," he said. "Finish up the report so I can present it to my Board."

"It will be incomplete," I reminded him. "We can't really finish it until we break in on the top floor to see where that concrete pillar goes."

He waved me off as though swatting an insect. "That's a minor detail. I can handle that. The important thing is that I have enough information to verify the feasibility of the renovation." He leaned towards me as though sharing a secret. "I'll be honest with you. The Board members don't have a lot of imagination between them. As long as the building is stable and the managing partners each get an office with a view, everyone will be happy. At this stage, they're not going to worry about a few square meters of space and whether it's usable or not."

Alex raised her eyebrows and flashed a grin at me. Under other circumstances, Moresby would be the ideal client, content with a big picture overview and not fussy about the details. But we had a bigger problem than that to deal with. What if Pieter Janssen decided not to sell now that Eline was dead?

I reminded myself that I didn't care about the fate of the project. The only concern was what effect it would have on Sam's future. If the project was canceled, it would be a disaster for him. But then so would dying. I really didn't know what to do but I was leaning towards doing everything I could to get him on the next plane to London.

"We can do this," Sam said. He checked his watch. "It's ten a.m., so I say we aim to finish everything by end of day, and then we can compile the documents into one report. Everyone all right with that?"

"You'll have plenty of drawings for me, won't you?" Moresby asked me. "Things that will show what the building could look like when it's finished?"

"That's my job," I said. "I have a lot of sketches ready. Do you want to take a look at what I've got so far?"

"Excellent idea." He sat down next to me and reached into an inside pocket of his jacket for a pair of reading glasses. Together, we huddled over my notebook, and I described the way I thought each floor could be used. Sam settled at the opposite end of the table, and Alex spread out her mechanical drawings next to him.

It felt strangely calming to be working again, as if nothing untoward had happened. But very soon my brain started to hum with questions. What was I going to do about Sam when we returned to London? What if the aura didn't disappear when we left Amsterdam? What if he was still in danger? Then what? I couldn't camp at Sam's grandmother's house. Trailing him to his office wasn't practical. Short of locking him in a padded cell, there was no way I'd be able to protect him.

"Kate?" Moresby glared at me. "Have you been listening to anything I'm saying? I asked if we could move the computer server room to the top floor?"

"What? Oh, well actually, it will be more... more cost-effective having it located it on the ground floor. But if you don't mind the costs, we can do it. The whole building will need new wiring anyway, apart from this apartment level of course."

I forced myself to focus on the work in hand, answering Moresby's questions while trying hard to push away thoughts of Sam's future. My body seemed to be mirroring my brain. One moment I felt hot and the next I was cold. I wondered if I was getting the flu. Just what I needed, on top of everything else.

A while later, Alex sat back in her chair and stretched her arms over her head. "I need a break," she said.

"Me too." Sam tapped his laptop. "Let's make some tea and review how far we've got." He stood up. "Are you still planning on flying back to London today, Mr. Moresby?"

Moresby shook his head. "No, I will stay to hear the outcome of Bleeker's meeting with Pieter Janssen. If there are any complications there, I'll need to know immediately."

"Excellent. We'll just keep pushing on then and assume that the project will go forward with minimal delays."

For a microsecond, a smile flashed across Moresby's face. He looked like someone's kindly uncle. But then it was over, and his mouth returned to a thin line over his set jaw.

"Jolly good, everyone," he said. "Fine work. Much appreciated. I'll be at my hotel if you need me."

Once Moresby had gone, the three of us sat and looked at each other.

"What now?" Sam asked.

"I say the first thing we do is eat." Alex switched off the kettle that she'd just turned on. "Let's get out of here and have lunch. We'll all think better when we're not starving."

That girl could eat ten times a day and not put on an ounce. Still, lunch sounded tempting, and getting out of the house even more so.

When we stepped onto the street, the wind had picked up, ruffling the surface of the canal. Pedestrians clutched at their scarves and hats to stop them blowing away, and cyclists bent their heads low over their handlebars. But it was pleasant to be out in the fresh air and I took a few deep breaths. We walked slowly, admiring the narrow houses and the many bridges, wide and thin, plain and ornate, that crossed the canals.

"I want to rent a bike," Alex said as several sailed past us. "Maybe we can do that tomorrow."

No way, I thought, but I didn't say it out loud.

For a while, it was peaceful walking along the water's edge but, as we got closer to the Rijksmuseum, the crowds thickened. Tourists followed guides with color-coded flags or umbrellas, and groups of school kids in matching sweatshirts swarmed everywhere.

Sam led us away from the busy area, along a quiet side street to a *rijsttafel,* an Indonesian rice table restaurant. I'd heard of them but never eaten in one. Dutch colonialism in the East had begun with the VOC. When the Dutch came home, they brought with them a love of the spicy foods they'd eaten in Indonesia. Like the Brits in India, I thought. Every small town in England has an Indian restaurant.

I wondered if Jacob Hals, the man who built the Janssens' house, had ever traveled on one of the company's big sailing ships. More likely he'd stayed in the safety of Amsterdam, reaping the profits made by the soldiers and merchants who worked for the VOC.

The restaurant was busy, but we got a table in a quiet corner and let Sam do the ordering. When the waiter brought a dozen small dishes of rice, satay chicken, spicy vegetables and pickles, I didn't think we'd get through it all. I shouldn't have worried. The food was delicious, and we emptied every plate.

While we ate, we formulated a plan of sorts. I wanted to talk to Eline's friend, the one she'd been staying with. I was hoping she would know something that might help me work out the threat to Sam. Alex already had plans to meet Willem for dinner and hoped he'd tell her more about the Janssens and the house.

"But now I'm wondering if there's any point," she said. "Maybe we should wait until we hear from Bleeker and whether the project is even going ahead. Whatever Willem knows about the house isn't much use if the project gets cancelled."

"No, but we still need to work out what it is that threatens Sam," I said. "And whether it is related to the house in any way. He might know something."

I glanced up at Sam to check on his aura. His lips were pressed tightly together. "I'm sorry," I said, reaching over to put my hand on his arm. "I know you don't like thinking about it."

Still scowling, he got up and walked off towards the loo.

"Poor Sam," Alex said. "But you're right. I'll keep my dinner date with Willem."

"I'll stay with Sam while you're out. One of us needs to be with him all the time."

Her eyes sparkled. "I'll take the night shift then."

We tried to keep our faces straight when Sam came back to the table, but Alex was still smiling when he sat down.

"I won't even ask," he said.

"Better not to," I agreed.

We were more somber by the time lunch was over, each of us ready to tackle our self-imposed task. First on my list was tracking down Eline's friend. I thought I remembered Eline saying her name was Karen. Or it could have been Catherine. Our only possible lead seemed to be Henk. He might know where Eline had been staying. So, we walked, more briskly now, back to the house, hoping he'd still be there.

We found him polishing the vast and empty dining table and left Alex to talk with him. She joined us a few minutes later.

"*Agh.*" She plopped down on a chair.

"No help then?" Sam asked.

"None at all. I think he's cut up about Eline's death, but insists he knows nothing. He just kept asking when we were planning to leave. I said I had no idea and told him we'll probably be around for the fore-seeable future. You should have seen his face."

"There has to be some other way we can find the friend," I said, watching as Alex jumped back up and started to make tea. The noise of clanking mugs must have woken Vincent, wherever he'd been hiding, and he wandered into the kitchen to rub up against Sam's leg. Dutifully, his on-call waiter went to the pantry to find a can of food. While the others were busy, I had an idea.

"Be right back," I said.

After checking that Henk was still busy polishing the dining table, I hurried along the corridor that led to Eline's bedroom. I grasped the crystal doorknob, trying to shake off the sense of guilt at what I was about to do, and then turned it. The room was empty, but I hesitated. This was Eline's personal space and I was intruding. It was all for a good cause though, so I put aside my reservations and took a few steps inside.

Heavy damask curtains were drawn across the window, allowing only a sliver of grey light to fall across the burgundy colored quilt, the packing boxes stacked against one wall, and the suitcases on the bed. I had the unnerving feeling that someone was in the room watching me.

The surface of the dressing table was almost invisible under stacks of papers, perfume bottles, and jewelry boxes. I flipped through a pile of papers, wondering what Pieter had taken. The papers weren't revealing much. They were all in Dutch. I straightened the pile and moved on to another one, only to find the same problem. Frustrated, I opened the largest of the jewelry boxes. It was crammed full of rings and earrings, all glittering with precious stones and gold. As I closed it and slid the clasp back into place, I heard a noise in the hallway outside. My hands began to shake so badly that I almost dropped the box. If Henk discovered me in here, what would he say?

I backed away from the dressing table and crouched down behind the huge four-poster bed. Ducking down as low as I could, I held my breath. Light from the hallway fell across the room as the door opened. I waited, hearing Henk's wheezy breathing but no footsteps. He had to be standing at the door looking in. Time seemed to slow, and then the light faded, and I heard a click as the door closed. Wary, wondering if he had come in and closed the door behind him, I waited for another few moments.

Focused as I was on controlling my breathing, it took me a few seconds to realize I was staring at a leather-bound book on the floor under the bed. Next to it was a pile of envelopes of different colors and sizes. I reached in and pulled out a couple. They were condolence cards, I realized, judging from the somber colors and the images of flowers on the front. I slid them back under the bed, picked up the book and carried it to the window. It appeared to be an address book, with entries in neat handwriting on each page. None of it made sense to me, but I guessed Alex might be able to decipher it.

I slipped out of the room, pulled the door closed, and dashed to the kitchen, where Sam and Alex were at the table, drinking tea. I could practically see a fluffy pink cloud enveloping them, all warm and mushy.

"Where did you go?" Alex asked, sliding a mug towards me.

"Take a look at this," I replied, handing her the book. "Can you read it?"

She flipped through a few pages. "Yes, it's an address book." She looked up at me. "Did you go through Eline's things?"

"Never mind that. Can you see if there's a Karen or Catherine in there?"

"We don't have a second name."

But she was already turning more pages. It seemed to take forever until she paused. "Karen Visser," she said. "She's the only Karen listed in here and there's no Catherine."

"Is there an address? A phone number?"

"Both. I'll write them down. Shall I call her?"

I thought for a second. "I'd rather talk to her in person. I think I'd learn more that way."

"But what if she doesn't speak English?" Sam asked. "You'd better take Alex with you."

He had a point, but I had no intention of leaving him alone. On the other hand, three of us turning up on Karen's doorstep would be overkill. I'd have a better chance of winning her confidence if I went by myself.

"I'll hope for the best," I said. "If it turns out I need Alex, we'll go back again later."

We agreed that Sam would do background research on the

nephew while I was gone, and Alex would have a go at coaxing Henk
into telling her more about the building and its occupants. With his
years of service at the house, it seemed that he had to know something useful that might help us work out what happened to Eline. We
weren't confident he would give us any information, but it was worth
a try.

12

Ten minutes later, after a fast walk towards Rembrandtplein, I stood in front of a modern redbrick townhouse with a green front door. Each of four doorbells had a name next to it. I located Karen's, the third one up, and rang the bell. After a long silence, the speaker crackled, and a female voice said something in Dutch. Leaning closer to the speaker, I introduced myself. "I'm Kate Benedict, one of the team working on Eline Janssen's house. I'd like to talk to you about her," I said.

There was a long pause. Had she not understood? I was about to reword my request when the buzzer sounded, and the door clicked open.

I stepped into a narrow lobby with a black and white tiled floor. Three bikes leaned against one wall and on the other side was a wooden staircase with a wrought iron banister. Karen's flat was on the second floor, according to the bell push, so I started up. On the first landing, I was met by a tall, thin woman with flaming red hair that fanned out around a pale face with high cheekbones. She was wearing dark jeans and a skinny green top and had to be about the same age as Eline.

"I'm Karen," she said.

Without another word, she turned and climbed the next flight of stairs. I followed her through an open entry door into a cozy living room lined with bookcases.

"Please sit," she said, pointing to a white sofa in front of an unlit fireplace. "Oh sorry. Hang on." She hurried over to remove a pile of books, which she put on the floor. "Tea? Coffee?"

"Tea, thank you. Can I help?"

She didn't answer, and I soon heard the clink of cups in the adjacent kitchen. I looked around the living room, which was well lit by two tall windows on one wall. My attention was caught by an oil painting propped against one of the bookcases. In it, two women in long silk dresses sat together on a chaise, their bodies turned towards each other as though in conversation, their hands busy with needlework of some kind.

"Eline gave me that painting," Karen said as she came in and handed me a delicate teacup and saucer. She sat down beside me. "She said it looked like the two of us together. Happy and always talking. We never stopped talking, although I probably did most of it."

"You've been friends for a long time?" I asked.

"Since forever. We met at university in Rotterdam and then both moved here to Amsterdam. I teach here at the university now." She waved her hand towards the bookshelves. "Political science. Eline worked as a hospital administrator. Before she met Tomas, that is. Then things changed for her. With all his money, there was no need for her to work, of course, and Tomas didn't want her to."

From her tone of voice, it seemed that perhaps Karen didn't like Tomas, or his lifestyle, much. I wanted to ask her more about him, but her eyes had filled with tears. Her hand shook as she put her cup down on the coffee table. "I'm going to miss her terribly."

"I'm very sorry," I offered. "I only met Eline once, and she seemed very nice." It was a weak word, I knew, but Karen seemed to accept it.

"Eline liked you too," she said, blinking away her tears.

"She did?" I was surprised. We'd hardly spoken enough for her to form an opinion about me, I thought.

"Eline had a sense about people. That's what made her so good at her job at the hospital. She told me about you." Karen tilted her head, her red curls bobbing. "She thought you had, what did she call it? Insight. A way of knowing things that other people don't. Was she right?"

I hesitated, wondering how much to say. If I confided in Karen, would it help me identify the threat to Sam?

"That's why I agreed to see you," Karen went on. "Because Eline liked you. And because you might know what happened to her last night."

I shook my head. "I don't know anything. I was hoping you would have some answers."

"Why does it matter to you?" she asked. "As you say, you only met her once."

This was it, my opening to explain about the auras and about the danger my friend was in. I took a swallow of tea and then plunged in. Karen listened without interrupting as I told her about my strange gift and about the threat to Sam. "We met Tessa on Monday morning," I added. "I saw an aura over her then and she died that afternoon."

Karen took my hand in hers. "Eline was right about you."

I exhaled a sigh of relief. At least Karen didn't think I was crazy.

"But I wish I'd been able to warn her," I said. "I wanted to let her know she was in danger."

"She already knew," Karen said. "Not about the aura of course, but that there was a threat. She didn't know what it was, though. There was a man she was convinced was following her. Wait a moment." She let go of my hand and leaned forward over the coffee table to sort through a pile of papers. After discarding a few magazines and newspapers, she handed me a sheet of white paper with a pencil drawing of a man on it.

I recognized him at once.

"That's the man with the grey hoodie," I said. "I'm sure he's been watching us."

"Eline sketched it. She was planning to go to the police with it. She told me he'd been following her for a couple of weeks."

"Wait. You think this man had something to do with her death? They told us it was an accident."

Karen gazed at the sketch in my hand for a long time before speaking. "Yes, it was an accident. Still, she was very nervous about this man for some reason. And, after the break-in at the house, she was so distressed that she asked to move in with me. Which made me very happy. I felt I could look after her better if she stayed here." She took the drawing from me and put it back on the table. "And in that, I failed."

"You said there was a break-in?"

"It happened the week after Tomas's funeral." Still talking, Karen got up and went to the kitchen, raising her voice over the tinkle of glasses. "Eline and I had been out for dinner. I made her do that a lot just to get her out, you know? Someone broke in through the back door and turned over the apartment as though they were looking for something specific."

She came back with two sherries and handed me one. "I know it's early, but I need something to help me calm down," she said. "I'm a wreck. Anyway, nothing was taken, but there was a lot of damage— vandalism really. Knifed cushions, drawers pulled out and emptied, broken glass. It really upset Eline, especially coming so soon after Tomas's death."

"I can imagine."

But my mind was whirling. Eline hadn't mentioned the break-in when we talked. I wondered if she had reported it to the police.

"There's no sign of the damage now," I said.

"There wouldn't be. Eline hired a man to clean and fix everything. It had to be picture-perfect to show to potential buyers."

"Last night, Eline was supposed to meet us—my friends and me —for a drink," I said. "But she didn't come. Do you know why?"

Karen's already pale face blanched, highlighting the dark shadows under her eyes.

"We ate dinner here together before I went out," she said. "She told me then that she was planning to meet you, so she must have changed her mind, although I don't know why. That's been bothering me. Why would she agree to see you and then cancel?"

"So, she didn't mention any other plans? Did she say she was going to meet Pieter? Or go to a meeting with the lawyer?"

Karen's eyebrows shot up. "No. I didn't even know Pieter was in town."

I couldn't be sure the man we'd met was indeed Pieter. "Would you recognize him if you saw him?"

"Of course. He came to Tomas's funeral."

"Tall, slim, dark hair going grey? Mid-forties maybe?"

Karen nodded. "Yes, that's right. Why?"

I told her about the man who'd come to the house and looked around. "He could have been Pieter or an imposter. Either way, it seemed that he lied about seeing Eline later in the day."

"How strange. She certainly didn't mention him. She just seemed happy she was going to see you, excited that you and your colleagues were working at the house. She said it was a big step towards making the sale happen. That was good. It made me less concerned about..."

She put her hand to her chest and took a deep breath.

"Less concerned about what?" I prompted.

"About suicide. There, I said it. I didn't want to acknowledge it while Eline was alive. But I was afraid she might take her own life. She seemed so depressed and lost. She'd given up her career for Tomas and then he was gone. Of course, she had all the money in the world, but that's not what makes people happy."

After a long silence, I continued. "Eline rang me at about nine, an hour after we were supposed to meet."

"Could you tell if she was outside when she called? Was it noisy?"

I thought back but couldn't recall any sounds that might indicate where Eline had been.

"She could have dozed off on the sofa," Karen went on. "She hasn't slept properly for weeks, not since losing Tomas. Or maybe she just decided she was too nervous to go out by herself after all. I know she was scared of that man with the beard."

"She must have gone out after she called me, so something made her change her mind. But what and when?"

"I wasn't home, so I don't know what time she left. I was moderating an evening symposium at the university. I thought it would be okay to leave her, particularly as she would be out for part of the evening with you. Not that I had any choice, not without seriously ticking off my department head and the guest speakers I'd invited. I left at seven, and Eline said she'd watch television until it was time to see you. When I got back, at about eleven forty-five, she wasn't here. I rang her mobile a dozen times but there was no answer. Then I called the police." Karen snorted. "Fat lot of use they were. Said she'd probably gone for a walk." She knocked back the contents of her glass. "I called them several times after that, but they were no help."

"So you have no idea where she went, if she met someone, nothing?"

"Nothing."

She nodded at my glass. "Drink up. I'll get us another one."

I never drank sherry. And I didn't drink at this time of day usually, but I swallowed it down anyway and handed over my glass.

While Karen was in the kitchen, I thought about Eline's evening. Had she gone to meet Pieter?

"When do you think Eline would have gone out?" I asked when Karen came back.

A silver mobile lay on the coffee table. Karen picked it up and showed me a screen full of texts.

"I sent her a message when I got to the university," she said, pointing. "Just to check in with her. She replied straightaway." Karen's eyes misted as she read the text. It was in Dutch, which she translated. "Good luck," Eline had typed. "Give no quarter."

I raised an eyebrow.

"It was a private joke." Karen sighed. "Two of the guests on the panel are old adversaries of mine. One tore my last book to shreds. Eline had told me to take control and make them answer the hard questions. To show no mercy." She smiled. "I actually did a pretty good job. I was excited to get back and tell her about it."

She carried on scrolling. "I texted her again at nine during a short break. She said she was watching *Casablanca*, her favorite film. She's an incorrigible romantic."

"That's when she called me," I said. "Anything after that?"

"Nothing." Karen gripped the phone in both hands, her last link to her friend. "At eleven, I let her know I was on my way back but she didn't respond. I assumed she was already asleep."

We didn't speak for a while. Karen cried quietly, her falling tears forming dark spots on her green shirt. After a minute or two, she grabbed a tissue from a box on the table and blotted her face. Then she took a deep breath and lifted her chin. "I may never know what made her go out alone or how she ended up in a canal. I hope you can look after your friend better than I did mine." Her voice was still raspy from crying.

"This isn't your fault," I said, taking her hand in mine.

"Maybe not. I'm glad we met." She looked up, gazing at me with tear-swollen eyes. "Are you in danger too? Would you know if an aura appeared over you?"

I shook my head. "No. I can't see them in mirrors or photos, so there's no way of telling."

Just wondering if I had an aura made my stomach tighten into a painful knot.

Karen bit her lip. Her eyes brimmed again. "You look after yourself."

13

I walked slowly back to the house, pondering what Karen had told me about the man who'd been following Eline, and the break-in Eline hadn't mentioned. That wasn't so surprising. It probably wasn't good practice to advertise a burglary in the property she was intent on selling.

What was surprising was that, according to Karen, nothing of value had been taken. Had the burglars been looking for something in particular and, if so, had they found it? Was the man in the grey hoodie involved? I glanced around but saw no sign of him. He hadn't gone out of his way to remain hidden over the past few days. In fact, his presence seemed almost blatant, and Eline had seen him as well, sufficiently close up to make the sketch of him.

When I reached the Janssen house, I rang the doorbell. The door opened immediately, and Henk stood there with his coat on, apparently ready to leave for the day. His eyes, faded brown and cloudy with cataracts, rested on my face for a few seconds, making the heat rise in my cheeks. I took a step back to give him room to pass, annoyed with myself for letting him bother me. He couldn't know I'd been in Eline's room and, even if he did, why would it concern him?

As he shuffled past me on the front doorstep, his coat gave off a musty odor. My heart softened. After all, he was just an elderly man with a job to do. He probably lived alone in a poorly heated flat that didn't let his clothes air out. And his aura still circled.

"Henk," I called, and he turned around. "*Fijne middag!*"

I'd practiced a few phrases I'd found on a language app. 'Have a good afternoon' was the only one I remembered.

He nodded in acknowledgement and carried on walking.

"What are you up to?" I asked Alex when I reached the living room. She sprawled on a sofa with her laptop resting on her knees. I heard Sam talking in the kitchen, on his phone again.

Alex blushed. "Taking some time out." She turned her laptop towards me. "Looking at Eddie Redmayne pictures. I've seen all of his films. Look at this one. Doesn't he look just like Sam?"

"He does actually."

Alex lowered the lid on the computer. "Don't tell Sam. He thinks I'm working."

"I very much doubt that he cares whether you're working or watching cat videos. Or ogling Eddie Redmayne."

"No need to watch cat videos." Alex pointed to a gilt side table on the opposite wall. Between two bronze statuettes of naked Greek youths, Vincent sat, one leg up in the air, cleaning himself.

"I was sure he'd knock something over, but he didn't. Henk glared at him when he walked through, but Vincent just out-glared him. He's got attitude, that cat." She stood up and stretched.

"Did you have any luck talking with Henk?" I asked.

"Some. I can't tell if he really doesn't know much or if he's hiding something. He confirmed that he's been working here for eons, well before the Janssens moved in. He said the previous owner never actually lived here and just paid him to keep the place clean. He got a check every month."

"The previous owner was Martin Eyghels, right? That was the name on the sales deed when the Janssens bought the house."

Alex swung her legs off the sofa and sat up straight. "Yes. Henk said Eyghels' name was on the checks he received. He never met him though. Seems like no one did. The neighbors were increasingly irritated at having this chunk of real estate sitting empty. A huge house that's always dark can really weigh on a neighborhood. Henk said some of them started sending written complaints to the city council and the building department and posting copies of the letters through the front door here."

I nodded. "Sounds like London."

"Yeah, one of my friends is an estate agent in Knightsbridge. She says some areas are like cemeteries. Deathly quiet, which might be a benefit for some, but people don't usually choose to live in London for its peace and tranquility."

"So did the complaints do the trick? Eyghels decided to sell up?"

"It seems like it. Apparently, the house was sold privately to the Janssens, so they must have known Eyghels. And they asked Henk to stay. Henk said they were happy to have someone who knew the house as well as he did. He acted as a sort of security guard during the initial construction phase, and then stayed on when they moved in."

"Did Henk mention a burglary? Here, just after Tomas Janssen died?"

Alex's eyebrows shot up. "No, he didn't say anything about that. What happened?"

I related what Karen had told me. "Oh, and Eline drew a sketch of a man who'd been following her. It's the same one, the lovely chappie who's been watching us."

A flush of pink crept up Alex's neck. "Oh heck, Kate. I'm sorry. I thought you were imagining things. Well, I didn't really, but I didn't want to believe some creep was following us around in nice, friendly Amsterdam. I think we should confront him next time we see him and tell him to shove off."

"Or just tell the police," I suggested.

Alex smirked. "Not as much fun, but yeah, we should do that." She stood up and stretched her arms above her head. "Did Karen say anything about Pieter?"

"Not much. She only met him briefly at Tomas's funeral, but she thought my description of him sounded right. Apparently, Eline never mentioned the appointment she and Pieter were supposedly having with Bleeker yesterday evening."

"Which means Pieter did lie about that meeting?"

"It seems like it." My head was aching. Nothing made any sense. "Who's Sam talking to?"

"TBA's legal chap, Terry. Again." She looked at her watch. "We've got time before my dinner with Willem so let's all get out for a while. Sam wants to visit the Rembrandt museum. It's only a short walk."

We waited for Sam to finish on the phone. He didn't take long and soon wandered into the living room.

"Terry's anxious to get the feasibility study wrapped up. He wasn't thrilled to hear about the missing data on the upstairs floors. In fact, he said we should go ahead and break through the panels to see what's on the other side. TBA will cover all the costs for repairs if the sale doesn't close."

"I don't know, Sam," Alex said. "Bleeker was very specific about not making any material changes to the house until he's got the paperwork sorted out."

"I know. But on balance I think Terry is right. We need to see that space for ourselves in order to finalize the plans. If TBA's willing to take responsibility for any damages, I'm okay with that."

"Should we warn Bleeker we're going to do it?" Alex asked.

"No way," I said. "If we were to do everything at lawyer speed and abide by every dot and comma, the world would grind to a halt."

"I didn't think of you as a lawbreaker." Sam smiled.

"Yeah, well, I do my best. But my inner felon needs to be let out occasionally. Please don't tell my dad I said that. He's a barrister—retired, but he still does everything by the book. He'd be horrified."

Just thinking of Dad made me feel tearful. What the hell was wrong with me? Eline's death had unnerved me, perhaps more than it should have, given that I hardly knew her. I thought of Karen's anguish over losing her friend. I imagined the pain of losing Sam, the overwhelming grief of his grandmother and sister. Well, it was up to me to make sure that didn't happen.

I found myself not caring about the house or the project. Every time I looked at Sam and saw that swirling air, my heart ached.

"Give me a moment," he said. "Let me call Terry back. Get him to say that he's absolutely up for it. If he says it's okay, then we'll do it."

Sam's words faded and blared like a radio with a broken volume dial. My head pounded, my skin felt hot, my stomach hurt. I sank into the nearest armchair as Sam headed back to the kitchen.

"Are you all right?" Alex asked. She knelt down next to me.

"Not really. Eline died. Tessa died. Sam's in danger. I'm scared because I have no idea what's going on."

I had rarely felt this out of control. In the past, I'd managed to focus on the task in hand; this last couple of days, I seemed to be working hard but not making any progress. I'd failed Eline. Would I fail Sam too? The thought ricocheted around inside my head, lighting up sections of my brain that seemed to have gone dormant.

Falling back on old practices, I closed my eyes and took several deep breaths in an attempt to calm myself. Alex's hand was cool against mine when she took my fingers in hers and squeezed. It reminded me of how my mother used to console me when I was sad, holding my hand, binding us together, stronger as a single entity.

"This isn't all on you," Alex said. "You're not responsible for Eline's death. Or Tessa's. You can't hold yourself accountable for Sam's safety. Or Henk's, come to that." She sat back on her heels but kept hold of my hand. "Just because you see it coming doesn't mean you can stop it."

"Then what's the point?" I asked. My throat hurt. "Why do I see these signs if I can't do anything to help?"

"You are helping. We know that Sam is threatened and we're doing what we can to protect him."

I thought about what Karen had said about Eline's depression. Was it possible she'd committed suicide? That her death was completely unrelated to whatever threatened Sam? But what about the man in the hoodie? He'd been following Eline, and I was sure he was watching us. There had to be a connection. And then there was Pieter. Where did he come into it? He'd lied to us about the meeting, using it as an excuse to take a document from Eline's room. He certainly couldn't be trusted.

"I think we should talk to the police," I said.

Alex tilted her head and stared at me. "About what?"

"All of it. The man who was following Eline. Pieter's little charade here yesterday. Something's not right."

"I doubt the police would take you very seriously. Pieter is Tomas's family and he is inheriting the house. I think he had every right to come in and take anything he wanted."

"And lying about the meeting with Eline and Bleeker?"

Alex shrugged. "I'm sure there's a logical explanation. And the police can't arrest someone for lying, you know."

"Lying about what?" Sam walked back into the living room, mobile in hand.

"Pieter and that non-existent meeting with Bleeker," I said.

"What did Terry say?" Alex asked.

"No answer. He's in a meeting."

"Let's wait before breaking in then." Alex stood up. "I'd feel better knowing someone else is taking responsibility. Besides, I'm done apart from that one area. I think we should get out of this gloomy old building for a while."

"Good idea," Sam said. "I'm sure to hear from Terry sometime today. Assuming he confirms it's okay, we'll come back early tomorrow, break through the panel and update the drawings. Then we can hand the keys over to Henk and skedaddle by about ten."

"That'll give Henk time to have his morning coffee," Alex commented. "So, what do we do now?" Her eyes lit up. "I know. Let's go for a bike ride."

"How about a museum?" I suggested, thinking that would be a safe place for Sam.

"Bikes," Sam said. "Come on, Kate. Let's live a little."

Living was precisely what I had in mind, which meant not riding bikes on busy city streets.

Five minutes later, we were all outside, wandering slowly along the canal side. The waterways were pretty, I thought, but deadly. Eline had drowned in one. I wondered when her funeral would be. Who would organize it? Karen? I would make an effort to come back for it because I'd like to see Karen again. I hoped she was coping with the loss of her friend and decided to call her later to check on her.

"Watch out!" Sam grabbed my arm and yanked me out of the path of a cyclist, who flew past in a flurry of bike bell ringing and a torrent of impenetrable Dutch. So much for me looking after Sam.

"Good grief, Kate. You almost got hit. Be careful," Alex said. She gave my arm a squeeze.

"I will. Those bikes are scary."

"We'll be safer on a bike than walking," Alex said. She pointed to a bike rental place on the other side of the street. "Amsterdam is one of the safest cities in the world to ride a bike. Come on."

Sam overruled my second round of objections and we were soon equipped with bikes and maps. We rode towards the Jordaan quarter, once working-class and now gentrified, with pretty houses, art galleries and boutiques. It was interesting to see the world from the seat of a bike, zipping past pedestrians and keeping pace with the slow-moving traffic. Amsterdam was incredibly flat, we realized, apart from a few humpback bridges over the canals. But I found being in the bike lane nerve-wracking as experienced cyclists sped past, weaving impatiently through clumps of novice riders like us. My close encounter with a speeding bike had made me jumpy.

I pulled slightly ahead of Alex and Sam when they slowed to examine the brightly-lit window of a chocolate shop. The aroma of chocolate and vanilla was enticing, but I was intent on overcoming temptation. I rode on and, moments later, heard the trill of a bike bell, yelling, and the clatter of metal hitting asphalt.

Braking hard, I turned to see a crush of people twenty meters back and glimpsed a bent bike frame lying on the road. I jumped off my own bike, left it leaning against a railing, and ran, pushing my way through a circle of stationary cyclists.

A woman with nurse's scrubs under her coat crouched on the

ground. Kneeling opposite her, Alex gazed down at Sam's prostrate figure. She looked up when I called her name, her face a white oval in the encroaching dusk.

14

The next few minutes were chaotic. The nurse wasn't speaking English, so I couldn't tell if she was saying that Sam was okay or had been critically injured. His eyes were open, but he was very pale. Blood trickled from a cut on his cheek. His aura, barely visible in the fading light, still circled.

"Alex." I squeezed her arm. She appeared to have gone into shock. "What is the nurse saying?"

"What? Oh. She thinks he may have a concussion."

I knelt down next to Alex and gripped Sam's hand, which felt cold and damp in mine.

"Sam?" I said to him. "Can you hear me?"

He turned his head to look at me. "Of course I can. I'm not dead."

"The nurse thinks you have a concussion," Alex said.

Sam moved to get up, leaning his weight on one elbow. The woman gently pushed down on his chest.

"She said you shouldn't move yet until they check for broken bones," Alex told him.

Someone in the crowd must have called for an ambulance because we soon heard a siren wailing up a nearby street. Finally, it pulled up close by, and three men ran towards us, two of them carrying a stretcher, and the other a large bag. They cleared a space around Sam, making us move back to give them room to work. One of them leaned over him and checked for broken bones while another taped the cut on his cheek.

A uniformed policeman turned up and talked with the ambulance crew and then with Alex. Once he'd ascertained that no car had been involved in the accident, he hopped back on his bike and rode away. I doubted that every bike crash in the city warranted a police report.

"I don't need to go to the hospital," Sam protested when they started to load him onto the stretcher. "Truly, I feel fine."

"It's just a precaution, for some X-rays and to check for concussion," Alex told him.

He was still grumbling when they carried him away.

Alex thanked the nurse before pulling her own bike up from the ground. "Lucky she was riding past when Sam fell," she said to me. "They're taking him to the emergency room at the OVLG on Oosterpark."

Around us, the crowd was dispersing, people wandering away on foot or remounting their bikes to continue their journeys.

"I need my bike," I said, hoping it would still be where I'd left it. It was, and with some trepidation, I got back on it and followed Alex. The ride only took ten minutes along the Amstel river and we soon braked to a halt outside the hospital.

At reception, Alex explained who we were looking for, and we were told to wait for more information.

"What happened?" I asked Alex, after she'd pushed euros into a vending machine and carried two bottles of water over to where I sat on the edge of a hard, plastic seat.

"I'm not sure. It happened so fast. Someone cut in front of us and snagged Sam's front wheel. It twisted sideways and the bike went down."

"Was it an accident? Did you see the other cyclist?"

She unscrewed the top off her water bottle but didn't drink. "No, I didn't see his face. And I don't know. It could have been an accident.

But it's too much of a coincidence, right? That Sam is in danger and some maniac knocked him off his bike?"

I nodded.

Alex sighed and stood up to pace around the waiting room. I took a few big swallows of water, hoping it would calm the cramping in my stomach. It worried me that the emergency crew had insisted on bringing Sam here. Did they find signs of an injury that we couldn't see?

My mind full of bleak imaginings, I massaged my aching temples. Each time a door opened I looked up, hoping to see a doctor who would tell us what was happening. I'd just finished my water and was contemplating getting another when the door swung open again and a nurse strode towards us.

As she spoke to us in Dutch, I saw Alex's face relax. She waited until the nurse had gone and then threw her arms around me.

"He's all right. No concussion and no broken bones. He hurt his knee and has a few scratches. They'll be releasing him soon."

I felt weak with relief and tried to sit calmly while we waited. Still, another twenty minutes ticked by. Twenty minutes in which I berated myself for going along with the idea of a bike ride in what turned out to be rush hour. I was supposed to be protecting Sam and I was doing an awful job of it. Whether it was deliberate or an accident, Sam had come to harm. On my watch.

My dark thoughts evaporated when the door opened and Sam appeared. Alex jumped up and ran to him. He had a small dressing on his cheek and seemed to be limping slightly, but I was elated to see him on his feet. His aura still circled though, bursting my little happiness bubble almost at once.

"No real damage done," he announced with a grin. "I banged up my knee, and grazed my hand, but my head's in one piece. I think the bike got the worst of it."

"Ah, the bike. We just left it there," Alex said. "I suppose we should head back to retrieve it and turn everything in at the rental shop." Her bottom lip quivered. "It's all my fault. It was a stupid idea to rent bikes in the first place."

"Don't be daft," Sam said, wrapping an arm around her shoulders. "It's okay."

"Did you see who hit you?" I asked, as the hospital doors swished closed behind us. It was dark now, with a sliver of moon barely visible between the clouds.

"Not really. Someone, a man in jeans and a dark anorak, swerved in front of me, probably to avoid someone else. I didn't see what happened. But his front wheel hit mine and I ended up on the ground."

"Did he stop? Was he one of the people helping back there?" I thought back. Had I seen the man in the grey hoodie anywhere amongst those cyclists? I didn't think so, but the light had been dim, and I'd been moving too fast.

"I don't know," Sam said. "The fall took the wind out of me for a minute or two. But the way everyone was driving... is that the right word? Riding, I mean. It was so crowded he probably didn't even realize he'd knocked me over."

I wasn't so sure. But, then, if someone was trying to kill Sam, knocking him off a bike was a rather feeble way to go about it. Was it supposed to be another warning, like the fallen chandelier? If so, would there be another one? Was Death going to have another go at Sam, and not give up until something fatal happened? I'd let myself hope for a short few minutes that this was a turning point, that because Sam had survived this accident, he was out of danger. But then his aura would have disappeared. And it definitely hadn't. It was still there, rotating, sickly yellow under the hospital entry lights.

We collected our two bikes and pushed them to the nearest metro station, where we loaded them on to a train. After a short ride, we walked back to where Sam's bicycle waited, bent and abandoned. Someone had leaned it up against a wall, where it couldn't cause any more accidents. At least no one had taken it.

Our conversation with the rental company didn't take long. I suspected they were used to dealing with damaged bikes. Sam paid the bill and we flagged down a taxi to take us back to the Janssens' house where we'd all left our laptops and bags.

"I should cancel my dinner with Willem," Alex said as Sam unlocked the front door. "I don't want to leave you, Sam, not after what happened back there. Besides, there's not much point."

"You should go," Sam encouraged her. "He's a friend of your parents and you said you liked his company. It's not really polite to cancel..." He checked his watch. "With only thirty minutes' notice."

"That's very proper of you," Alex said. "But you're right. Don't have too much fun without me then."

While Alex got ready, Sam and I debated what to do with our evening. Takeaway food and television easily won the argument. We'd go to the hotel and hang out there, waiting for Alex to come back from her dinner. I tidied up the kitchen while Sam put out some dry food for Vincent. On my way to gather my things from the dining room, I heard my phone beep with an incoming text. It was from Karen. She asked if we could meet because she'd been thinking about something Eline had told her.

I hesitated before answering. Whatever Eline had said to Karen, it probably wouldn't make any difference to the future of the project. That now seemed to rest in the hands of the mysterious nephew. But Sam was still in danger. The bike event, whether an accident or deliberate, was a stark reminder of that, and I had to follow every lead possible to discover the source of the threat to him. If Eline had said something that would cast any light at all, then I had to know about it.

Besides, I liked Karen and wanted to see her again. I texted back and suggested that Sam and I meet her in our hotel bar in an hour. We could have a drink with Karen before settling into our takeaway food and television night.

When Karen confirmed the arrangement, I went into the kitchen to let Sam know. He wasn't there. The living room was empty too. I did a quick sweep of the guest bathrooms but didn't find him. Every empty space made my skin prickle. Where was he? Had he left something upstairs?

I hurried to the staircase, but it was in darkness and there were no lights on at the top, which meant he couldn't be up there. Glad I didn't have to investigate the creepy upper floors, I retraced my steps to the kitchen. On the counter, the dish of cat food sat untouched, and I realized we hadn't seen Vincent since coming back from the hospital. I guessed then where Sam might be. After taking the lift down to the lobby, I found, as expected, that the back door was wide open.

For a moment, I stood on the doorstep, waiting for my eyes to adjust to the darkness. The sky was still cloudy, offering only sporadic glimpses of a crescent moon. The only real light came from a street lamp that hung over the farthest corner of the garden, where overgrown shrubs clambered over the fence as though trying to escape. It was surprisingly quiet, considering we were in the middle of the city. An occasional car rumbled past. The breeze rustled the leaves of trees and bushes close by.

And then I heard Sam's voice. "Vincent, come on. Time for dinner."

I called out to Sam and jumped when he suddenly appeared in the rectangle of light from the lobby.

"I'm worried about Vincent," he said. "I hate to leave for the night without knowing he's okay."

"I'll help you look, but there's no way we can find him out here if he doesn't want to be found. Don't you have your phone? Turn the light on."

"Yes, but he won't like the bright light. It'd probably frighten him off. It's better if we just keep calling him. And I have a handful of kitty treats that should entice him out."

When he turned and wandered off, I hurried after him. From my quick reconnoiter the day before, I remembered that the garden was huge, as wide as the house from side to side, and perhaps a hundred feet long. At the far end was an iron fence that formed the boundary between the garden and a neighboring property, a commercial building that faced out on to a different street. We had a lot of ground to cover unless Vincent decided to come out of his own accord.

A prickly bush snagged my shoulder and I pulled my sweater free. Once again, I wondered why the garden was so neglected. Very few of the house windows overlooked it, and it wasn't really visible from the street that ran along one side, but I'd have thought that Tomas and Eline would have wanted to use it occasionally.

I looked up at the small house next door, where a window on the top floor was lit with a warm yellow glow. The people who lived there had surely been some of the neighbors who'd complained about the empty building. They may have been happy when the Janssens moved in, but it was sad for them that they still overlooked an unkempt garden.

Just then we heard a yowl. It had to be Vincent. He had a low, throaty voice that was quite distinctive. Sam headed towards the noise and I followed in time to see him scoop the cat up into his arms. Relieved that Vincent was safe, and eager to get out of the chill and dark, I turned back towards the house, careful to stay on the flag-stones between the uncut lawns and untamed shrubs. It took a few seconds for me to realize I'd taken a wrong path and was walking away from the light coming through the back door. As I was about to turn around, something rustled in front of me. A muffled footstep made me freeze.

"Sam?" I whispered.

In the darkness, I was sure I heard breathing. Then another foot-step. And then everything went quiet.

"Sam!" I called.

He materialized at my shoulder, still holding Vincent. "Are you all right?"

"I don't know. I thought I heard someone, just here."

Sam cradled Vincent in one arm while he dug in his pocket for his mobile and handed it to me. I blinked in the sudden bright light, feeling silly that I'd left my own phone on the kitchen table. I turned in a slow circle, the light hitting the leaves of bristling undergrowth and the gnarled bark of trees choked by climbing vines. There was no sign of a person, though.

"Wait," Sam said, "Look over there."

He guided my hand to lower the light and pointed to a corner formed by the back of the house and a dense hedge separating the

garden from the property next door. Among the shadows, I saw a
green light blinking. It was small, the size of a pound coin, and
seemed to be attached to the house.

"Is it an alarm?" I asked.

Vincent was squirming and suddenly launched himself from
Sam's arms. Thankfully, he made a dash for the open door. At least
we wouldn't have to find him again.

Sam and I moved towards the green dot, which pulsed steadily.
When we were closer, I saw that it was set in a steel panel screwed to
the wall of the house. It seemed like an odd place to be part of an
alarm system, far from the back door.

"What do you think?" I asked Sam.

He moved closer and examined the wall. "I don't really understand why it's here. There are no doors or windows close by."

I moved along the brick wall of the house until I reached the
hedge that separated the property from the one next door. Half as tall
again as I was, and very thick, the brambly foliage created a
formidable obstacle. It was hard to see through the thicket of shrubs
and weeds.

"Come on," Sam said. "There's nothing there."

But then the light reflected on something and I pushed the phone
up closer to peer in through the leaves.

"Look at that," I said. "There's a piece of metal in the ground
behind the hedge."

"It's just a manhole cover," Sam said. "Maybe part of the sewage
system."

We retraced our steps towards the back door, but something was
nagging at me. "Sam, I was sure I heard someone out there, just
before you showed up with Vincent. There's a flashing green light in
a strange place and I'm not convinced that piece of metal is a
manhole cover. It's square and about two meters wide. Can we go
back and take another look?"

"Whatever makes you happy," he said. "But we've only got five
minutes before I turn into a werewolf... always happens when I'm
hungry."

"Five minutes, I promise."

With the faintest of sighs, Sam followed me back to the hedge. Sharp twigs caught at our clothes and scratched our hands as we forced our way through the undergrowth to get a better view of the metal sheet. Sam tried to help by pushing ahead but accidentally let go of a branch, which rebounded and hit me on the cheek. The shock and the stinging pain that followed brought tears to my eyes. With my arms held up to protect my face, I wiggled the rest of the way through.

Beyond the spiky shrubbery, there was a strip of bare soil where the metal sheet lay, and then a six-foot-high concrete wall. If I had heard someone in the garden, it was unlikely that he or she had disappeared next door. The property line was impenetrable.

I knelt down to examine the metal while Sam held the light. "It's not solid," I said. "It's slotted."

The slots revealed nothing however, just darkness. When I ran my hand over the metal, I thought I felt a faint movement of air. That would make sense if the metal was covering a ventilation shaft of some kind. Half-expecting Sam's sewage theory to be correct, I breathed in, but the air smelled fairly fresh, tinged with a hint of damp. Sam crouched down next to me and took a sniff.

"It's probably just part of the house's heating and cooling system," he said. "We can ask Alex. She probably already has it marked up on her plans."

"Oh." I sat back on my heels. "That doesn't explain the flashing light, though."

"No, but I'm sure there's a reasonable explanation." Sam pushed to his feet, grimacing slightly. He massaged his injured knee for a few seconds and then straightened up. "Let's go, shall we? I want to make sure Vincent found his food."

Although there was no chance Vincent wouldn't remember where his food dish was, I stood up, ready to follow Sam back to the kitchen. As we emerged, scratched and scraped, from the jungle-like foliage, Sam's light hit the back wall of the house.

"Look at that," I said, pointing.

Sam went over to look more closely. Then, reaching up as high as he could, he ran his fingers along the wall and down to the ground. "Huh. It looks like there used to be a door here. See this line?"

I copied him, sweeping my hand along the wall, until I felt a distinct indentation that didn't follow the lines of grout between the old bricks. Instead it formed a door-sized rectangle just to the left of the green light.

"It's been closed up like that for some time, don't you think?" I said. "It's barely visible to the naked eye. I wonder if there's any sign of it from the inside?"

I hurried through the back door into the lobby. Sam came in more slowly and stopped to lock the door, sliding the bolt into place. "Dinner," he said. "Now, or I can't be responsible for my actions."

"But that bricked-up door..."

"The door can wait. It's been closed off for years."

15

The cat rescue mission and subsequent foray into the bushes meant we were running late to meet Karen.

"We can still make it," I told Sam.

"That sounds good," Sam said. "Because I really need to eat something very soon."

We locked up and decided to take a taxi to the hotel. I could tell that his knee was bothering him.

The hotel cocktail lounge could have been in London, New York, or Singapore. It was modern, all steel and glass, with cushioned bench seats and low lighting, aiming for sophisticated but settling for bland. Still, it was nice to sit down in a quiet corner where I felt myself relax, the tension of the bike incident and the garden exploration draining away in the candlelight.

Sam soon came back to the table with our drinks and several bowls of nuts and crisps and a plate of cheese. He tucked in immediately while I nibbled my way through a handful of nuts.

"Tall with red hair?" Sam said, looking at the door.

I saw Karen at the entrance. She scanned the tables, gave me a little wave and made her way over. This evening, she was wearing a green dress that brushed her calves and matching green suede flats. I introduced her to Sam, who asked her what she'd like to drink.

"Gin and tonic," she said. "Thank you."

While Sam went to the bar, I asked her how she was doing.

"Not so bad, I suppose. I had classes all day, which was a good distraction. Anything new with you?" She glanced over at Sam, who was chatting to the bartender, his aura eddying blue under the LED lights above the bar. "How is he doing?"

"He's doing okay. He had a bike accident earlier this evening that freaked me out, but there was no serious damage."

Sam came back with the drinks and we chatted for a few minutes about Karen's class at the university.

"So, you had something you wanted to tell us?" I asked finally.

"Yes, I've been thinking about it all day. About three months ago, Eline said something that I didn't pay much attention to at the time. She thought that Tomas had got caught up in some business deal that had gone bad. Well, I don't know much about business, so I didn't have a clue what that meant and didn't pay much attention. But she mentioned several times that Tomas seemed very stressed although he wouldn't talk to her about it. I wondered later if that stress contributed to his heart attack."

"Before you go on," Sam said. "I think we should tell you that the house project has been put on hold while the lawyer sorts out the paperwork. It could take months, and we're not even sure the house sale will go through. Which means I'm not sure how relevant this stuff about Tomas is, to be honest."

Karen's neck flushed red, and little circles of pink bloomed on her cheeks. "Well, I don't want to waste your time," she said.

Sam looked mortified, his eyes lowered like a little boy who'd broken his mother's favorite plate. "I didn't mean that we don't care about what's going on," he said. "And I am truly sorry that Eline died."

I leaned towards him and put my hand on his arm. "The issue for me, Sam, is that we may be out of the picture on the house development, but you are not out of danger." I spoke as gently as I could. "Your aura is still there. Maybe it will go away if the sale is officially canceled and you go back to London. I hope so, but I can't count on it. I still believe that Eline's death and your... situation are connected. Any information we can gather on Tomas and Eline might be helpful in uncovering the source of the threat to you.

He frowned, drawing his brows together. "I wish..." He looked at Karen. "I'm sorry. I wish none of this was happening."

Karen nodded. "Me too. This is all so far outside my usual routine and experience that I barely know what I'm doing or saying. I didn't mean to criticize you."

"So, back to the business deal gone bad," I said. "Did Eline say anything more?"

"She mentioned several times that she was worried about Tomas. He took a lot of phone calls in his office, where he couldn't be overheard, and went out for hours at a time without telling her where he was going. It wasn't that unusual, of course, for him to be busy. He was on several company boards and attended a fair number of meetings. But Eline thought this was different. He never talked about where he'd been." Karen took a sip of her drink. "Eline was very smart. But Tomas treated her like a child in my opinion. I know he loved her deeply, but there was a paternalism that irritated me. He was older than she was by about ten years and that age gap sometimes showed. He paid all the bills himself, for example, as if he didn't trust her to do it, even though she'd successfully run an entire hospital department for years before they met."

"Or maybe he just didn't want her to see his financial details?" Sam suggested.

Karen looked thoughtful, running her finger around the rim of her glass. "It's possible. They had several bank accounts. She had her own for buying clothes and jewelry and they shared one for joint expenses like travel. But once, when I asked her if Tomas had a big mortgage on the house, Eline said she didn't know. She didn't even know about any of their investments. So, yes, I think he kept his financial situation pretty close to his chest. Eline was stunned when she got a valuation on that house of nearly ten million euros. She had no idea it was worth that much."

Karen drained the last of her gin and tonic, and Sam jumped up to order another round.

"Oh, and there's something else," she said. "Eline and Tomas had a safety deposit box. She gave me a key and, about two weeks ago, she had me go to the bank with her to sign some forms so I can have access to the box."

That was a surprise. "What's in it?"

"I have no idea. I haven't looked yet."

"Do you know why? I mean, do you know why she did that?"

"I've never married. Never seemed to have the time or the inclination. But Eline was really happy to be a wife. She loved having a life partner and called Tomas her soulmate. After he died, she was distraught. She told me she felt as though she'd been marooned on an island, alone. That upset me, of course. I told her she had me." Karen smiled. "Anyway, she said she'd feel better knowing I had a key and access to the box. It has some of her mother's jewelry in it, she said, and she wanted me to have it if anything happened to her. But I don't know the legalities of it all." She sighed. "I suppose I should contact her lawyer and find out."

"Probably," agreed Sam. "It's possible that Pieter is entitled to half of whatever's in that box, depending on how the will was drawn up."

"Do you think we should ask Bleeker some questions about Tomas?" I asked. "If Eline was right about him being involved with something shady, perhaps Bleeker would know."

"I doubt it," Sam said. "If Tomas was stupid enough to get himself caught up in something illicit, would he talk to someone in the legal profession about it?"

"He might, if he needed legal advice," Karen said. She stared off into space, biting her lower lip. "Eline was really upset yesterday," she said after a long silence. "What if she'd found out why Tomas was so stressed? Uncovered some sort of crime?"

"I suppose it would be very distressing to learn that your husband was doing something illegal," Sam said.

"Distressing enough to commit suicide?" Karen shook her head. "I can't imagine that. But none of it makes sense. Where was Eline going last night? And why didn't she tell me?" Her hands cradled her stomach as though it hurt. "What on earth happened to her?" She took a deep breath.

"Have you had a look around the house? I'm wondering if Eline left anything that might give us a clue about what Tomas was up to."

"Kate would know that better than me," he said with a smirk. "She's had a good rummage through Eline's room."

Karen raised her brows. "Did you find anything?"

"Just your address. Which is all I was looking for, Sam. I didn't dig around more than I needed to."

"Hey, it wasn't an accusation. Just a statement of fact."

"Shall we take a look then?" Karen said.

Sam swallowed the last of the peanuts. "I'm not sure about that. We're supposed to be out of the house in the morning. We have to give the keys back to the janitor or whatever Henk is."

"Well, we still have access to the house this evening," she said. "I'd really like to get to the bottom of this thing about Tomas." She clasped her hands in her lap. "Will you help me?"

I was torn. I wanted to find something that might explain what was going on because that could save Sam. But poking around that old house at night seemed unnecessarily risky. What if we were being watched? I thought of the hoodie man with the blond goatee. A glance around the bar assured me there was no sign of him. And this was our last chance. We wouldn't have time in the morning, and Henk would almost certainly be around then. If there was a clue in Eline's room, we'd never know.

And I needed that clue, anything that would point me in the right direction. Sam's life depended on it.

"I say we do it," I said.

Sam looked unhappy. "Is this a good idea?"

"It's not a good idea to sit back and wait for whatever threatens you to happen," I said.

Sam ran his hand through his hair, something I'd noticed him doing more each day. A nervous tic, or an unconscious attempt to detect the aura over his head perhaps. "All right," he said. "I'll get the bill and we'll go."

Twenty minutes later, the three of us stood on the doorstep of the old house. The street was quiet. An older couple strolled past, arm in arm, but there was no one else around. A fine drizzle shrouded the streetlights in yellow mist.

"Hurry up, Sam," I said. "I'm getting wet."

We dashed in as soon as he had the door unlocked, and Karen led the way to the lift. When we reached the apartment, we turned on all the lights, which made me feel better about what we were doing. We'd been working here late the last couple of evenings, I reasoned. This wasn't so different.

"Where shall we start?" I asked.

"Let's take a look at the room that used to be Tomas's office," Karen said, moving off along the corridor. Sam and I followed.

When she opened the last door on the right and turned on the light, we found a sparsely furnished room: a black desk under a window that looked out over the street and a bookcase decorated with a few leather-bound books, a marble bust that may have been of Beethoven, and a small gilded globe.

"It looks as though it's been completely cleaned out," I said.

Karen went to the desk and pulled open each of the drawers. "Empty. I was hoping we'd find something."

"Let's go through Eline's room," I said. "She had piles of papers and stuff in there."

When we walked into Eline's room, my throat flushed warm as I thought of my earlier search in here. I was my father's daughter. I usually played by the rules and didn't even jaywalk, but when there were lives at stake, I'd been known to step out of bounds, sometimes in fairly dramatic fashion.

Karen gazed around the room and then pointed to the mounds of paper on the dressing table. "Let's look at those."

Sam and I stood by as Karen rifled through the first stack. "Mostly bills," she said, turning her attention to another pile.

"Pieter's already been through those papers," I said. "Maybe he took what you're looking for."

"I hope not," she muttered, moving papers around.

I picked up a few envelopes that were lying on a chair but none of the words made sense to me. We weren't going to be of much help, I realized.

"I'll go make some tea," I said.

Sam must have felt the same way. "I'll come with you. If that's all right with you, Karen?"

When she muttered in response, we wandered towards the kitchen and I put the kettle on.

"I have a feeling this will be a waste of time," Sam said.

"But if it makes Karen feel that she's doing something that might help, it's worth it. Pass me the teapot, please."

We poured tea and sat at the kitchen table. Vincent padded in moments later. He jumped up on the counter and glared at his empty bowl.

"You'll get fat," Sam told him, but he stood up to open another tin of food.

"Did you text Alex to let her know we won't be at the hotel after dinner?" I asked.

Sam frowned and took his phone out of his pocket. "I did it before we left. But I haven't heard anything back yet."

"Well, she's probably still eating."

Karen came in just then, breathless and flushed. "I found something. Before Eline's mother died a year ago, she wrote to Eline every week. Eline kept all her letters in an old chocolate box. I found this in it, deliberately hidden, I think."

She sat down and spread a piece of paper on the tabletop. "This is a photocopy of a letter addressed to someone called Martin Eyghels. Tomas signed it."

"Martin Eyghels is the previous owner of the house," Sam said. "His name is on the deed."

"Well, he and Tomas must have had some kind of agreement about the house, because this letter says that Tomas is asking to be released from it."

"What?"

"It says here that Tomas understands he had agreed to sell the house back to Eyghels if and when the occasion arose. But, Tomas says here, he has decided he needs to provide a permanent home for Eline, that she loves the apartment and would be heartbroken if she had to leave it." Karen looked up at us. "Huh, didn't I tell you that Tomas never really understood Eline? She did love the apartment but only because she was in it with him. When he died, she could hardly wait to move out. The place is vast and, quite frankly, unsettling. It has a malevolent feeling to it."

I thought about the falling chandelier and the broken picture chain and the empty spaces upstairs. Not to mention all the auras over people connected with the house. Karen was right about it being sinister.

"What else does the letter say?" Sam prodded.

Karen skimmed the words again. "Tomas says he has rewritten his will, leaving the house to Eline and to his nephew, having already agreed with Pieter that he will allow Eline to continue living in it for as long as she desires. But..." She frowned. "Really?" Screwing her eyes up, she read the typed text again. "But Tomas goes on to say that he is wiring eight million euros to Eyghels as a penalty for reneging on the agreement."

"Eight million?" Sam asked.

"How much did he pay for it in the first place?" I asked.

Sam thought for a second. "I can't remember the exact figure, but it was about two million, I think."

"That sounds about right," Karen said. "It needed a huge amount of work. It was only barely habitable when Tomas and Eline moved in."

"But I don't get it," I said. "Why would anyone have an agreement to sell a house back to its original owner?"

"Perhaps it was a complicated leaseback situation," Sam mused. "Maybe Eyghels provided the financing for Tomas to buy it and renovate it at some preferential rate because he knew he'd get a good deal on repurchasing it once all the renovation work was done. But, in order to buy his way out of their agreement, Tomas pays Eyghels the eight million in lieu of returning the house to him. I'll do some digging around. I'd like to find out more about Martin Eyghels. When was this letter dated?"

Karen checked. "Four months ago. It's odd. Eline never mentioned any of this to me, about this agreement to sell back to Eyghels."

"This must be the deal Tomas was worrying about," Sam said. "Maybe Eyghels turned down Tomas's offer of the eight million euros. Perhaps he wanted more. Or he didn't want the money at all. He just wanted the house back." He ran his hands through his hair. "You know, it's possible Pieter discovered that Tomas had originally agreed to sell the house back to Martin Eyghels? He might feel he has to honor that agreement and offer Eyghels right of first refusal, at least."

"Even if that's true, he should still have the decency to let us know what he's doing and to let Bleeker know too," I said. Pieter's behavior was getting under my skin. Didn't he realize that we needed to hear from him?

"That agreement would be void if Eyghels accepted Tomas's payment of eight million euros, wouldn't it?" Karen asked.

"It would." Sam frowned.

"Well, in order to work it out," I said. "We need to find out if that money was sent."

Karen nodded. "I'll go look through the rest of the paperwork. Can you give me just half an hour? And then we can go home."

Sam looked at me. "What do you want to do?"

"Let's go downstairs and check out that flashing green light and closed-off door."

"I don't think we should leave Karen here alone."

She put one hand on her hip and glared at Sam. "Oh please. I'm a big girl."

Karen didn't have an aura, which meant she'd be all right. "We'll be back in ten minutes," I promised.

16

D ownstairs, I pushed the door open to the original kitchen. The odor of old smoke and grease hit us as we walked in. Sam fumbled around until he found a switch. Old-fashioned fixtures came on, casting a dim light, barely enough to see by.

"The location of the bricked-up door should at the end of this hallway." I led the way past the ancient tiled counters and the soot-covered fireplace into a long corridor. Something moved in the darkness and I froze.

"Mice," Sam said, taking my hand. I saw one then, scampering along the grimy floor in front of us. I wasn't keen on mice. "Come on." He tugged gently on my arm.

We walked to a door at the far end of the hall. Sam pushed it open, and we found ourselves in what must have been an old scullery. The walls were lined with shelves, empty for the most part, except for a broken pot here and there. Spider webs glistened in the corners.

I focused on what we were doing, trying to ignore the mice and spiders. "It should be on this back wall somewhere, although it might be covered up by this shelving," I said.

Sam took a few steps forward and tripped over a metal bucket.

The noise was deafening. "Who'd leave a bucket in the way like that?" he grumbled.

"There is a door." I pointed to white-painted wood barely visible behind a run of shelves. "Do you think that's the inside of the closed-off entry?"

"Give me a hand moving this." Sam started pulling a section of the shelving unit away, and we dragged the rest of the greasy shelves off their supports until we had access to the door. Sam tried to open it, but found it was either stuck or locked.

I held my phone light up close. "This door appears to be fairly new," I said. "It's not from the nineteenth century like the rest of the kitchen, that's for sure."

"This wasn't on any of your sketches or plans?" Sam asked.

"No. Alex and I assumed this rabbit warren of rooms and pantries was just going to be torn out, so we didn't draw in the details, just the basic measurements."

Sam rattled the knob again. "Any good at picking locks?" he asked.

"I skipped that class." I looked around for something we could use to break the door open, retraced my steps, and found an old copper skillet.

"Give it a bash with this." I handed it to him. "In for a penny, in for a pound," I added when he looked unsure. "We're almost certainly breaking a half-dozen laws already. May as well add trespassing and vandalism to the list."

"But what if..."

"Go on. No one ever comes down here."

Sam whanged the pan against the lock. It took three tries, but finally the knob fell away. He pulled the door open.

"Are you seeing this?" he asked, holding up his phone to shed light on the dark room. We were staring into what seemed to be a wiring closet. Hefty bunches of cables of different colors were neatly tied along the walls, some of them disappearing up through the ceiling, while others led to a large white metal cabinet in the corner.

"This is modern." I ran my hand along a loop of wires. "And there isn't a speck of dust in here. What do you think? Perhaps the whole thing is a huge alarm system. But still, the flashing light outside is in an odd place."

"So is that." Sam pointed to the dark corner of the closet. "There are stairs going down."

We moved towards it. When I stared down into inky darkness, my heart raced, and my palms started to sweat.

"Let's take a peek," he said, one foot already outstretched to take the first step down.

"No, let's head back. Come on, Sam."

"Wait for me here then." Sam went down two steps.

"Absolutely not."

The steps were metal and curved in a gentle spiral. I gripped the handrail and followed him. After descending ten or twelve steps, we found ourselves in an unlit tunnel about four feet wide.

"There was no basement marked on the plans," I said. "So, this is really weird."

Sam wasn't really listening. He'd moved forward to examine a shiny steel door set in a brick wall. "It's locked with a keypad," he said. He punched a few keys. Nothing happened. "Let's see where the tunnel goes."

He took a step towards it, but I pulled him back. "Wait. It could be dangerous."

Sam rolled his eyes. "Life is dangerous. I don't skydive, you use hand sanitizer. We each do what we can to reduce our risk. But death can come from anywhere or from nowhere. A distracted driver. A falling tree. My feeling is that the more we uncover about what's going on here, the closer we'll be to understanding why Eline died and who or what is threatening me."

I blinked at him, amazed by this turnaround. Earlier in the day, he'd been so resistant to digging around for more information.

He threw his hands up in the air when he saw the expression on my face. "Look, I'm trying to say I'm sorry. I should have trusted you completely and followed your lead. It's taken me longer than it should. Shall we do this?"

"Definitely."

I followed as he led the way along the tunnel. The lights from our phones bounced off brick walls and a ceiling that curved gently over our heads, reminding me of the wine cellar in my dad's Italian farmhouse. When a puff of fresh air briefly cooled my skin, I glanced up to see the vent we'd found earlier. The tunnel, I realized, ran under the house and along the edge of the garden, presumably all the way to the back fence.

We'd only been walking for a minute when Sam slowed down and held his hand up, warning me to be quiet. Not that I'd been making much noise. I was tiptoeing along and not speaking, trying not to even breathe too hard. We'd reached the end of the tunnel. Ahead, a set of metal stairs ran up to a steel door like the one we'd just passed. My chest was ready to burst with pent-up tension as Sam eased his way up the steps.

"Please come back now," I whispered.

He kept going however, and I hurried to catch up. My boot caught the edge of a metal tread and I fell forward, my hand slamming onto the step above with a noisy thud.

"This one has a keypad too," Sam said from the top.

"Ok. There's nothing we can do then. Let's go."

As I turned to descend the steps, lights came on, illuminating the staircase and the tunnel. I yelled at Sam to run, certain someone would burst through the steel door. We slid down the steps and dashed along the tunnel. It was easier to move fast now that we could see where we were going. We raced up the spiral staircase at the other end, through the wiring closet, and into the old scullery. There we paused for breath, and I leaned over with my hands on my knees.

"What the hell was that all about?" I asked while Sam pushed the door closed and hauled one of the heavier bits of shelving in front of it.

"We don't want anyone getting into the house from the tunnel," he said, as he positioned another unit in front of the first one. "And it would be best if no one realizes we know about this place."

"That's a cheery thought." I took a deep breath. "What do we do now?"

"There's something I want to check out. Follow me."

We walked back through the lobby to the back door, which he'd secured earlier. He unlocked it, stepped outside and led the way along the back wall to where the light blinked.

"Oh God, the light isn't green any longer. It's red." I grabbed Sam's arm.

"And it's right outside the wiring closet."

I closed my eyes, mentally reviewing the layout. Sam was right. "So, at some point, an old door was closed off and the wall sealed to create a closed-in space."

"Come on, I have an idea."

"No, wait. We probably triggered some sort of alarm when we broke into that wiring closet, or when we entered the tunnel, or both. I think we should go back in the house and lock the doors."

Ignoring me, he set off towards the iron fence at the back of the property. My eyes were more used to the darkness this time, and I managed to avoid any painful confrontation with the spiny shrubs that overhung the flagstone paths.

The windows of the three-story office block on the other side of the fence were unlit and there were no signs indicating what kind of business it contained. From where we stood, it was just a dull and innocuous-looking modern structure. But it seemed that the steel staircase at the end of the tunnel led into that building somewhere.

Sam turned around and leaned against the fence, facing towards the house. He moved a few feet further along and then turned again. "There," he said, pointing.

When I caught up with him I saw that the red flashing light was clearly visible. "What does that mean?" I asked.

"I'm not sure. Maybe some kind of visual warning system?"

He turned and pointed to the car park on the other side of the fence. It was no more than a square of asphalt with a few marked parking spaces right behind the building. "It would be seen easily from the car park there."

The roar of a car engine drowned out his last words, and white light filled the street beyond the building. When I heard the squeal of brakes, I grabbed Sam's arm. "Let's go. We can easily be seen from over there too."

We dashed away from the fence along a winding flagstone path that led back to the house. When the vehicle turned into the car park next to the modern building behind us, Sam stopped and pulled me down to the ground, where we crouched in the shelter of an overgrown shrub. For a few seconds, the car's bright white high beams shone like searchlights on the wall of the house before they snapped off.

Peering through the tangle of branches, I saw a man get out of the vehicle, a BMW, I thought. He walked to the fence and stared into the garden. It was too dark to see his features, but his build made me think it could be the goatee man. Although there was no way he could get through that fence, my palms grew damp and my skin crawled.

We waited in the shadows until he turned away from the fence and went into the commercial building through a side door. As soon as he was out of view, we jumped up and ran to the house, leapt across the step and slammed the door closed.

Without pausing, we ran across the lobby, up the stairs to Eline's bedroom. Karen was still there, reading papers. She flung them on the bed when she saw us.

"Thank God! Are you all right? You seemed to be gone forever."

I let Sam do most of the talking while I caught my breath. He described the wiring closet downstairs and the tunnel that led to the commercial building.

"We must have triggered an alarm," I said. "Someone drove into the car park over there. It might have been the man who was following Eline, the one she made the sketch of."

"Do you know what they do in that building?" Sam asked. "What sort of business is it?"

"No idea, but it'll be simple enough to find out," Karen said. "I'll check it online. Come and sit down. You look as though you could do with a cup of tea." She led the way to the kitchen.

Karen did some research on her phone while Sam made tea. "I found that building," she said. "It's rented to a graphics design firm called Alpha Design." She looked up at us. "What do you think is going on? The tunnel is a secret passageway between that office building and this house? But for what purpose?"

"I've no idea," Sam said. "But it can't be anything good."

17

The tea finally settled my nerves enough that I stopped shaking.

"I think we should tell the police about the tunnel and the alarm system," I said.

"It could be nothing," Sam said. He stood up and leaned against the counter. "But I agree. The tunnel doesn't show up on the plans. None of the paperwork mentions an alarm system or any hint of a connection to the office building. All of that should have been detailed in the preliminary inspection reports."

"Eline mentioned once that the business must be doing well. There were always cars parked in front and people going in and out," Karen said.

I thought about that. Did those employees know about the secret tunnel? And what was the point of it if it only led to a wiring closet in the abandoned kitchen downstairs? I was wondering if there was another entrance into the house that we hadn't seen when Sam waved his hand in front of my face.

"Hello? Are you still with us?"

"Yes. And thinking of strange items not shown on plans, we still don't know what that concrete pillar is for," I said.

"What pillar?" Karen asked.

Sam quickly described the mysterious concrete structure that he'd found behind the walls.

"So maybe the next logical step would be to go up to the top floor and break in through the paneling there," Karen said. "That might explain what it's doing there."

Sam checked his watch. "We'll do that first thing in the morning. It's almost one, and I'm knackered."

"Perhaps we should just stay here for the night?" I suggested. I was worried about Sam's leg. His limp had become more pronounced. Far from resting it as advised by the doctor, he'd been running around on it all evening. It seemed best to get him to sleep on one of the comfortable couches.

"So, is it okay if I stay too?" Karen asked. "I'd really like to get to the bottom of all those papers and I want to be here when you investigate upstairs."

I felt uncomfortable about sleeping in a guest bedroom because I'd be separated from Sam, so I suggested we both camp in the living room. Karen said she'd work on the papers for an hour or so before taking a nap on Eline's bed. Sam and I collected some blankets and pillows and settled on the cushy sofas. After making sure our phones were being charged up, we checked our messages. Sam said Alex had texted to say she was going straight to her aunt's house after dinner and would see us first thing in the morning. Josh had texted me several times over the course of the evening, so I responded to all of his messages, wishing we were at home together. There was no point in worrying him with stories of secret tunnels and alarm systems, so I stuck to the basics and told him we were doing fine and that I'd be home on Friday.

As I fidgeted on the sofa, adjusting my pillow and trying to stop the blanket from falling off, I thought wistfully about my own comfortable bed with Josh in it. About our Saturday morning routine of coffee at our favorite cafe, before wandering through the market to buy provisions for a nice dinner. Every week, Josh bought me flowers from the same stall. For a minute, the sweet fragrance of last weekend's white roses floated around me. Then I breathed in again and smelled only dusty fabric and lemon-scented furniture polish.

From where I lay, the sky filled the window, but it was overcast, tinged orange from the city's streetlights. Occasionally, a sprinkling of stars twinkled for a moment before being blotted out by swollen purple clouds.

Sam seemed to fall asleep quickly. His breathing was soft and regular. I remembered a camping trip we'd taken to the Brecon Beacons in Wales. There'd been six of us, looking forward to a weekend away from London, planning to roast chestnuts on blazing fires under a full moon. But we'd never even seen the moon or managed to light a fire. For two days, cold rain had inundated our campsite, filling the fire pit with grey, ashy water and washing away one of our tents. Determined to make the best of it, we'd huddled together inside the remaining tent, sipping tea made on a thermos stove and telling scary stories. At night, while the rest of us struggled to get any sleep at all, Sam had slumbered peacefully, as he did now.

I moved my pillow around and willed myself to go to sleep. But the more I tried, the more awake I felt. A floorboard creaked, and I bolted upright, my heart pounding. It took a few seconds to recall that Karen was in the house. Maybe she couldn't sleep either.

I eased myself off the couch and, using the light from my phone screen, I tiptoed into the hall. All the doors were closed. Reluctant to disturb Karen if she was asleep, I turned back towards the living room.

I'd only taken two steps when the sound of another creaking board froze me in place. My heart pounded so hard against my ribs that it hurt. Willing myself to calm down, I strained to listen. There it was again, another creak. It came from the staircase at the end of the corridor. Someone was in the house. Had they come through the tunnel? I couldn't imagine how. I was sure that Sam had secured the entrance to the wiring closet with all that heavy shelving.

Moving on legs made of cement, I walked towards the nearest light switch, near the kitchen.

And then someone grabbed me from behind. A hand went over

my mouth, muffling my scream. The smell of musty wool filled my nostrils while Dutch words whispered in my ear.

I struggled, twisting my head to face my attacker.

It was Henk.

He let go of me and put a finger to his lips.

"What the hell are you doing?" I kept my voice low although I wanted to scream at him. He whispered back in a torrent of Dutch that made me throw my hands up in frustration. I needed Karen to sort this out.

Grasping his coat sleeve, I guided him along the hallway to Eline's bedroom door. His eyes widened but he kept quiet as I knocked and then pushed the door open. Karen was still sorting through papers by the light of a table lamp.

She jumped when she saw me. "What's the matter?"

I opened the door wider so she could see Henk. They seemed to recognize each other. Henk inclined his head in acknowledgment.

"Can you ask him why he's back in the house and wandering around in the dark and why he grabbed me and scared me half to death?" I asked Karen.

Shivering with cold and the residual panic of being grabbed in the dark, I pulled my cardigan tighter around me while the two of them talked.

"Henk says he came to warn us," Karen said finally. "He says we should leave now and never come back, that the house is evil and will hurt us."

"Oh, not that again," I said. "He told us that when the chandelier fell from the ceiling. Why now though? In the middle of the night?"

Karen shrugged. "It's hard to understand some of what he says. He speaks in riddles half the time. To be honest, I think he's a little crazy. He says the house has ears, and that it's watching us. And he seems to know about the broken panels on the second floor."

"So, he's been walking around, checking up on us," I said. "But maybe he knows something useful. Can you ask him about the concrete pillar? Does he have any idea why it's there?"

Karen talked to Henk. I watched for a reaction. Even though he shook his head, I didn't believe he didn't know something. He blinked several times and shuffled backwards a few inches.

"Henk," I begged. "Please tell us what you know."

When Karen repeated my words, he lifted his eyes to stare at me. In the lamplight, they were amber, like Vincent's. I stared back, noticing that his aura was moving faster. Not a good sign.

He spoke to Karen again and then turned away, shuffling along the hall towards the stairs.

"Is that it? That's all he's going to say?" I asked Karen as we heard the front door open and close. I was wide awake now, adrenaline still pumping through my body. "I need a cup of tea."

"He's a strange one," Karen said, as we walked to the kitchen. "I never did understand why Tomas kept him around. Still, he was always kind to Eline." She looked over at me as she filled the kettle. "Do you believe all that about the house being evil?"

I thought about it. "I think this house has secrets."

My eyes drifted to the sledgehammer leaning against the wall. "You saw how Henk reacted to the question about the concrete pillar?" I asked. "It means something. I think we should find out what. We need to break into the top floor, to see if the damn thing goes all the way up. Or if it is a structural support for something up there."

"Like what?"

I'd had an idea but decided to wait to see for myself. "Let's do it. Now."

"I'll go put my shoes on," Karen said.

"I'll wake Sam."

It took a couple of firm shakes to awaken him. When his eyes opened, he bolted upright, looking panicked.

"It's all right," I rushed to reassure him. When I explained the plan, he jumped up and followed me. We stopped to collect the hammer.

Five minutes later, we stood facing a green wood panel in one of the two vast chambers on the top floor. The portable lamp threw hard white light against the faded paint.

"Do you think it will be the same as the one below?" Karen asked. "With all the old pipes and cables?"

That seemed the most likely, but I was still hoping for an answer to the question of the concrete pillar.

"Alex will be gutted to miss out on all this," Sam said. "But the time has come." He lifted the sledgehammer, steadied himself, and banged it into the wall.

Karen and I took a few paces back as splinters of wood flew from the paneling. With just three more blows, which were deafening in the echoing, empty room, he'd made a sizable hole. He put the hammer down and stood back to examine his handiwork. "We need a bigger hole," he said with a grin. He seemed to be enjoying the destruction.

After another few hits, the hole was big enough to walk through. We carefully peeled away jagged pieces of heavy wood, surprised to see that the back side of the paneling was lined with sound-deadening insulation and painted white.

"That's different," Sam said, passing a piece to me. "The wall downstairs was just plain wood."

I turned on my phone light and pointed it through the shattered panel. Crowding together, we all peered in.

"What the heck?" Sam asked. In the darkness beyond, a strip of blue and green lights flickered on and off. A soft hum emanated from the space. And there was warm air in there, far warmer than the chilly damp chamber we were standing in.

"Shall we?" I asked, already stepping carefully through the opening Sam had created. He stopped to reposition the portable lamp so that it shone through the hole. The bright light illuminated the center of the room, leaving the edges in deep shadow.

We were in an area roughly eight feet wide and twice as long, similar to the space we'd found behind the painted panels on the floor below. Above, a row of skylights offered glimpses of the night sky. Those windows were invisible from the garden, I realized.

Four sleek black and chrome desks and office chairs were lined up along one wall. Each desk held a computer keyboard, a mouse, and three large monitors.

"Good lord," Sam said. "I didn't expect to find an office in here."

"A functioning one," I said, pointing to a six-foot tall glass cabinet housing what looked like a computer server, with its green and blue lights winking on an array of black boxes. At one desk, a coffee mug sat on a coaster, and a jacket lay draped over a chair, but there were no piles of papers, no photos in frames, no topical cartoons taped to the monitors as there were in our offices in London. I picked up the cup. A half-inch of coffee sloshed around in the bottom. It was cold but seemed fresh, not something that had been abandoned days ago.

"What do you think they do up here?" Sam asked.

"And who are 'they'? This seems like a very high-spec technology set-up."

"Software development? Financial trading?" Sam suggested as I followed Karen towards a hefty steel door at one end of the room. It appeared to be the main entry into the office, and it was protected with a keypad. She pulled on the handle, but the door didn't budge.

"Interesting that you need a code to get out," I said, inspecting the keypad.

"Interesting and scary," Karen said. "Why all the security?"

We'd reached the end of the office, so we turned back to walk slowly past the desks and the server. We joined Sam at the other end of the room, where he was examining a fancy coffee maker in a small, neat kitchen space.

He opened the fridge and pulled out a carton of cream, which he sniffed. "Still good," he said. "It seems that people are currently working here."

Karen glanced around nervously. "We shouldn't stay long then. What if someone comes back?"

I lifted my phone to illuminate the space beyond the kitchen. There was nothing but a wall with a single door, with WC initialed on it.

No sign of the concrete pillar, or anything to explain its presence on the floor below.

Sam pushed open the door. Inside was a narrow landing and, to one side, was another door that opened, predictably, to a loo. But, ahead of us, the space widened. In unison, we shone our lights into the shadows, and my breath caught in my throat. My guess had been right.

We were standing in front of a huge vault.

Although the exterior steel door lay open, an inner iron gate with multiple locks protected the safe. I moved closer and looked in through the bars. Against the far wall, gold bricks were stacked from floor to ceiling. Grey metal boxes occupied a corner of the vault floor and a half dozen red cases sat on a long shelf that was otherwise empty.

Tearing my eyes away from the glittering stash, I examined the complex system of locks and levers on the vault door. The safe was an antique, I thought, although not as old as the house, obviously. I remembered from an architecture class that it was only in the late 1800s that vaults of this kind had started to be installed. Several years ago, I'd worked on the design for a remodel of a historic building in London that contained an early-model safe like this one. All the new construction had to be done around it. The thing was practically indestructible.

This explained the massive concrete pillar on the second floor. It and all the reinforcements below it were essential to support the tremendous weight of the steel vault.

"What the heck is that doing here?" Sam murmured.

A thousand questions milled around in my head as I gazed at the vault. Even though I'd conjectured that the pillar might support a heavy safe, I hadn't imagined it would be in use. I'd thought it might be an artifact of the past life of the house. But here it was, guarding its treasures, alongside the very present-day computing array.

It took a minute for me to realize that I was shivering. Ice water trickled down my spine. I grabbed Sam's sleeve. "We need to go."

"Hang on." Sam snapped some photos of the vault and the stacks of gold bars. As we hurried back into the office area, he took more pictures.

We scrambled back through the breach in the paneled wall and stood for a second, staring at the hole and the shards of wood lying on the floor.

"I think someone will notice they had uninvited guests," I said, with an attempt at humor. I had goose bumps all over. We'd thought we were breaking into an old and abandoned part of the house, something that had seemed perfectly reasonable in the context of drawing up anatomically correct plans. But we'd stumbled into something that was clearly supposed to be secret. Someone would be very unhappy.

"I think we need to call the police and tell them what we found and how," I said. "We can explain it before anyone else reports the break-in."

"But wait," Karen said. "We didn't do anything wrong. It seems to me that these people, whoever they are, are trespassing on the Janssens' property. Eline had no idea this was here. I think we should contact her lawyer first thing in the morning and tell him what we've found. He can advise us on the best way to proceed from there."

Sam nodded. "Karen's right."

"I suppose so. We were just doing our jobs," I said. "But we should still get out of here. We don't want to risk a confrontation with anyone. Let's grab our things and go."

We hurried down the stairs to the kitchen and began gathering up our plans and laptops. Karen collected the documents she'd been reading in Eline's room.

"We should leave the keys on the table for Henk, as Mr. Bleeker instructed," I said, taking one last look around to make sure we hadn't left anything behind. Apart from a huge hole in a wall.

"Done," Sam said, putting a bunch of keys on the kitchen counter. "But I can't find Vincent. I hate to leave him here alone."

"I'll come back for him tomorrow." Karen held up a keychain. The fob was a pretty silver heart and it held three keys. "These are Eline's spare house keys," she said. "She gave them to me so that I could help with picking up boxes and suitcases."

We hurried down the stairs and out into the night. At two in the morning, the streets were deserted. It was cold, made worse by a brisk wind that ruffled the surface of the canal.

"Why don't you come to my place?" Karen suggested. "It's much closer than your hotel, and I'm not sure we're going to find a taxi around here at this time of night. And, let's be honest, I could do with the company. I don't really want to go home alone. The couches are quite comfortable."

Sam nodded. "I agree. And I can sleep anywhere. All right for you, Kate?"

"Definitely." I'd be happy for the three of us to stick together until we could talk to the lawyer in the morning. Besides, I wouldn't sleep much. The sight of the office and the vault had set my mind racing. They had to be connected to the danger to Sam.

Half an hour later, Sam and I settled on the white sofas in Karen's living room. The adrenaline rush of our discovery was wearing off. But, although my pulse was back to normal, my mind wouldn't stop churning. Who owned that office? Clearly, Tomas Janssen must have known about it, maybe even used it. Karen had told us that he was on the boards of several companies, so perhaps that office belonged to one of them. It could be a perfectly legal enterprise. Yet the contents of the vault made me doubt it. What kind of company kept gold bars on hand like that? Or hid itself behind a bricked-up wall accessible only through a tunnel? If Tomas hadn't passed away, it's unlikely it would have been discovered. The fact that he hadn't renovated the upper floors was starting to make a lot more sense. Exhausted, I closed my eyes and willed myself to get some sleep.

When I woke up, grey light filtered through the window. A quick glance at Sam assured me he was still sleeping. Even in the gloom, I could see his aura swirling. Anguish swelled like a wave crashing on a beach. Why Sam? Why hadn't I saved him yet? More to the point, had we just made things worse by blundering into the secret office?

Tired and aching, I staggered into the kitchen where Karen was already making coffee and toast. I was helping to set out plates and cutlery just as Sam wandered in, his hair sticking up in all directions, his usually pristine shirt creased and untucked.

"Comfy sofa," he commented, accepting a mug of coffee from Karen. "I slept like a baby."

"I slept a little," I said. "But it wasn't exactly restful."

I'd had nightmares about tunnels and vaults, and I'd been dreaming about searching for a key in a bank when I woke up. My dad said that waking up in the middle of a dream was your brain's way of sending you a message, something it wanted you to think about. He said he'd come up with some of his best legal arguments that way. While I made tea, I thought about my strange dream and realized there was something Karen had said that bothered me.

"Yesterday, when you told us that Eline had given you a key for her safety deposit box, you said she did it in case something happened to her."

Karen nodded. Her skin was so pale it was almost translucent, and she had dark circles under her eyes that looked like bruises. "Yes, that's what she said."

"Why would she think that anything would happen to her?"

Karen wrapped her hands around her mug. "I don't know. I suppose after Tomas died, she felt vulnerable. It's probably not that surprising."

"Let's go take a look at the box this morning."

She nodded. "We should do that. I'll cancel my morning class. And I'll call to make an appointment with the bank."

While Karen sorted out her schedule, Sam typed on his phone.

"Anything from Alex?" I asked.

"Not yet. But it's still really early. I'll let her know where we are."

"I carried on looking at those papers last night," Karen said, spreading butter on her toast. "I found a stack of bank statements with Tomas's name on them. No sign of a large payment of any kind, and certainly not one for eight million to Martin Eyghels or anyone else."

Sam looked up. "It's not definitive. There could be other accounts Tomas might have used, but it's a good start at least."

"But if Martin Eyghels didn't get any money from Tomas, then the house is still officially subject to the agreement?" I asked. "Eyghels still has the right to buy it back? If that's the case, why didn't he approach Eline and show her the contract? Why let her get as far as putting the house on the market and accepting an offer from TBA?"

We all fell quiet. My head was so fuzzy with fatigue, it was a struggle to think clearly. "What time do you think lawyers start work?" I asked.

"Not yet," Karen said. "But let me be sure I have Bleeker's number so we can call him at eight."

As she picked up her mobile, it rang, filling the kitchen with the sound of The Clash's *London Calling*.

She raised the phone to her ear and listened, the color draining from her face. She didn't say anything more than "I understand" before the call ended.

"Is everything all right?" I asked as she sank back into her chair.

"That was Mr. Bleeker. The police have opened an enquiry into Eline Janssen's death."

"It wasn't an accident?"

"They just got the autopsy results. They're saying she was murdered."

18

Eline was murdered. The words echoed around the kitchen. Karen stood up suddenly and rushed to the bathroom. I felt nauseous too. With my head in my hands, elbows on the table, my thoughts rampaged. This changed the stakes for Sam. I was sure now that Eline's death and the danger to him were linked. But who would want them both dead? Pieter, or someone claiming to be him, had come to the house and taken away some paperwork. Was he Eline's killer and the threat to Sam?

I stood up to pour a glass of water for Karen when she came back. She looked wretched, her eyes red and her skin ashen.

"Bleeker said the police will want to talk to us all," she said. "Everyone involved in the house sale."

"We have a lot to talk about," I said. "We'll have to tell him about everything we've discovered over there."

Karen's mobile rang again, the brash music jarring after the shock of the first call.

She listened for a while. "Yes, we'll be here," she said.

"The detective will come in an hour." She pushed her mobile to the middle of the table as though wanting it out of her sight. "He suggested Moresby and Alex join us here."

Sam sent another text to Alex and rang Moresby while Karen and I cleaned up the kitchen. In the bathroom, I washed my face and tamed my tangled hair into some semblance of order. With the help of an airline travel kit that Karen had given me, I brushed my teeth and slicked moisturizer on to my pallid cheeks.

Feeling somewhat refreshed, I returned to the kitchen to find that Moresby had already arrived. He was sitting at the table, talking with Sam, whose aura was moving ever faster. My heart rate climbed. The fact that Eline had been murdered changed everything, but I didn't have much time to think about it. The doorbell rang, loud and insistent.

Karen went downstairs to let in our visitor. After a couple of minutes, we heard voices, and then she reappeared, accompanied by a man in jeans and a brown leather bomber jacket. He was in his early forties, I guessed, tall with fair hair cut short. His eyes were startlingly blue, the color of Delft china. With him was a young woman dressed in leggings, desert boots and a fisherman's sweater.

"Ivo Nouwen," the man said, shaking hands with each of us. "And this is Detective Lange." The young woman raised a hand in greeting.

Moresby glared at him. "You're a policeman?" His gaze shifted to Nouwen's feet, which were clad in black sneakers.

Nouwen smiled. "I'm a chief detective."

"Take a seat," Sam offered, pulling out a chair for him.

"I prefer to stand, thanks."

Unsure, we remained standing until Nouwen urged us to sit down. Sam took the chair next to Karen's. Moresby sat next to me.

"Just a few questions," Nouwen said in nearly flawless English. "This won't take long."

If he was aiming for intimidation by towering over us where we sat, he succeeded. My stomach was doing flips, even though I'd done nothing wrong.

Using his phone, he took note of our names, where we were staying, our home addresses and our reasons for being in Amsterdam. Behind him, Lange scribbled notes with a pencil in a beaten-up notebook.

"The incident took place very close to your hotel," he commented, tapping keys. "Was there anyone else working on the project?"

Sam told him about Alex and gave him her mobile number. "She's staying with her aunt somewhere in the city, but we don't have an address for her." He stared at his mobile. "She should be in touch very soon."

The reminder that Alex had been out of touch for twelve hours stirred butterflies in my stomach. Where was she?

Nouwen spoke in Dutch with Karen, presumably asking some of the same questions. They talked for several minutes, while we waited impatiently for more information about Eline.

Karen sat erect and seemed to be having a hard time holding back tears.

"What happened to Eline?" I asked the detective when he'd finished talking with her. "They said she drowned. But it wasn't an accident?"

Nouwen tapped something into his phone and then looked down at us. "We believe it wasn't an accident."

Then he asked which of us had met Eline and where we were on Tuesday night.

"Kate, Alex and I were at a nightclub until about one in the morning," Sam said.

"And you were all together the entire time?"

"Well, Alex and I were." Sam looked uncomfortable. "Kate left earlier, around midnight."

I didn't have an alibi. The hotel didn't track the coming and going of its guests. Nouwen made a note and said something to Lange.

"And you, Mr. Moresby?" he asked.

"You can't seriously believe that any of us had anything to do with Eline Janssen's death?" Moresby said. "We have no motive. Just the opposite, in fact. Her demise is putting my project at risk, jeopardizing weeks of work. It's the same for everyone here."

Decent of him to stick up for us, I thought. But Nouwen didn't look convinced.

"You need to talk to Pieter Janssen," Moresby went on. "If anyone has a motive, it's him. He is now the sole inheritor of the property."

Nouwen's face remained blank. He'd probably be a good poker player. "We'll be talking to him," he said.

"He came to the house on Tuesday afternoon," I said. "At least, we think he did." I related the story of Pieter's arrival, his search for a document, and the appointment he said he had with the lawyer.

"So, you spoke with him and helped him find the papers he was looking for. Do you know which paperwork he took?"

"Actually, I didn't. Alex volunteered, because she speaks Dutch and could help with searching through the papers. She said he took a copy of the original house deed, but I didn't see it, to be honest. I should have paid more attention, I'm sorry."

"That was irresponsible," Moresby said. "Letting a stranger walk around the house and take things."

Nouwen cleared his throat. "As I said, we will be talking with Mr. Janssen."

The detective wrote more notes and then looked up at Moresby. "Your movements on Tuesday night, please?"

Moresby sat upright, bristling with indignation at being questioned. "When I left the Janssen house, I went to my hotel and called my Managing Director in London. We talked for twenty-five minutes. You can check records, I'm sure. Then I called my wife. I ate dinner by myself in the hotel restaurant, had a brandy in the hotel bar and went to bed at ten."

Nouwen made a note. "Thank you."

"Eline was supposed to meet us for a drink at eight on Tuesday evening, but she didn't come," I said. "She called at nine to say she couldn't make it."

Nouwen turned his brilliant blue eyes on me. "What else did she say?"

"Just that. It was very short, only that she couldn't come and was sorry for standing us up. She said she'd see us over here today."

"And you're sure it was Eline?"

I thought about it. I'd only talked with Eline for a few minutes two days ago. She spoke English with a fairly strong accent, and it had certainly sounded like her on the phone. I showed Nouwen my mobile. "This is the number she gave me, and that's the number the call came from."

"I appreciate it, thanks." He tapped on his phone. "Interesting that she was supposed to be at a meeting with Pieter Janssen at the lawyer's office, yet she said she'd come out with you for a drink."

"There was no meeting with the lawyer," Karen said. "Not that Eline was aware of. Pieter told Alex and Kate that he and Eline had an appointment, but Eline didn't know about it. She was home with me at that time."

Nouwen typed more notes and then looked up at us. "And, just for my records, give me a summary of what you did yesterday, please?"

Between us, we gave an account of our meeting with Bleeker and the agreement that we could finish our study with the understanding that the purchase would be delayed until the inheritance issues were resolved. Karen confirmed that I'd come to talk to her about Eline.

"And in the evening?"

"Alex went out for dinner with a family friend." Sam said. "Karen, Kate and I stayed at the Janssen house for a while."

This would be the moment to tell Nouwen about the secret office and the vault. I waited. Sam got to his feet, probably having reached his sitting-down limit. While Nouwen watched him, he stalked around the tiny room and then came to a halt at the window, where he leaned back against the sill. "We should tell you that we found some interesting things on the top floor of the house."

Nouwen nodded. "Go on."

Sam did his best to provide a succinct description of the house, with its renovated apartment and the abandoned upper floors.

"As part of our survey of the property, we removed some paneling on each of the two upper floors to ascertain what was behind them."

That was a delicate way of describing the havoc we'd wreaked with a sledgehammer.

"And on the top floor, we found an office with a lot of high-tech equipment and a large vault full of gold bars," Sam continued.

"There's a keypad-protected steel door which must lead to another set of stairs. None of it is on the house plans." He pulled his phone from his pocket. "Here, I took some photos."

That certainly caught Nouwen's attention. He and Detective Lange spoke in Dutch and then she left the kitchen. I heard her talking on her phone in the hall.

"Anything else?" Nouwen asked.

Sam told him about the tunnel he and I had found, and the blinking light that seemed to be an alarm system. "There were some other things that happened there," he went on. "We thought of them as pranks, but in light of Eline's death, perhaps they were warnings."

Nouwen's eyes lit up. "Go on."

Sam looked at me. "Kate saw more of them than I did."

I jumped in, describing the painting falling off the wall and the chandelier crashing to the ground.

"And do you have any idea who could be behind these incidents?" Nouwen asked.

"It could be the caretaker," Sam offered. "He's there every day."

Nouwen checked the notes on his phone. "Henk Mayer?"

"Yes, but I don't think he would harm Eline," I said. "She was very fond of him, she said."

Nouwen eyed me for long enough for me to feel uncomfortable. "You had a long conversation with Mrs. Janssen?" he asked.

"Not really. We chatted for a few minutes. I asked her about a stray cat."

"What else did you and Mrs. Janssen talk about?"

"I told her about the incidents. She was surprised to hear about them but didn't have any answers. She said she'd be coming in and out to collect some of her things. That was all."

Nouwen stared at me for a few more seconds but said nothing.

"There is one more thing," I added. "I'm sure that we're being watched. There's a man in a grey hooded sweatshirt. I saw him in a bar on Monday night and he was outside the house yesterday evening. He has a goatee beard and is probably in his thirties."

Sam flicked a look at me. Neither he nor Alex believed that we were being followed, especially since my overreaction when I'd accosted the poor tourist who happened to be wearing a grey sweatshirt. But I still had a feeling there was someone watching us.

"Could you describe him? Recognize him in a photo perhaps?" Nouwen asked.

Karen got up, went into the living room and returned with the sketch that Eline had drawn.

"He was following Eline around as well," she said, handing it to him.

"There's something else," I said. "Eline's assistant, Tessa De Vries, died on Monday afternoon after falling down the stairs at her apartment. Apparently, it was an accident. But, perhaps, it wasn't. Now that we know Eline was murdered, it makes me wonder."

Nouwen gazed at me for long enough to make my cheeks warm. But the more I thought about it, the more unlikely it seemed that Tessa and Eline would die within a day of each other and there not be a connection.

"We met Tessa on Monday morning. She was at the Janssens' house." I glanced at Sam, looking for his support. "She seemed... nervous. And she warned Sam to be careful."

"About what?"

"I don't know. She just said she hoped nothing would go wrong. I planned to ring her to ask her some questions but then we heard that she was dead."

Again, Nouwen and Lange exchanged glances. Lange wrote something in her notebook while Nouwen put the sketch of the goatee man and his phone in his pocket. "Thank you for letting me know. I'll be back in touch again soon. I assume you are all staying in the city?"

Moresby raised his arms in a gesture of frustration. "Are you treating us as suspects? This is ridiculous."

"As witnesses, for now," Nouwen said calmly. "I expect to have more questions for all of you and need to know where to reach you. Do you still have access to the Janssen house?"

"We've collected all our things and locked up," Sam said. "We're waiting to hear from the lawyer about whether Pieter Janssen wishes to proceed with the sale of the house." He rubbed his eyes. "Which I sincerely hope he does. At that point, we would be able to resume working again."

"Sit tight for now," Nouwen said. "As part of our murder investigation, we will conduct a search of the house. Detective Lange will stay to explain the details to you. And she'll give you my direct number. If anything happens, or if anything occurs to you, call me at once."

With that, he turned and left.

Detective Lange sat down on Sam's empty chair. She explained that, as the Janssen house wasn't the scene of the crime, the search would simply be for any evidence that might cast light on Eline's murder.

"What about the tunnel and the office?" I asked. "Will you try to find out who's using them?"

"We'll need to hear from Pieter Janssen, as the house owner, in order to initiate any enquiries in that direction. There's no law against tunnels, you know, or having an office in your house."

"But what if they are connected in some way to Eline's murder?" I asked.

Lange tilted her head. "What makes you think that?"

I wanted to tell her that Sam was in danger too, and to explain my theory that the house was the source of the threat to him. But I couldn't talk about auras, especially with Sam listening, so I shrugged and said nothing. Lange closed her notebook and pulled a piece of blue elastic around it to keep it closed. "We'll be in touch."

While Karen walked her back downstairs, we sat in silence for a while. I was still coming to terms with the fact that Eline's death wasn't an accident.

"This is all very irritating," Moresby said at last. "We have to keep the pressure on Bleeker to get the paperwork sorted out."

Sam and I looked at each other. It was as if Moresby hadn't heard a word about Eline being murdered, he was so focused on the project.

Sam nodded. "Well, we'll know more today after Bleeker's meeting with Pieter Janssen. We'll either be closing down the project or setting things in motion again."

"Closing the project down is out of the question," Moresby objected.

"I hope you're right. I'll do everything I can to keep things moving forward, I promise."

"I'm going to my hotel. I can work from there," Moresby went on. "Let's plan on reconvening when we hear from Bleeker."

He must have passed Karen on the stairs as she came back up after seeing Lange out.

"That man is quite rude," she commented. "Listen, we have the bank appointment at ten, so I'm going to do a bit of work here until it's time to leave."

"We probably should have mentioned the safety deposit box to the police," Sam commented.

Karen shrugged. "I think it will contain her mother's jewelry. They don't need to know about that sort of thing. And once we've done that, I think we should do some more research."

She raised an eyebrow at me, and I nodded. "We need to dig around for info on the nephew," I said. "And track down the grey hoodie chap."

Sam was aghast. "What? You have to be kidding. Let the police do their job. There's nothing we can do."

"We can't rely on the police to move quickly enough to protect you," I said. "We need to get involved and learn everything we possibly can."

"You're not a detective, Kate. How can you achieve anything faster than the police can?"

"I've had some practice. And I'm far more motivated than Nouwen. I know there's another life at stake—yours—and he doesn't."

"I want to find out who killed Eline," Karen went on. "And if that helps us work out what threatens Sam here, all the better."

"The police are working on it," Sam said. "They'll find the killer. They just need some time."

Karen muttered something in Dutch. "I wouldn't even trust the police to solve a crossword puzzle," she translated for us.

"I've never heard anything bad about the Dutch police," I said.

Karen shrugged. "I'm sure most are good. But not all. About ten years ago, my brother-in-law was accused of theft, a heist from an art gallery in The Hague. He wasn't even in the city the night it happened and he's a law-abiding citizen. They arrested him anyway and held him in a prison cell. Eventually, they let him go, when their so-called eyewitness turned out to be highly unreliable. But the experience traumatized him. I prefer to keep my distance from the police, and I don't like that detective, Nouwen. What did you think of him?"

"Seems like a good chap," Sam said.

"Maybe we should tell him about the danger to Sam?" Karen said to me, but there was a tone of doubt in her voice.

I thought back to my previous encounters with the police. There was the officer in London who'd thought my active participation in the investigation was a sign of guilt; for a while, I'd been the prime suspect in a murder case. I shivered at the memory. More recently, a dour Scottish detective had done his best to relinquish his preconceptions and had accepted, more or less, what I told him about auras and the imminent danger they represented. It had been a blessing to have his support. But Nouwen didn't seem the type to collaborate, and his main objective right now was to find out what happened to Eline, a wealthy Dutch citizen. I doubted he'd pay me any attention or worry very much about Sam, a very alive Brit who happened to be passing through Amsterdam.

"Not yet," I said. "Let's see what happens if we meet him again."

"If I get a vote," Sam said. "I'd choose not to say anything to him. I don't want him looking at me like a victim." He raised his chin and stared at me. "I don't want *anyone* to treat me like a victim. I've been through that once and that was enough."

Karen glared at him. "Don't be hard on Kate," she said. "That's like shooting the messenger. She's just doing her best to save your life."

19

In the aftermath of the detectives' visit, the flat felt very quiet and none of us seemed to want to talk much. Karen said she was going to mark papers in her room, and Sam went off to ring Terry, so I settled at the kitchen table and opened my laptop.

A deluge of work emails from my colleagues had flooded my inbox. There were several from Alan, too, asking how the project was going. I sent a vaguely worded response, saying that the client liked my designs so far, which was true, and that we were on a temporary hold while the lawyer looked into some estate planning issues, which was sort of true. I decided it was all right to withhold the whole story until we knew more. At least until we could work out what came next.

With my emails answered, my eyes came to rest on the papers that Karen had found in Eline's safety deposit box, still neatly stacked on the kitchen table: the copy of the letter Tomas had written to Martin Eyghels, and the bank statements that didn't show any large money transfers. Who was this Martin Eyghels? I wondered if he could be the man with the goatee who was following Eline and watching us.

I opened my browser and googled his name, expecting a handful of entries. Most people had some sort of online presence but, strangely, Eyghels didn't. In fact, his name only showed up once, on a Dutch history website, as a merchant trading with the Dutch East India Company, or the VOC as Sam called it, in the mid 1600s. He had sailed to Batavia where he stayed for almost ten years before traveling back to Amsterdam. I stared at the screen, bemused. Had he known Jacob Hals, the man who'd built this property? Could there be a modern-day Martin Eyghels who'd bought the house because of some centuries-old connection to it? Or was it just an assumed name? That was an interesting possibility.

An alarm on my phone pinged. It was time to leave for the bank. I closed my computer and went into the living room to find Sam. He was standing at the window, staring out, and not on his phone for a change.

"Are you all right?" I asked.

He turned to me. "I'm worried about Alex. It's gone ten-thirty. She must be awake by now but she's not answering my texts."

A cold puddle of unease sloshed around in my stomach. Where was Alex? It didn't seem like her to disappear on us, but then, I reflected, I didn't really know her that well. Could it be that I'd misread her? She'd told us she acted in a theater group. Had she been playing a role here? Did she know more than she was letting on? Or was something really wrong?

Summoning a forced smile, I joined Sam at the window. "Try not to worry. She's probably doing something with her aunt."

"On a workday?"

"She doesn't have an aura, Sam. That means she's going to be all right."

I wasn't feeling as confident as I tried to sound. We'd stumbled into something frightening: the old house with all its secrets, Eline's murder, Tessa's death, the strange behavior of Pieter Janssen.

"Come on. It's time to go the bank," I said, pushing those dark thoughts away.

"You don't need me for that. I'll wait for you here."

"No. You're coming with us. We need to stay together until this is all sorted."

I didn't mean to, but my eyes drifted up to the space over his head. "It's still there then."

I nodded.

Karen came in, buttoning up her wool coat. "Time to go."

I was tying my scarf around my neck when Sam's phone pinged. "It's a text from Alex." He smiled and lifted the screen for me to see.

"Sorry I'm running late! Be there soon as I can!!"

"I'll tell her not to rush, that we'll be back here at midday." Sam said, typing the message.

Karen had ordered a taxi to take us to the bank, an impressive building, with stone steps leading to a columned porch. Glass doors opened to a marble-clad lobby filled with people. It was very different from the local branch of my bank in Bayswater, crammed into a sad building from the 1970s.

Karen went off to find the manager and soon came back, accompanied by a middle-aged woman with cat-eye glasses. "I will take you down," she said. "But only two of you, for security reasons."

"Sam, you go with Karen," I said. "I'll wait."

Sam would be safe in a bank vault, I reasoned, more than he would be in this busy lobby with so many people coming and going. I was sorry to miss the experience of opening a safety deposit box, but I settled on an upholstered chair in a corner and flipped through a glossy magazine, looking at pictures of elegant homes without understanding a word of the articles.

Several minutes later, the skin on the back of my neck prickled. I looked up and glimpsed the man with the goatee beard. Dressed today in a black anorak, he was leaning against a marble pillar, pretending to look at his phone, but he wasn't. He was scanning the lobby. When he saw me watching him, he gave a slow smile. More of a smirk really.

I shivered. His eyes were very light, not blue like the detective's, but almost colorless. I gripped the pages of the magazine so that my hands wouldn't shake. The place was crowded. He wouldn't dare to try anything here, surely. I looked for a security guard and saw two, one near the front door and one closer to the teller windows.

I relinquished the magazine and pulled out my phone. Quickly, I texted Detective Nouwen. When I looked up, the goatee man had disappeared. *Damn.* I should have kept my eyes on him. This might have been a good place to confront him, to demand he tell me why he was following us. I hurried to the doors and peered along the crowded street. There was no sign of him. As I walked slowly back to my seat, my phone pinged with a message from Nouwen, telling me not to follow the man and to stay safe.

A few minutes later, Sam and Karen appeared.

"That man was here," I said at once. "The one with the goatee. He's definitely following us."

Karen grabbed my hand. "Are you all right? We should tell the police."

"I did."

"Good, because we have things to tell you. Let's go get a coffee."

Opposite the bank, we found a bright, modern cafe furnished with white tables and lime green chairs. The smell of coffee and sugar blended with the scent of dozens of vanilla candles lit along the bar and on each table. We sat in a corner and ordered coffees and poffertejs, those delicious little pancakes covered with powdered sugar.

While we ate, Karen showed me a photo of some expensive-looking jewelry. "This was all in the box. I know Eline intended me to have it, but, really, what would I do with it? I left it there for now. But there's also this."

She lifted a large white envelope from her bag and showed it to me. Some Dutch words were neatly hand-printed on it. "It says 'Important. Do Not Throw Away.' And that is Tomas's writing, not Eline's."

Sam held out a small velvet box. "We found this in there too." He opened it to reveal a man's signet ring.

"That was Tomas's," Karen said. It was a simple platinum band with a small, square face bearing a heraldic design of some kind.

"He wore it all the time. I assume Eline put it in the safety deposit box after he died. Maybe at the same time as she wrote this note to me." She showed me a lavender-colored envelope. "I haven't read it yet." Her voice broke.

I put my hand on her arm. "I'm so sorry you lost your friend."

Karen pushed her plate away and wiped her fingers on her napkin. "Well, let's take a look, shall we? There's no point in putting it off."

She slid a sheet of notepaper from the lavender envelope and read it slowly. "It starts off by saying... well, I won't read it out loud. It's just a personal note to me. But then Eline goes on to say that she's worried that before he died, Tomas had got caught up in something bad."

"We already knew that, didn't we?" I asked through a mouthful of pancake. "That she thought Tomas had a problem with a business deal—the agreement to sell the house back to the previous owner?"

She shook her head. "No, this is different. Eline says that she'd overheard Tomas talking on the phone about someone called Zeckendorf. Tomas seemed very upset, she said. He begged whoever was on the line to tell Zeckendorf to get off his back."

"Who is he? This Zeckendorf? Wait, I'll take a look online." I fished in my handbag for my mobile. "No first name?"

"No—" She was interrupted by Sam, who'd jumped to his feet. Startled, I looked up to see a big grin on his face as he waved to someone across the room. Alex was making her way through the tables. But, when she came closer, my heart clenched. Under the bright lights of the cafe, her blonde hair shimmered. And over it, the air fluttered and coiled.

20

The sounds of the cafe receded, drowned out by the rush of blood pulsing in my temples. My heart raced. Alex had an aura. She hadn't before, so something had to have changed. It must have something to do with her prolonged absence. After several deep breaths, my heart rate settled. The clink of china and cutlery came back into focus, mundane sounds against a soft hum of Dutch conversation.

"Tell me everything you've been up to," she said, beckoning a waiter over to take her coffee order. "I bet you missed me."

"We did." Sam was gazing at her with his puppy-dog eyes and a broad smile. How could I tell him about her aura?

"Did you hear about Eline?" Karen paused and took a deep breath. "She was murdered. A detective interviewed us all this morning. He wants to talk to you as well."

"Murdered? But I thought she'd drowned."

Sam told her what we'd learned from the detective, which wasn't much really. "And we have other news," he said. "We broke into the top floor of the Janssen house last night. You won't believe what we found up there."

He waited when the waiter came by with Alex's coffee and then told her about the office and the vault.

Her eyes went wide. "Oh my god. That's incredible. I'm gutted that I missed it." She picked up her cup and wrapped both hands around it, tapping her fingertips against the white china. She seemed upset.

"I'm sorry you weren't there," I said. "We couldn't wait. There wasn't much time. If we hadn't broken in when we did, we'd have missed the chance completely."

"Of course, I understand. Did you tell the detective about it?"

"Yes," Sam said. "But before they investigate, they want to hear from Pieter Janssen—who seems to have gone missing."

"Missing?"

"Well, no one has heard from him since we saw him on Tuesday."

"That's strange." Alex sipped her coffee. "What now? We can't work on the project anymore? Are we leaving?"

"Kate and I are planning to stay for another day or two at least to see if Pieter confirms that the sale can go ahead. Bleeker, the lawyer, will let us know as soon as he hears anything. The detectives suggested we hang around in case of further questions, so Moresby is hanging out at his hotel."

Sam looked exhausted. He'd put so much work into the building renovation, and now it seemed to have fallen apart. I knew he was worried about the money too.

Alex put her cup down and rubbed her eyes. She seemed to be on the verge of tears.

"Is everything all right?" I asked her.

She shook her head. "No, my aunt isn't well, which is why I was late. I stayed home with her until I was sure she could manage by herself."

"What's wrong with her?"

"I think it's migraines. She's had them before."

"That's too bad. I hope she feels better soon." I pushed my last piece of pancake around on my plate. "How was last night? Did you see Willem? Did he have anything useful to say?"

Sam shot me a look. "The Spanish Inquisition ended a long time ago," he said.

"Sorry. I was just interested, that's all." And desperate for any information that might cast light on why Alex was suddenly in danger.

"It's okay." Alex smiled at me to show she wasn't offended. "He didn't say much, to be honest. He said he'd heard rumors that Tomas was in trouble financially, but he didn't know whether that was true."

"Eline never said anything to me about any money problems," Karen said. "But she seemed to think that Tomas was having problems with this Zeckendorf fellow."

"Zeckendorf?" Alex asked.

Sam put his hand over hers. "Are you feeling okay? You look a bit pale."

Alex conjured up a smile that didn't reach her eyes. "Of course. I'm super tired. I got home late last night, and then this thing with my aunt... I'm worried about her. But I'm fine."

"You know that name, Zeckendorf?" Karen leaned forward across the table. "You looked as though you recognized it?"

"Willem mentioned him over dinner, but I can't really remember the context. He might be another wealthy client or something like that." Alex tapped her lip, thinking. "Yes, I think that was it. He's a client of Willem's. What did he do to upset Tomas so much?"

"We don't know," Karen said. "Eline just overheard a phone conversation and the name came up. She mentioned it in a letter she left in the safety deposit box."

Our waiter came by and asked if we needed more coffee. We all said yes. While he collected our cups, I played with my unused knife, spinning it in circles on the table. Its silvery blade caught our reflections, our faces ghostly circles. I shivered and put my hand down on the knife handle, stopping it dead. Sam talked quietly with Alex, gripping her hand in his.

My thoughts whirled, reflecting the swirling air over his head. The puzzling thing to me was that he still had an aura. If my theory was correct, that the danger was linked to the house, he should be safe now that we'd given back the keys and put the project on hold.

But his aura was still there, and now there was Alex's aura to worry about. The two had to be linked somehow. I stared at the space over her head, thinking of possible connections. Things were not going well.

Karen nudged my arm. Alex was looking at me, eyes wide with alarm. Sam was, too.

"Don't tell me Alex has an aura," he said.

Damn. I'd been staring too hard. Swallowing, I nodded. "I'm very sorry, Alex. I don't understand why. It means that something has changed since we saw you yesterday. Can you think of anything that happened that might have put you in danger?"

"Something that made the invisible wheel of death appear over my head? No." She looked at Karen and then at me.

"Karen doesn't have an aura," I confirmed. "And, no, I don't know if I have one."

Alex sat up straight. "Well, I don't intend to shuffle off this mortal coil any time soon, so what are we going to do about it?"

"It's not fair." Sam's voice was rough with emotion. "Alex shouldn't have been caught up in any of this. It has to be the project, right? I should have pulled out days ago. It's just one stupid consulting gig, not worth anyone's life."

"It's not your fault." I rushed to assure him. "We didn't understand the scope of the threat. We've hardly had time to absorb the reality of Eline's murder and we only just found the secret office."

"Do you think that whoever owns that space is going to come after us?" Alex asked.

"Maybe."

"Why would they?" Sam asked. "They must know that we'd have reported it to the police. It's not exactly a secret anymore."

"But you and Alex are still in danger. So there has to be more to it," I said. "Something else they think we know, or that we're going to discover somehow."

"They?" Alex asked.

"They, he, whoever is using the office."

Alex nodded. "What do we do then?"

"I think we should disappear for a while. Until the lawyer tells us what's going to happen to the house, and the police have chance to pursue their investigation."

We fell silent while the waiter set down our coffees.

"I have an idea," Karen said when he'd left. "A friend of mine has a houseboat on the Brouwersgracht, a canal in a quiet neighborhood. He wouldn't mind if you camped there. I've got the key, I think." She dug around in her oversized bag and pulled out a laden keychain. She sorted through them and held one up. "That's it."

I raised an eyebrow at Sam. He nodded. "Thank you, Karen." He turned to Alex. "What about you? Will you come?"

"Of course."

"What about your aunt?" I asked. "Aren't you worried about leaving her? Won't she wonder where you've gone?"

Alex shrugged. "I'll let her know I need to work for a while. She'll understand."

I wasn't convinced about Alex's story of a sick aunt but decided to let it go for now. She'd just learned she had an aura. Self-protection was probably kicking in, and the prospect of her own death almost certainly overruled any concerns about a relative's headache.

"Good," Sam said. "I'll feel better if we all stay together. So we'll go to the boat and lay low there while we get this thing sorted out." For a moment, he sounded determined, almost forceful, but then his face slackened, and he looked at me. "Right?"

"I hate to whine," Alex said. "But this goddamned aura is weighing heavily on me." She glanced at Sam. "And I'm afraid for Sam. Is hiding going to keep us safe? What about that man with the goatee you thought was watching us?"

"He *is* watching us. He followed us to the bank this morning." I looked out through the cafe windows at the crowded street beyond. Was he out there right now? "I don't know how safe we can be, but we'll do what Karen suggested. We'll check out of the hotel, maybe even take a taxi to the airport to make it look as though we're leaving.

Then we double back to the houseboat. After that, we'll work it out as we go along."

My stomach started to churn even as I said it. I liked to plan ahead, to weigh and minimize the risks. Running headlong into a dangerous situation without a proper strategy was terrifying, like leaving a life jacket on the beach before wading into rough water.

"Let's go," I said, standing and picking up my bag before I could change my mind.

Karen gave us the location of the houseboat and said she'd meet us there in an hour. Unease fluttered in my chest like a trapped butterfly. Karen was going out of her way to help us, claiming she wanted to find Eline's killer. What if that wasn't her real goal? She had been Eline's best friend. Eline was dead. I pushed the cafe door open and was slapped with a sharp blast of cold air. Pulling my scarf tighter around my neck, I followed Karen outside.

I had to trust someone.

21

S am, Alex and I walked in silence past canal houses that stood straight and tall, their myriad windows like blank eyes watching us. I shivered in the chill of the late winter sun, aware of the water that ran alongside our path, flat and dark and hiding secrets of its own.

It only took us twenty minutes to pack our bags and check out of the hotel. From there we took a taxi to the airport and got out at Departures. After mingling with the crowds inside the terminal for ten minutes, we walked to the Arrivals hall, where we exited and got into another taxi.

By the time we reached the houseboat, Karen was there waiting. Her cheeks were ashen, the dark circles under her eyes more pronounced. Still, she waved cheerily when our taxi pulled up alongside the canal where the boat was berthed. It was a beautiful little vessel, its wooden hull gleaming. A few shy winter pansies bloomed in pots on the deck and red gingham curtains adorned the windows.

We hurried inside and carefully descended a short flight of wooden steps. Below, the interior was far bigger than I'd imagined. Beyond a well-fitted kitchen with a table and four chairs was a roomy seating area.

"The couches turn into beds at night," Karen said. "There's bedding in the overhead lockers."

She set a kettle of water on the gas hob and pulled out some cups while Sam and I stashed our luggage in a cupboard under the beds. Alex settled at the table.

"It's cozy," I said, "So nice of your friend to let us stay here."

Karen nodded. "He's a good man and he'll be very discreet. I didn't tell him your names or why you're here. He trusts me to look after his little treasure."

Once we were seated around the table, Karen brought over mugs of tea and sat down.

"Time to take a look in here," she said, picking up the big white envelope with Tomas's writing on the front. "I'll read and translate as I go, if that's all right."

First, she showed us a three-page typed document with Tomas Janssen's signature on each page and a notary seal stamped in blue. "This is an addendum to Tomas's will," she said. "And it's all related to the house."

Sam shifted on his chair. There wasn't much space for him to stand or pace around. That would drive him mad after a while. He chewed on a fingernail.

Karen murmured to herself as she read through the document. "All right. The summary is that Tomas wrote this up to give the house jointly to Eline and to his nephew Pieter. It says that this will supersedes all other documents including the addendum dated October 17, 2018." She rustled through the papers in the envelope. "I don't see that addendum here, though."

She picked up another sheet of paper. "This is a photocopy of a handwritten letter from Tomas." She held her hand against her chest as though she had a pain there. "What did poor Eline get mixed up in?" She looked up at us. "I'll just translate it out loud."

"Gezagvoerder,

Accept this letter as proof of my good intentions regarding the property..."

"Who's Gezagvoerder?" Sam asked.

"It's not a name, it's a title," Karen replied. "It usually means captain of a ship or commander."

"Weird," he muttered.

Karen continued.

"I am protecting it as you directed me to. It no longer sits empty, the object of speculation among the neighbors. It has become a home, and as such, my wife deserves to have the option of continuing to live it in should I predecease her. While I hope that to be an event in the distant future, I feel compelled to make arrangements now to be sure Eline is provided for.

"Following our recent discussion, I now agree to add my nephew, Pieter, to the will as co-inheritor. He will ensure that the property's interests are always protected. Nothing will change with regard to the upper floors. I deeply respect the property's centuries of history and its association with Zeckendorf. My wife knows nothing of that. Those secrets remain yours and mine alone. I am sending this letter by trusted courier for you to share with those who need to know. I hope this will bring an end to the recent unpleasantness."

In the ensuing silence, the boat creaked and rocked gently in the wake of a tour boat chugging by. The amplified voice of a tour guide echoed over the water. Sam couldn't sit still any longer. He jumped to his feet and leaned against the fridge door. Alex was staring down at the table.

"Bloody hell," Sam said. Like me, he seemed stunned by the revelations.

"Zeckendorf sounds more like a company than an individual," I said. "But what do they do?"

"Obviously something to do with those computers on the top floor," Karen said.

"Hang on," Sam said. "This implies that the house belongs to Zeckendorf. So, who is Martin Eyghels? His name was on the purchase document."

I explained the research I'd done. "Eyghels might be an assumed name," I said. "Or maybe just someone that works for them. So, the house belongs to the company, but they put an individual's name on it, maybe for tax reasons?" Flummoxed, I stared at the papers on the table. "If Zeckendorf cared so much about the building, why didn't they just buy it back from Eline once she put it on the market?"

Alex lifted her head. "Maybe they don't have ten million euros."

Karen snorted. "They have hundreds of millions in gold up in that vault. I'm sure they could afford it."

"Because they knew that if they got rid of Eline, Pieter would inherit," I was thinking out loud. "Pieter must work for them? He'll hand the house back to them. Why would they want to give Eline all that money if they could get it back for free?"

"More to the point, why did they let Tomas buy it in the first place?" Sam asked.

"Perhaps they were short of money back then," Karen suggested. "They needed the two million Tomas paid for it."

"I don't think so." The details were becoming clear in my mind. "The sale was a sham," I said. "Henk told Alex that the neighbors were complaining about the house sitting empty for all those years, right? The last thing Zeckendorf would want was for the house to draw attention to itself. So, they moved someone—Tomas—into it to stop the complaints. And to make it look official, they created a fake sale document with Eyghels' name on it."

"Which means that Tomas was really just a tenant," Karen tapped her fingers on the letter. "But then he decided he wanted to actually buy the house so Eline could stay in the event of his death."

"That would have upset the apple cart," Sam said. "To the point where Zeckendorf insisted that Pieter be named as a co-inheritor."

Karen laid the letter on the table with trembling hands. "So Zeckendorf killed Eline. Pieter inherits and the house is safely back in Zeckendorf's hands."

"Do we have any proof though? Alex asked. "Anything we can take to the police?"

Karen slipped several more sheets of paper out of the envelope. "Maybe this," she said. "It's a letter to Tomas, accepting his arrangement that Pieter inherit the entire estate in the event of anything happening to Eline."

"Who is the letter from? Is it signed?" Sam asked.

"There's no letterhead, no name."

Karen held up the paper and Sam leaned forward to take it from her. He stood and went to lean against the counter before peering at the piece of paper. "Just a squiggle of ink as a signature," he said. "That doesn't help much. In fact, I'd say that none of this paperwork gives much away. No addresses, phone numbers, or names. But maybe the police can make something of it all."

"Did Zeckendorf kill Tomas?" I wondered out loud.

Karen thought for a moment. "I doubt it. If his death had been expected, don't you think these people would have had a plan in place? It seems to me that he had a heart attack, died suddenly, and they were all taken by surprise. And then Eline had the house on the market before they could come up with a strategy."

I looked at Alex. "Remember when Pieter said they didn't have time to plan? Maybe this is what he meant."

She nodded. "It seems like it."

I stood up to make more tea, nudging Sam aside so I could get milk out of the fridge. "We should talk to Detective Nouwen," I said. "And show him that letter, if that's okay, Karen?"

"Of course."

As I held my hand out for it, I changed my mind. "I'll just take a photo of it for now. I can show that to Nouwen and he can come here if he wants to see the original. I don't fancy walking around in public with it."

"But I still don't understand why they continue to threaten us," Sam said. "We've stopped the project. The sale may never happen. Haven't they won already?"

"Maybe they think we know too much. That we've worked it all out," I said as I took my mobile from my bag and snapped a shot of the letter to Tomas.

Karen stowed it back in the envelope and looked around. "Where's the best place to keep this safe?"

"I keep my jewelry in my sock drawer," Alex said. "But how about the microwave? No one would think to look in there."

While Karen closed the envelope, I dialed the number Nouwen had given us. He picked up on the second ring and agreed to meet me at a coffee house nearby. I'd already decided to go by myself. I needed to tell the detective that Sam and Alex were in danger. If that meant telling him about my strange ability, then I'd have to, but I'd rather have that conversation with him alone. Who knew how he would react to stories of auras?

"I'm seeing Nouwen in fifteen minutes," I said. "Alex, you look exhausted. Maybe you can take a nap? Sam should stay with you."

"I'll stay too," Karen said. "I can keep an eye open for anyone loitering nearby."

With a last glance at Sam and the aura that spiraled over his head, I hurried up the steps and unlocked the door that led to the deck. I was careful to close it behind me before clambering off the boat on to the cobbled road that ran alongside the canal.

A herd of tourists meandered past, following a guide with a rolled umbrella held high. Tagging along at the back, I examined the street in every direction to check whether the man with the goatee was around. When I saw no sign of him or of anyone else paying me any attention, I relaxed a little and hurried to the coffee shop Nouwen had suggested, thankful that he would see me on short notice.

The cafe felt like an English pub with its paneled walls and smoke-stained beamed ceiling. A boisterous group of young Americans crowded around a table in the center, with large glasses of Heineken lined up in front of them. I found a seat in a corner and ordered a coffee. The waitress soon came back with a mug of dark roast. "It's Douwe Egberts," she said in English. "We grind the beans ourselves."

The coffee was good and kept me company for ten minutes until Nouwen strode in through the front door. The animated conversation at the middle table calmed suddenly. Even in jeans and his leather jacket, Nouwen exuded authority. I wondered if that was a disadvantage at times when he might prefer to go unnoticed.

Within a few seconds, though, the hubbub resumed. Nouwen spoke to the bartender and came over to join me. He nodded at the mug in front of me. "Another?"

"No, thanks. This is fine."

"I'm sorry I kept you waiting, Miss Benedict. Do you have some information for me?" He sat down on on the other side of the table. His Delft blue eyes seemed even brighter in the subdued light.

"Please call me Kate. I do have some information. And I also have a couple of questions."

"Fire away," he said. His accent was strong, but his knowledge of English idiom was good.

"Did Eline Janssen report a burglary at her apartment a few weeks ago?" I asked.

Nouwen shook his head. "I don't know. Was there one?"

"Karen told us about it."

"She didn't mention a burglary this morning. Was anything valuable taken?"

The waitress approached with a mug similar to mine and put it down in front of Nouwen. She didn't bother to tell him about the coffee beans which made me wonder if he was a regular here.

"Karen said not. Just a lot of damage—broken glass, ripped cushions, that sort of thing, but we think maybe he was looking for this." I handed him my phone to show him the letter Karen had found in the deposit box.

Nouwen took it from me but didn't look at it. "Remind me. How do you know Karen Visser?"

Memories of sneaking into Eline's room made me fidget on my chair. "I went to find her after we heard about Eline's death. Eline had mentioned she was staying with her."

"And Eline also mentioned Karen Visser's address?"

"Not exactly. I did some research. And Karen was kind enough to make time to talk with me."

"Enlighten me. Why would you need to talk with Eline Janssen's friend?"

"Because I thought someone wanted to stop the house from being sold," I said. "I'd hoped she might know something about it."

Nouwen seemed to think about that for a moment. "You believe the house sale is the motive for Eline Janssen's murder?"

"Possibly." I didn't say any more, hoping to draw him out on any theories of his own. But he said nothing and took a long swallow of his coffee.

"Ok. There's something screwy going on with the ownership of the house," I said. I told him about the letter from Tomas to whoever *Gezagvoerder* might be and was happy to see a spark of interest in his blue eyes. I nodded at the phone screen. "If you read that now, you'll see why we think Zeckendorf might have had a motive to kill Eline."

"Zeckendorf?" Nouwen leaned across the table, his eyes lasering in on mine.

"You've heard of them? Do you know what they do?"

The detective leaned back in his chair. "I can't talk about it, sorry. But text me that photo and I'll follow up." He handed me back my phone, and I sent him the photo. When his phone pinged, he stared at the image of the document for a moment, his forehead furrowed. "No identifiable names or signatures," he commented finally. "But I'll get someone to take a closer look. Was there anything else you wanted to tell me?"

I tapped my fingers on the scarred and stained tabletop, thinking about how to enlist his help. I decided to be direct. "I think there may soon be another death."

That got his attention. "What makes you say that?"

"Let's say I'm right about Eline being murdered because of the house sale. Now that Eline is dead, Pieter inherits the entire property."

"So, you think Pieter Janssen could be in danger. Given what happened to Eline." He scrolled through some notes on his mobile. "Ah, William Moresby," he said. "Mr. Moresby seemed convinced this morning that Pieter Janssen is our prime suspect, as he now inherits everything."

"It's possible," I agreed.

"But *you* think Janssen is a possible target?"

"I don't know, to be honest. It's not him I'm thinking of. It's Sam Holden, whom you've met. And Alex Hart."

One of Nouwen's eyebrows arched. A nifty trick that conveyed surprise, disbelief, an invitation to say more. I complied, wishing I didn't have to. But I couldn't think how else to explain about Sam and Alex.

"I can tell when someone is in danger," I said. "More precisely, when they're about to die."

Nouwen looked as though I'd just claimed Bigfoot had killed Eline.

"Really, Kate? Are you going to solve the case for me?" He gave me a weak smile, looking disappointed. At least he wasn't hostile, but he wasn't taking me seriously.

"Listen. I know it sounds mad." I held up a hand when he started to speak. "But please hear me out. No, I don't think I can solve your case. In fact, I need your help. There's real urgency in finding out who killed Eline, because I think her killer might go after Sam next. And Alex."

"So, what? You read tea leaves?"

I breathed in, reminding myself to stay calm. I needed Nouwen on my side.

"I don't read leaves," I said. "I see air circling over the head of the person who's going to die."

"Oh, that's a relief," Nouwen said. "Much more scientifically accurate than tea leaves, I'd guess." The grin had faded, replaced by a deep crease between his brows.

In the silence that fell between us, I heard the buzz of voices from the table of Americans, a guffaw of laughter and a high-pitched giggle, the thud of a beer glass put down too heavily. Then the coffee bean grinder started up, drowning out everything else. When it stopped, the silence was intense.

"Eline had an aura," I said. "I knew she was going to die."

"An aura?"

"I call it an aura, although it's not really that. Just moving air."

"We're all going to die. How does it help to see this aura thing?"

"The aura only appears when death is imminent, usually within a few days, or a couple of weeks at most."

"Did you warn her? Did you tell Eline what you thought you could see?"

"No. There was no time. I was going to talk to her about it, but…"

"What do you want from me?"

"Police protection for Sam and Alex, while you investigate."

"I'd need to justify that to my superiors, and they won't take kindly to a request based on swirling air."

"It's more than just that," I said. "We're being followed by the man with the goatee. I saw him at the bank this morning. And I think he caused an accident in which Sam was injured last night."

"Sam didn't mention an accident when we met this morning. Was he hurt?"

"Not badly, but he could have been. Listen, the point is that we discovered that secret office, and the goatee man is following us. We're in danger."

Nouwen's blue eyes widened. "You too?"

"I don't know. Probably. But I'm mostly concerned with the others. I hoped you might share information with me. If I knew how Eline died, perhaps that would make it easier for me to protect Sam."

To give myself something to do while I waited for Nouwen's response, I pulled my bag closer and retrieved my hand sanitizer. Its lavender smell rose faintly when I rubbed it into my hands, calming my nerves. As Nouwen watched, he seemed to come to a decision. He leaned forward and spoke quietly.

"Eline Janssen was knocked unconscious and then tipped or thrown into the canal. She was still alive when she hit the water, so the official cause of death was drowning."

"Was it supposed to look like an accident?"

Nouwen shrugged. "I don't think so. There were signs of blunt trauma on her skull. And a few other injuries."

I thought about poor Eline's last hours. What had led her to be out alone after telling Karen she'd be home watching television?

"She must have gone to meet someone she knew," I said. "Did you find her mobile? Maybe there were texts to indicate where she was going?"

Nouwen shook his head. "We're dredging the canal to see if we can find it. There are no guarantees. You can't imagine the stuff that turns up. Bikes, of course, by the hundred, but also bottles, shopping trolleys, false teeth." I raised an eyebrow. "No, really," he said. "And hundreds of historical artifacts. It's quite fascinating. But we rarely find what we're looking for."

For a moment, Nouwen appeared far less intimidating, but then the frown returned. "I'll do what I can to get you some protection. But I'd advise you to leave the city if you are truly concerned for your friends' safety. I know I asked you to stay, but under the circumstances, that might not be the best option for you."

I wondered if he just wanted us off his territory. Having British visitors die in his jurisdiction would be rather embarrassing.

"I have a good team working on this," he said, clasping his hands on the table on front of him. I noticed how surprisingly delicate they were, smooth and long-fingered. "We are talking to everyone who knew Eline Janssen and we're looking for eyewitnesses, of course."

"What about Tessa? Did you look into her death? I can't believe she just fell. It's too much of a coincidence."

"Yes. We're reviewing the autopsy report."

"You'll talk to Pieter Janssen? He's up to something, for sure."

"When we find him, yes." Nouwen sighed. I knew I was wearing out my welcome.

"And Henk, the caretaker at the house. He knows more than he's saying. He must be a Zeckendorf employee, don't you think? He's been working there for decades, even when the house was empty, so someone must have been paying him."

Nouwen held up both hands to stop me. "We are following every lead, I promise." He checked his watch. "I need to go. You have my number and you can ring me anytime. I will be back in touch very soon. For now, just be patient."

Patient. The one thing I couldn't afford to be. Time was running out for Sam and Alex.

22

I walked away from the cafe, wondering if I'd achieved what I'd gone for. Nouwen had been courteous, even quite charming, but had he really internalized anything I'd said about the danger to Alex and Sam? Would he act in time to save their lives?

Feeling the urgency of getting back to the boat to make sure they were okay, I dug in my bag for my mobile to check the map. At the same time, I felt that familiar prickle on the back of my neck, a sudden awareness of someone standing too close. I turned to see the man with the goatee at my shoulder. He dug something sharp into my ribs.

"No noise," he warned. "I'll use the knife. And things will go badly for all of you. Now come with me."

I stumbled a few steps forward, steadied by a hand that gripped my elbow. Within seconds, my attacker had shoved me into the back seat of a car, a BMW, probably the one that had come rushing when Sam and I had triggered the alarm in the tunnel. He climbed in beside me and tapped the back of the driver's seat.

"Let's go."

In front, the driver revved the engine and we sped off.

"Who are you?" I twisted to look at the man with the beard. "Is your name Martin Eyghels?"

He laughed. "Martin Eyghels died a long time ago. You can call me Max."

His English was good, with a hint of a British accent, which sounded a little put on. In the rearview mirror, I saw the driver glance back at us, chuckling. I doubted Max was my abductor's real name.

"Where are we going?"

"You ask too many questions. That's been the problem all along. Prying, poking around, getting into things you shouldn't. Irresponsible behavior has consequences. Oh, and give me your phone."

When I didn't immediately offer it up, Max sighed. "Don't be stupid. I will take it from you if I have to."

I handed it over, my only link to Sam. It hurt.

"We were planning to leave the city," I said. "I was calling for a taxi to the airport when you so rudely interrupted me."

He turned his head to gaze at me. He wasn't particularly evil-looking, although those colorless eyes were cold. The blond, trimmed goatee and neat haircut showed he was more concerned with his appearance than his shapeless black anorak suggested. In his early forties, maybe, he had a strong build, with thigh muscles that strained his dark-wash jeans.

His thin, pale lips moved upward into a smile, that same smirk he'd given me in the lobby of the bank.

"Too bad for you, Kate, that I don't believe you."

My stomach filled with ice. He knew my name.

"And I do appreciate your going for a walk just now," he said. "I'd tracked you to this area but you did a good job of disappearing and I'd lost you. So, you can imagine how happy I was to see you coming out of that café. Now you can tell me where Sam is."

He didn't know where Sam was. I exhaled a breath of relief.

"Did you kill Eline?" I asked, to change the subject.

"It's my turn to ask a question, and I have several. First, tell me what you found in the safety deposit box."

So that was what he was after. "There were several things in there. What were you interested in, specifically?"

He leaned over and grasped my arm. His accent slipped a bit, rougher, less refined. "Don't mess with me. You'll tell me, or I can ask your friends. I'm sure Karen would be happy to talk to me."

Once you find her, I thought. And I wasn't going to help with that. I'd do anything to keep this creep away from the others.

He kept the pressure on my arm. "Well? What was in the box?"

I had to tell him something to get him to back off. "There was an addendum to Tomas's will adding Pieter Janssen as a co-inheritor with Eline."

Max released my arm, and I rubbed my wrist to get the blood flowing again.

"Ah, Pieter," he murmured.

"Do you know where he is? Have you taken him too? Or is he working with you?"

My questions seemed to amuse Max. He smirked and then leaned over to tousle my hair as though I was a little kid who'd just said something silly. I pulled away, horrified, my heart racing.

Afraid of provoking another weird reaction and worried that he would touch me again, I stayed quiet, wondering about Pieter. He could be dead. That would explain his absence and his silence, but I wasn't sure why Max would think that what I said was funny, even in the alternate universe that he lived in. And Pieter hadn't had an aura when I saw him. But then, Alex didn't have an aura earlier this week either.

"Do you know about Zeckendorf?" I asked, which caused Max to lean over and grip my wrist again.

"What do you know about them?"

"Enough to know they're up to no good."

"You shouldn't be so quick to judge us." He let go of my arm and settled back in his seat. "You have no idea what you're talking about."

"Why don't you tell me then? What it is that you do?"

He chose to ignore me, so I gazed out of the window in an attempt to work out where we were going. The area seemed familiar, but we'd walked everywhere, and everything looks different from a car.

When we stopped at a red light in heavy traffic, I seized the chance. Unlatching my seatbelt while pulling on the door lever, I braced myself, ready to jump. But the door remained closed, the handle useless.

"Child locks," Max said.

Of course. I should have known. He hadn't bothered to tie my hands. I was a prisoner in the BMW. But maybe I could attract someone's attention. Beating my fists on the window next to me, I yelled for help, willing a bored driver to look my way, to no avail. The young man in the car nearest to us stared straight ahead, bobbing his head up and down, presumably in time to music I couldn't hear.

"I wouldn't do that if I were you." Max's voice was low and threatening. I looked back to see him extract his knife from his pocket. With an ornate, carved black handle and a long blade tapering to a vicious point, it was a nasty-looking thing that could have come from a medieval torture museum.

Defeated and furious, I turned away from the window.

"Sensible move." Max tucked the weapon back inside his anorak. "Now tell me where the others are."

I didn't respond even though my heart was pounding. I couldn't betray them. They'd soon work out that I wasn't coming back, then they'd call Nouwen and move somewhere else. I just had to play for time.

Max clenched his fists until the knuckles went white. "I can force you to tell me," he said. But he didn't follow up. Instead we rode in silence for five minutes before he spoke again. "We're here."

The car turned into the empty parking area behind the building that housed the graphics design firm and pulled up close to the entrance. I noticed a bike rack against the wall. It, too, was empty.

"We'll walk calmly into the office and you'll follow my lead," Max instructed. He seemed to have regained his composure and his fake British accent. "One squeak from you, I will hurt you. Understood?"

With the knifepoint at my ribs, I stumbled up the entry steps into a spacious lobby, its white walls decorated with colorful framed prints of product adverts, none of which I recognized. The place was empty, and a notice on the desk instructed visitors to ring the bell for assistance.

Standing at a door to the side of the reception area, Max entered numbers on a keypad. With a beep, the door opened to a narrow landing at the top of the staircase I'd climbed with Sam twelve hours ago.

Max walked me down the stairs and then at a brisk pace through the tunnel. It was probably just over a hundred meters at most, but it seemed to take a long time to cover the distance between the commercial building and the Janssen house. Plenty of time for me to grow increasingly apprehensive.

Finally, we reached the other end, where the spiral staircase wound up to the wiring cupboard in the old kitchen of the house. Set in the wall next to the stairs was the steel door that Sam had tried to open last night. Tears of frustration clogged my throat. Letting myself get abducted wasn't going to help him at all.

Maintaining his grip on my arm, Max used his other hand to enter a code on the keypad. The heavy door eased open to reveal a brightly illuminated room lined with metal filing cabinets, all painted grey and numbered. In one corner, a metal staircase led upwards. That had to be the way up to the secret office on the top floor. Staring at it, I was taken by surprise when Max shoved me forward, making me stumble on the uneven cement floor. I fell to one knee, jarring every bone in my leg.

"Brute," I muttered.

His grin was menacing. "You have no idea."

Fear paralyzed my brain, raised goosebumps on my skin, and set my heart pounding like an engine piston. Under the strong white lights, Max's features became sharp angles. He rested his pale eyes on me for a few seconds as though considering what to do to me. Then he shrugged. "Get up. Let's go."

A few deep breaths helped to clear my mind, just enough anyway, to take note of our route as we passed through the cabinet-filled room to yet another keypad-protected door. My knee ached but I tried hard not to limp. I didn't want to give Max the satisfaction of seeing I was hurt.

Once we were through the door, and it had clanged shut behind us, Max let go of my arm. "Follow me," he said.

Overhead, a bare bulb hung from a wire, forming a puddle of light rimmed by dark shadows. It took time for my eyes to adjust to the semi-darkness, but Max marched on. On heavy and unwilling legs, I followed, peering through the gloom, gauging the size and shape of the space. We must be in a series of cellars under the house, and this one was massive, I soon realized, mirroring the spacious rooms of the apartment and the empty expanses of the upper floors. It was rough and unfinished, the stone walls exposed, and it reeked of damp and mold.

Max stopped at a small door of dark wood with iron hinges. No keypad here, just a rusty old bolt which he slid open. He pushed me inside. A single bulb hung from a low brick ceiling, casting an anemic light over the cramped space. The walls and floor were made of stone and there were no windows.

It was a prison cell, and it already had an inmate. To my astonishment, Henk was there, his aura rotating rapidly over his thin grey hair. He sat hunched over on a bed that was pushed against the back wall. He glanced up with an expression of shock when he saw us, but he didn't speak.

"What's going on?" I projected more assurance than I felt. Even when Sam contacted the police, they'd have no way of finding me down here.

"From you, I need information and then you can leave," Max said, which I knew was a lie from the way his eyes shifted when he said it. He had no intention of letting me go. "And for Henk here, well, it's the end of the road. He betrayed us and from that, there's no going back."

"Betrayed you how? What did he do?"

Max tilted his head. "Oh, come on. He told you about the upper floors, about the vault."

"No, he didn't. He never said a word. Just the opposite. Even when we asked him questions, he didn't say anything. And we think he staged a number of... pranks, in an attempt to scare us out of the house,"

Max smiled. "Really?" He turned to Henk and spoke in Dutch. Henk nodded once or twice.

"Well, you're right about the incidents," Max told me. "He was indeed trying to get you out of the house, out of harm's way. So very noble of him. Now, tell me where the others are."

"No."

"Okay." He grabbed Henk by the arm and pulled him to his feet. "Both of you come with me." He frog-marched Henk out of the cell and across the gloomy outer chamber. "Keep up," he warned me.

Max prodded Henk along as the old man's breathing grew more labored, making me worry he might have a heart attack. Once or twice he glanced at Max with an expression of hatred on his face. Even in the dim light, I could see the air over his head swirling madly. Things were not looking good for the old man.

When we came to a stop in front of an arched opening on the right-hand wall of the chamber, Henk held his hands out in front of him as though warding off some unseen horror. Seeing his distress, I moved closer to him, ready to help him if I could.

The arch formed an entry into an alcove about four meters deep and built of brick that glowed red in the light from a small LED torch that Max was holding. He dragged the caretaker inside, all the way to the back, and played the beam across the walls. Many of the bricks were marked with scratched letters, but they were impossible to read from my position at the entrance. I had no intention of going in there. It smelled of damp stone and decay.

Henk, clearly agitated, pulled himself free of Max's grasp and put both hands over his face. When Max laughed and spoke to him in Dutch, the elderly caretaker sank to his knees and bent forward, his forehead on the stone floor. What the hell?

Max turned to me with that sardonic smile etched on his lips. "I was reminding Henk of the history of this place. Come over, take a look for yourself."

I took a reluctant step forward. The air inside felt heavy, saturated with despair. Up close, the letters looked like sets of initials, roughly etched into the brick.

"It's a burial chamber." Max pointed. "See here? These are the initials of those who died, the early ones at least. Later on, no one bothered to record the names."

I felt faint, horrified by Max's words.

"What people?" I asked. "How did they die?"

Henk started shuffling backwards out of the alcove. Max grabbed his arm, making the old man stop. Trembling, Henk bowed his head.

"People who betrayed us." Max traced a letter with his finger. "Including Henk's grandfather." He gave a deep sigh. "Now, we have other ways to punish traitors, using computers. That works too, but sometimes we have to do things the old-fashioned way."

My legs shook so badly that I crouched down, hoping to mitigate the damage to my head if I fainted and fell. Pain shot through my temples. Max was more dangerous than I'd even imagined. He was a psychopath.

Still, his comment about computers cast some light on the presence of that high-tech office upstairs. But how was Henk's grandfather involved in all of this?

Max talked to Henk for what seemed like a long time, his voice growing louder by the second. The old man spoke occasionally, but none of what he said seemed to please our captor. He yanked on Henk's elbow and turned back towards the cell.

As I slowly got to my feet, hoping for the dizziness to pass, Henk came to a sudden halt, planting his feet on the stone floor. Max muttered at him in Dutch, but Henk refused to budge, instead twisting his head to look back at me. He said something I didn't understand. Whatever it was, it made Max angry. He swung his fist and punched Henk violently in the stomach. Henk doubled over, clutched at his chest, and sank to the ground. The noise of his head connecting with stone took my breath away.

After a few seconds of being paralyzed by shock, I bent down beside him. His eyelids fluttered, his breath rasped in his chest. I held my fingers against his neck and felt a faint pulse. It faltered and, seconds later, it stopped.

"Come on, Henk," I shouted at him. "You're not going to die down here. Do you hear me?"

In horror, I saw the spinning air over his head slow and fade. He was dead. I unbuttoned his jacket, ready to start chest compressions, but Max grabbed my arm and dragged me to my feet.

"Leave him."

"You killed him."

Max shrugged. "He deserved it, believe me. Just like his grandfather, who told the authorities the house was being used to store weapons destined for delivery to the Nazis. No one betrays Zeckendorf and lives to talk about it. Henk's father was allowed to stay on, though. He was only too aware of the risk of crossing the organization. He was loyal. And I'd thought his son was too, but he obviously changed his allegiances." Max glanced back at the dreadful tomb. "We need to keep moving."

He marched me back to the cell, where he shoved me inside and made me sit on the cot. The fact that he hadn't already killed me made me feel a bit better. Still, my situation was dire. No one knew where I was, and there were steel doors with passcodes between me and freedom.

Standing over me, Max asked where Sam and Karen were. I was thinking it was interesting that he didn't mention Alex when he pulled his knife from his jacket and waved it in front of me. "Tell me where they are."

"I don't know."

"I don't want to hurt you, Kate." He gave me his serpent-y smile. "Actually, that's not true. Nothing would give me more pleasure. But there's a lot at stake here so I need you to cooperate, right now."

"Tell me why. What is it that you want? We've already told the police about the tunnel and the secret office and the vault. It's too late to stop us from talking about what we've found."

"I want the documents you found in the safety deposit box. And I want your friends to bring them to me."

"We showed the police photos of those too. There are no secrets left to protect."

Max thrust my phone back at me. "Show me."

I opened the phone and noticed there was no signal. Not surprising, given the mass of stone and concrete between me and the outside world. I pulled up the photo of the letter to Tomas.

"That's it," I said. "I showed it to a detective earlier."

Max contemplated the photo for a few seconds. "What else did you find?"

"Eline's mother's jewelry, a copy of the house deed and a note from Eline to Karen."

"What did it say?"

I thought back. "Something about being worried that Tomas was being hounded by Zeckendorf. Why? What were you and Tomas fighting about?"

"Nothing you need to know about. Was there anything else in the box?"

"A platinum signet ring, like the one you're wearing. What does that mean? Is it like some sort of weird club thing?"

Was Pieter wearing one? I couldn't remember, yet I was sure I'd seen another one in the last few days.

"You ask too many questions, Kate. Shut up and listen to me. This is what will happen. I'm going to send a message from you to Sam. Tell me your passcode."

I refused, but that earned me a slap across the face that made me think my jaw had been dislocated. I tasted blood in my mouth. "It's 5886," I said finally. My birthday. It struck me that I might not live to see the next one.

Max started scrolling. "I found Sam's number. And I see Karen's too. Thank you. So, this is what will happen next. I will send a message, from you as far as they know, telling Sam and Karen to meet me with the contents of the safety deposit box. The message will go out as soon as I'm upstairs. From that moment, they have one hour to comply. If they don't turn up at the specified place and time, you will die. I hope your friends care about you enough to save you, Kate. If you'd rather not take that risk, just tell me where they are, and I'll go pick the stuff up myself."

I took a surreptitious glance at my watch. How long before Sam would realize I wasn't coming back to the boat? It had only been ninety minutes. I wasn't certain that I'd been gone long enough yet for him to worry, to move on somewhere else. I looked up to see Max watching me.

"Your choice. Tell me where to find them and, when I have what I need, you'll all go free."

"You killed Henk. I can't trust you. I think you'll kill us all once you have what you want."

Max held his hand over his heart. "Not trust me? I'm wounded, Kate, I really am. But if that's the way you want to play it..."

He turned and walked out, bolting the door closed behind him.

After Max left, the silence in the cell was palpable. It hung over the cot and mingled with the shadows in the corners. I doubted I had ever heard absolute silence before. Even on occasions when I'd been alone, there had been traffic noise, or wind in the trees, or the call of an owl or songbird. In the void, my ears rang.

My blood pressure seemed to plummet, leaving me light-headed and dizzy. I gripped the edge of the cot, fighting off nausea and trying to order my thoughts. What would Sam do when he got Max's text? I hoped he'd realize it was a trap and just call the police. Karen and Alex would surely be able to persuade him not to rush over here, and it was obvious that Max didn't know where they were. For now, they were safe.

I got up off the uncomfortable cot and examined the cell. The solid walls of stacked stone were blackened with mildew and slimy with moss. It felt like a dungeon from the Middle Ages, only missing lengths of thick rusty chain and instruments of torture. The floor was laid with slabs of the same grey, mold-mottled stone.

I tapped my way along the walls, looking for a gap, a loose stone that might be pried out. But the walls, centuries old, were unyielding.

Then I attacked the door, first yanking on the door handle, then throwing myself against the old wood, hoping it would be rotten and give way under my weight. But the door remained sealed shut, an impossible obstacle. In a final desperate attempt to find an exit, I tried to slide the cot away from the wall, visions of a trapdoor dancing in my head. But the bed was immoveable, and when I wriggled under it to check, I found it was bolted to the floor.

Disheartened, I sat down on the cot and rubbed my knee, which was sore from when I'd fallen on it. My jeans were torn, revealing a glimpse of abraded red skin. I hated Max.

I wondered why he hadn't made a run for it when I told him about the police investigation. It wouldn't do him much good to kill me now the police already had the information about Zeckendorf. But he was still looking for something that had been in the safety deposit box. What had we missed?

I jumped up and paced to the door and back, fighting off the urge to scream. I was desperate to talk to Sam and Karen, to tell them to examine everything again. Was it the platinum ring? A document we'd overlooked?

A shortened version of my usual stretching routine did nothing to dissolve the muscle knots in my legs and the tension in my shoulders. I yawned, gulping in dank air. My watch showed five p.m. The day had started at dawn after a long, sleepless night. No wonder I felt exhausted. And thirsty. Fear and adrenaline had sucked up every drop of fluid in my body. My tongue stuck to the roof of my mouth, my lips were strips of sandpaper, the skin on my arms itched.

I dreamed of a jog through St. James Park, breathing fresh air, enjoying the spike of endorphins that would wake me up and clear my brain. The cell was barely ten steps across, though, so I stretched some more, determined to stay awake even though my eyelids were heavy.

But it was a losing battle. Perhaps if I lay down for a few minutes, a nap would help to fight off the exhaustion. I settled on the thin mattress and huddled under a damp-smelling blanket. After rubbing my sore knee for a minute, I soon fell into a troubled sleep.

My watch showed seven when I woke up, far later than I'd intended. I bolted upright, panicked. Max hadn't reappeared. What did that mean? That Sam hadn't responded to the text Max had sent?

Selfishly, a wave of self-pity engulfed me. If Max didn't get what he wanted, he would kill me. Or maybe he'd leave me here to starve slowly to death. I really didn't want to die in this godforsaken prison, cold and alone. Josh might never know what happened to me. My dad and my brother would be devastated.

Unwanted tears gathered in my throat and I swallowed them down. I pushed away the musty blanket and stood up, welcoming the twinge of pain in my knee. It was time to focus, to come up with a plan. Maybe I could outwit Max, take him by surprise. The bare bulb that cast its feeble light on the room was within reach, suspended from the low ceiling. I could unscrew the bulb and hide in the dark, then jump on Max when he opened the door. But a quick search for a weapon of any kind was fruitless. None of the stones in the floor and wall were loose enough to pry up. The bolts holding the bed together had fused into a rusty mess. I doubted I could overcome Max with my bare hands.

Just as I was sinking into further despair, a noise in the outer chamber sent a bolt of electric fear through me. Max was back. I didn't have time to think before the bolt slid back and the door opened. Alex and Sam were pushed into the cell, their auras eddying in the dim light.

Max remained at the door as Alex rushed forward to hug me. "Thank god you're still alive. He wouldn't tell us what he'd done with you."

"Such a touching reunion," Max commented with a sneer. He turned and closed the door. I heard the bolt being rammed back into place.

"What happened? How did Max find you?" I asked. "Where's Karen?"

Sam sat down heavily on the cot. "She's safe. She was going to get in touch with Nouwen while Alex and I went to meet Max to do a deal. We decided we would give him everything from the deposit box if he agreed to release you. We'd even chosen a hand-off location."

"That went well," Alex said. "As you can see."

"Did you ring Detective Nouwen?"

"No, but Karen will have told him everything by now. We didn't know for sure where Max was holding you, but she'll tell them to start with this house, as that was a likely option."

"You shouldn't have gone to meet Max." I crouched down in front of him. "Why put yourself in danger? What if Max had been keeping me somewhere else, where the police would never find us?" I looked around the dismal cell. "As if they could ever find us down here anyway."

"Water under the bridge. We did what we thought was right." Sam bowed his head. He looked and sounded defeated.

"Chin up." I reached up to give him a hug. "I'm sure the police will find us. Karen will tell them about this place. We'll get out of here."

I straightened up and moved to sit next to him on the bed. "Did you look through all the papers after I left? Did you find anything else? Because Max is obviously looking for something we either don't have or don't know we have."

"You saw everything we did." He checked off the items on his fingers. "The white envelope containing the addendum to Tomas's will, adding Pieter as co-inheritor. The copy of Tomas's letter to Zeckendorf requesting that they allow Eline to stay in the house. The return letter from Zeckendorf agreeing to the arrangement as long as Pieter inherited the estate if anything happened to Eline." He looked at Alex. "Anything else?"

"Tomas's platinum ring," she added.

"Like the one Max is wearing," I said. "It must be some sort of membership symbol. I've seen it somewhere else too, but I can't remember where. Anyway, Max insists there was something else in the box. I just don't understand what it can be."

Alex had been walking back and forth from one side of our prison to the other. Now she sat on the ground facing us, her legs pulled up in front of her.

"I have something to tell you," she said.

It must have been my imagination, but suddenly the cell felt colder. I huddled a little closer to Sam, feeling the warmth of his shoulder.

"I've been working for Zeckendorf." Alex lifted her eyes to meet mine. "I'm really sorry."

Beside me, Sam tensed but he didn't speak.

"Go on," I prompted her.

"They placed me on this project to keep an eye on things and report back. I was supposed to stop you and Sam from digging too deep, uncovering their secrets."

"But you didn't."

"Actually, I did try for a while. But I hadn't foreseen... liking you and Sam so much." Her gaze lingered on Sam, but he was looking down at the floor. "It was hard..."

"Have you always worked for them?"

"God, no. I only heard about them a week ago. My grandfather on my mum's side was part of the group back in the 1980s and 1990s. He tried to recruit my mum, but she was having none of it. That's the main reason she moved to London. But for all these years, they kept an eye on her. They knew where she lived, they knew about me. They even knew I'd graduated in structural engineering, so they told Mum they needed me for this job. If I didn't agree, they would... well, they would ruin our lives."

The oxygen seemed to leave the little room. Alex choked up and a tear slid down her cheek. I shifted on the thin mattress. Sam still didn't move.

"You knew Max before today?"

She nodded. "He was the one who gave me my instructions, but I could tell he didn't trust me. That's why he's been following us around, as a back-up."

"Did you meet him last night? Is that why you disappeared for a while?"

"Yes." Alex closed her eyes for a moment. "My aunt isn't ill. I went to see Max to tell him I couldn't do it anymore. I planned on quitting and going to London, providing I could persuade Sam and you to leave as well. But he told me I had to stay until he'd retrieved what he wanted from the safety deposit box."

"Which is what exactly?"

Alex clambered to her feet and leaned against the wall. "I honestly don't know. He wouldn't tell me. It was only when you all headed to the bank that he knew the safety deposit box even existed and now he's convinced that *it,* whatever it is, was in that box."

"And that's what Pieter was looking for, too?"

Sam finally lifted his head. "Pieter is part of Zeckendorf?"

"Yes," Alex said. "He may even be the *Gezagvoerder*, the commander, of it all. The name originated with the ships that the VOC sent to Indonesia. My mother told me that. Anyway, I think Max likes to think he runs the organization, but I suspect he's a little lower on the totem pole." She took a couple of steps towards Sam.

Instinctively, I jumped up and moved in between them.

"I would never hurt Sam," she said. "Never, I swear. That's why I'm in danger now, because I disobeyed Max's instructions. He'll kill me when he kills you. My mum..." She covered her face with her hands, her shoulders heaving as she sobbed loudly.

Sam stood up and gently moved me aside so he could face Alex. The look of hurt on his face made the blood pound in my temples. He cared for Alex. He'd trusted her. I had too.

"I'm sorry," she said again, staring into Sam's eyes. "Please believe me."

I wasn't convinced. She could be lying.

It seemed that Sam was feeling the same way. He went back to the cot and slumped down on it. I joined him, my mind in turmoil. I was still coming to terms with the fact that Pieter and Max were Zeckendorf. Tomas had been, too. In spite of my feelings about Alex, I agreed with her that Max was unlikely to be the leader. I doubted he had the skills needed to run the sophisticated operation that Zeckendorf appeared to be. He'd made clear his low opinion of computers as weapons; he was definitely a guns and knives kind of thug. Shuddering, I thought of the way he'd treated Henk in the outer chamber and wondered if the old man's body was still out there.

Despondent and suddenly shaking with cold, I dragged the old blanket up around me. The damp air had permeated my jacket and jeans, chilling my skin. It reminded me of the fog on the Scottish moorland surrounding the castle where I'd stayed last year. Another aura, another death.

Sam turned to me. "Are you all right?"

"Just giving into my worst fears for a moment." I took a breath. "What do we do now?"

"Karen will send help," Sam said with confidence.

"We came through at least two, maybe three, steel doors with keypads," I reminded him. "How do the police get through those? Even if they know to look down here. These cellars aren't on the plans."

"We told Karen about the tunnel. She'll make sure Nouwen knows."

I paused, not sure if I should share my reservations with him. "Do you trust Karen?" I asked, with a glance towards Alex.

When Sam raised an eyebrow, I explained. "She doesn't have an aura, so she's not in the same danger that we are."

"That doesn't mean she works for Zeckendorf," Sam said. "She'll be safe. Nouwen will look after her."

"You're right." I stared at Alex. "It's not as though having an aura signifies innocence."

She winced, and I felt a tiny bit guilty, but not much. She'd led us on, made me think she was helping me to protect Sam, when she was working for the very people who threatened us.

"Is there anything else you can tell us about Zeckendorf?" I asked her. "Not that it makes any difference, but I'm curious as to how exactly we all got here. And please sit down. You're making me nervous, looming over us like that."

"Before I left London, I convinced my mother to tell me what she knew." Alex sat on the floor again, her back against the wall. "Jacob Hals, who built this house, and a couple of his colleagues started the organization. Their first operations were fairly minor, siphoning off a percentage of goods imported by the Dutch East India Company and selling them privately. They moved on to insurance fraud, and then, basically, anything that made money. Over the centuries, they've been into diamond smuggling, gambling, drug dealing, insider trading. And worse. Collaboration with the Nazis and Mafia-style executions of their enemies. A lovely bunch of people. But Mum was scared to talk about them. When Max showed up, demanding my services, she was terrified."

"Aren't you worried they'll hurt your mother if you turn on them?" I asked.

"Of course I am. But there are no guarantees. They could decide to kill us both anyway, just to make sure we don't give them away."

From what I'd seen of Max, I thought that was possible, although the timing of Alex's aura suggested otherwise. She hadn't been in danger until she'd crossed them. Which almost made me believe she was telling us the truth. Almost.

"Max told me some things about the house," Alex continued. "He said I needed to know about the hidden places so I could try to keep you away from them." Her voice was low and faltering.

"When were the walled-off rooms created?" I asked.

"Right at the beginning, in the original construction. They were always there, to be used for secret meetings, storing illegal goods— and sometimes people. This house was built to conceal secrets, Max said."

"So you already knew about the concrete pillar, and the vault and the tunnel?"

She bowed her head. "Yeah."

"And what do they do up there in the office?"

"You know Max. He wouldn't give me straight answers, but it was something to do with developing cyber weapons that they sell to the highest bidder."

"Cyber weapons?" Sam asked, seeming to wake from a deep reverie.

"There have been some famous ones, like Stuxnet, that closed down the Iranian nuclear plants," Alex said. "I did some research to find out more. There are many, many versions. Bad actors use them to disrupt money markets, wipe out corporate data, mess with election results, or shut off ATMs like they did once in South Korea. That's what they were doing up on the top floor."

"This place is a nightmare," I said, shifting to try get comfortable.

Alex pointed to my knee, where the jeans had torn when I fell. "What happened?"

"Max," I shrugged. "Not that it matters now." I paused. "He killed Henk."

Alex's eyes widened. "What? Why?"

"He thinks Henk told us about the vault, which isn't true. But Henk did admit to staging those pranks, trying to warn us off."

"Poor Henk. I wish I'd liked him better." Alex sighed. "He said his father had told him once that being given residence in the house was a privilege, reserved for the more senior members of the organiza-tion. They were called owners, but in reality they didn't ever own the building. And, of course, working for them was considered a great privilege too."

"Henk knew you were working for Zeckendorf?" Another betrayal. It made me angry.

Alex's cheeks flushed pink. "Yes. We were supposed to cooperate, but I think he knew my heart wasn't in it. He was a lifer, and I'd been coerced into helping. We didn't get along."

Sam was quiet, staring at some fixed point on the stone floor.

"So now what?" I asked finally. "Max could be back at any time. Can we take him down between us?"

"Yes!" Alex scrambled to her feet. "There are three of us, only one of him. We can do it."

Sam looked up. "We don't know the codes for the keypad-protected doors, so we'd still be stuck down here."

"Not necessarily," I said. "There's a staircase in the cabinet room that must lead to the top floor."

"And a steel door between us and that room," Sam reminded me.

"But I suppose we'd be safe until the police work out how to break through."

We were about to test our theory. Footsteps echoed through the outer chamber, thudding to the same rhythm as my heartbeat. The bolt on the outside of the door shrieked like a human in pain.

24

Max walked in. From behind the door as it creaked open, I jumped on his back while Alex and Sam charged straight at him. Max teetered under the onslaught. Alex grabbed his left arm as Sam raised a clenched fist, aiming at Max's face.

But then Alex suddenly stepped back, leaving Max's left arm free to defend himself against Sam's blow. For a sickening moment, I thought she'd betrayed us.

And then I saw the gun in his right hand. He was pointing it at her. "Get back or I'll shoot her."

Sam took two steps back, and I followed suit, my body shaking with pent-up adrenaline. For a few seconds, I'd really thought we would succeed in overcoming Max and escaping. But the small black gun changed everything.

"Sit on the bed," he ordered. We did, the three of us shoulder to shoulder, with Alex in the middle. She was trembling, her hands clasped tightly in her lap.

"The interesting thing about this space is that it's totally self-contained," Max went on. "Whatever happens in here stays in here."

He chuckled and then pointed the gun at Sam. "You cooperate or you die, one by one. Where's Karen?"

"At the police station," Sam answered. "Talking to the detectives and beyond your reach."

"No. If she cares what happens to you, she's not. After I texted you from Kate's phone to set up our meeting, I sent her a message, warning her that I'll kill you all if she goes to the police. So, if she's smart, I'd guess is that she's hiding and that she still has everything you found in the safety deposit box. You just tell me where she is, and this can all be over."

"If we're going to die, will you at least tell us what it is that's worth killing us for?" Alex asked.

"Shut up. I don't talk to traitors." Max spoke without looking at her. His eyes and the gun were trained on Sam. He gave an exaggerated sigh. I saw his finger tense on the trigger. All the blood drained from my upper body, replaced by ice water. I felt numb.

"Wait!" Alex said. "I'm not a traitor. I know where Karen is. She's on a houseboat. I'll show you."

Max's colorless eyes shifted from Alex to Sam and back to Alex. She stood up to face him and spoke to him in Dutch while Max smirked with self-satisfaction. It seemed that he'd got what he wanted. She had betrayed us after all.

"You're coming with me," he said to her, in English for our benefit. "If you're lying, I know a lonely stretch of canal with your name on it."

Sam slumped over, his elbows on his knees, his head in his hands.

Without looking at us, Alex followed Max out. The bolt slammed into place, and silence fell on our little cell. I moved over to Sam and wrapped my arm around him. "I'm sorry," I whispered.

Sam lifted his head. "I can't believe she did that."

"Me neither. Do you think Karen's still there at the houseboat?"

He gave me a lopsided grin. "No. She has a friend, a big, strapping man friend, as she described him, who was on his way to meet her at the boat. They were going back to his place to lay low for a while." He took a deep breath. "But now Alex has put herself in real danger by lying to Max. I believed him when he said he'd dump her in a canal."

"Her odds are probably as good as ours, to be honest. At least she's not locked in a dungeon. That was brave of her, though."

"We have to use the time to find a way out of here." Sam unfolded himself from the cot and stood up.

"I checked every square inch of this place," I said. "Every rock and stone. It's impenetrable."

He went to the door and pulled on the handle. "It's bolted," I reminded him.

"Yes, but that bolt is ancient and rusty and the wood on the door is rotting. I had a chance to look at it when Max was bringing us in here. If we put enough pressure on it, it might give."

"Let's give it a try." I gathered the blanket from the cot and rolled it lengthwise to form a rudimentary rope. We wrapped it around the old door handle and pulled. Nothing happened. Sam pushed up his shirtsleeves while I grabbed the rope halfway along its length and we tugged in unison. On the fourth hard tug, the door shifted a tiny bit. On the fifth, the wood gave a loud crack, and I heard the old bolt hitting the stone floor outside.

We dashed out of the cell into the huge, badly-lit chamber beyond. My burst of euphoria faded. Just ahead, Henk's body lay, sprawled and abandoned on the cold stone. Sam and I stopped for a second, but we couldn't do anything for the old man right now. There was a password-protected steel door to get through, and no amount of brute force would get that open.

We moved towards the door anyway, lured to the idea of freedom like moths to a light. When we got closer, I heard a faint tapping sound—someone punching the keypad—and grabbed hold of Sam's arm. The tapping stopped, followed by a loud click.

"We can rush him," Sam whispered. "He won't be expecting us out here."

Light flooded the opening as the door swung towards us. My leg muscles twitched, ready to run, but it wasn't Max standing there. It was Pieter. He didn't look like the well-dressed businessman who'd come to the house two days ago. The tie was gone, his shirt and trousers wrinkled. He had more than a day's worth of stubble on his chin.

"How did you get out? Never mind, tell me later," he said. "We need to move before Max gets back." He beckoned us to follow him.

Not needing any more urging, Sam and I hurried out through the door. Pieter pulled it closed and checked it was secure before joining us for a dash across the room with the filing cabinets. Under the bright lights, a platinum ring gleamed on his finger. That's where I had seen it before, of course. My footsteps slowed. Pieter was part of Zeckendorf, perhaps even the leader of the organization. So why was he rescuing us from Max? Were we heading into something worse?

Sam grabbed my arm. "Keep moving," he said.

"Why is he helping us?" I whispered.

Pieter stopped and turned to talk to me. "It was never meant to be like this. You were supposed to be scared into abandoning the project, not kidnapped and threatened."

"What about Eline?" I demanded. "Was she supposed to die? What kind of monsters are you?"

"Let's talk about that later. We need to get out of here before Max comes back."

"Why don't you just tell him to stop, to back off? Doesn't he have to obey you?"

Pieter's head jerked back in surprise. "No. Max only answers to the *Gezagvoerder*. We all do. Now please, hurry. Max has a gun."

We knew that already, and I really didn't want another encounter with it. Pieter ran ahead and punched numbers into the keypad. The heavy steel door opened. Beyond was the tunnel, blazing with lights. He set off at a jog in the direction of the graphics design building.

"Where are we going?" Sam asked after a few steps. "We have to help Alex and Karen."

"Exactly," Pieter answered. "We're going to find Karen first and then we'll look for Alex."

His skin was pale, even under the ruby glow of the red-brick walls.

"Wait," I said, coming to a halt. Max or no Max, rushing off with Pieter seemed ill-advised at best. "You have to tell us what's going on."

He turned and raised his arms in a gesture of frustration. "I'm rescuing you."

"But why?"

His hands dropped to his sides. "I need your help."

"Help with what?" Sam asked.

Pieter glanced nervously up the tunnel. "They're going to frame me for Eline's murder. Tessa's too. I didn't kill them, I swear, but I won't stand a chance against Zeckendorf. They're too powerful. My only hope is to find the list first. If I give them that, I can prove I'm still loyal. So, you have to help me find it. Before Max gets his hands on it."

"What list? And why does Max want it?"

"He's in all sorts of trouble. Unauthorized hits mostly, because he's a violent and unstable man. He needs some leverage with the organization to keep his position. And his life."

"And the list is..." Sam started. A racket at the end of the tunnel stopped him.

Pieter swore in French and turned to run in the opposite direction, back the way we'd just come. I hesitated, staring in the direction of the noise. Could that be Nouwen and his men?

Seconds later, my question was answered. Four men in dark suits ran towards us, each one holding a gun. One of them yelled at us, in Dutch I assumed. None of them looked like police officers.

I glanced back to see that Pieter had reached the steel door into the cabinet room. He jabbed at the keypad and shouted for us to join him. But I couldn't move. Fear and indecision had cemented my feet to the stone floor. Sam stayed with me.

The four men stopped in their tracks suddenly, like disconnected robots. In the eerie silence, I heard a single set of footsteps coming closer. Soon, a suited figure came into view, striding towards us. The four men fell in behind him.

"You?" Sam sounded as shocked as I felt.

Bleeker inclined his head and spoke in his well-enunciated English. "Delighted to have arrived in time."

As on the previous occasions when we'd met, he was dressed in an expensive suit, dark grey today, with a starched white shirt and blue silk tie.

"Arrived in time for what?" I asked.

"To save you from poor Pieter. I'm afraid he's completely out of control."

A metallic thud echoed along the tunnel. I looked back to see that the steel door had closed, and there was no sign of Pieter. He had locked himself in the filing cabinet room. When I turned around, Sam and Bleeker were talking. Sam said something to me, but I didn't hear what he said. My attention was on his aura, which still circled over him. That was weird. It should disappear now that he was safe.

"Don't worry. We'll get Pieter the care he needs," Bleeker was saying.

Confused by the presence of the aura, I took a deep breath. Maybe it would take another minute or two for the moving air to go away.

Bleeker held up a hand to beckon one of his men over and I found myself staring at the platinum ring on his finger. Now I remembered noticing it when Bleeker first came to the house. At the time, I'd had no idea what it signified.

"You're Zeckendorf," I said to him.

His expression didn't change, but I noticed a faint twitch under his right eye. "Zecken who, my dear?"

"Are you the leader? The commander?"

Sam moved close to me, his hand seeking mine. He gripped my fingers tightly.

Bleeker shook his head as if bemused. "Let's get you upstairs. It's been a terrible ordeal, I'm sure. But you're quite safe now."

He whispered to the man next to him, who came over and cupped my elbow in his hand, applying gentle pressure.

"Run, Sam," I whispered.

"Not so fast." Bleeker motioned another man forward. This one was less subtle. He stared at us like a predatory animal eyeing its next meal. His shaved head gleamed as he grabbed Sam's arm and bent it up behind his back.

"So, what we need is your help in finding Karen," Bleeker said. "We think she has the list. Once that is safely in my possession, you will be free to leave. Where is she?"

That word 'list' again. Pieter had said it and now Bleeker. But what list? There hadn't been anything like that among the papers Karen had picked up from the safety deposit box.

Bleeker repeated his question. "Where is Karen?"

"We don't know," I replied. "But Max went to look for her. He works for you, doesn't he?"

"Max is an idiot," Bleeker said. "But that does add some urgency to the situation. Where is Alex?"

"She's with Max."

He nodded approvingly. "Good. That will make things easier."

Easier for whom? To do what? While I pondered those questions, Bleeker turned to talk in Dutch to his men. The two already holding Sam and me tightened their grip. The other two ran along the tunnel to the steel door. One of them pressed buttons on the keypad and they slipped in before the door was fully open. I wasn't sure what to make of Pieter, but I didn't think he'd easily evade the two thugs. Each of them was twice his size. He didn't have an aura, though, so maybe I was underestimating him.

"Off we go then," Bleeker said, turning to lead the way towards the exit through the graphics design office. "You can talk while we drive."

25

A s we marched through the tunnel, I listened carefully, straining to hear any noise that would indicate the presence of Nouwen's team, but I only heard Bleeker's elegant leather wingtips tapping on the stone floor.

We reached the end of the tunnel and climbed the stairs to the design firm's lobby where another henchman in a suit waited, one hand tucked inside his jacket. A wire ran from his ear and he was talking on a mobile. He finished the call immediately, his eyes scanning us, assessing us for threats, I supposed, and he stayed at Bleeker's shoulder as we headed to the exit.

My captor pushed me out through the door towards a flashy black Mercedes parked outside. And then he yanked me back in as sirens screamed on the street beyond. Within seconds, two police cars sped into the car park, tires squealing and lights flashing. Officers in bulletproof jackets poured out of both vehicles.

Bleeker and his men retreated rapidly, hauling us along with them. They slammed the office door closed and bolted it. Then we scrambled back down the metal stairway and began a hundred-meter dash along the tunnel.

The bald man holding Sam let go of him and sprinted ahead to

enter the passcode for the steel door at the far end. It slowly swung
open. I guessed we'd all head for the cabinet room and use the
metal stairs to reach the top floor. From there, we could get into the
house through the hole we'd made in the wall, then run down the
stairs and out through the front door. I could only hope the police
would be guarding the front of the building by the time we
got there.

But no one had followed the bald man into the cabinet room.
Instead, Pieter came out, accompanied by the other two thugs. I didn't
know what to make of the nod Pieter gave me. Was he sending a
message? I couldn't decipher it, if so.

All three men were carrying grey metal boxes like the ones we'd
seen in the safe upstairs. They contained ammunition, it turned out,
which was quickly distributed to Bleeker and the others. Baldy gave
Pieter a handgun. Together, they joined the other men to form a solid
line in front of Bleeker, facing in the direction of the design office,
waiting for the police to break through the steel door.

The prospect of a gun battle turned my legs to water. Standing
next to Bleeker, as instructed, I leaned against Sam, glad of his
shoulder against mine.

"We're going to get out of this," I said without much conviction.
"The police will rescue us."

A deafening bang surged through the tunnel like a tidal wave.
The clatter of boots on the metal stairway sounded like a death rattle.
It was going to be a bloodbath down here if Bleeker didn't call his
men off. But they were showing no signs of backing down. Guns
raised, feet braced, they waited.

I realized that their attention was focused on the tunnel in front
of them, as was Bleeker's. No one was watching us. Taking hold of
Sam's hand, I inched backwards. None of them paid any attention.
We took another couple of steps and then froze as the first of the
police officers came into view. Bleeker said something to his men and
they all lowered their guns. I sagged against Sam with relief.

But the moment lasted only a couple of seconds. Bleeker turned,
reached out to grab my arm and put his gun against my temple. He

shouted at the officers. One of them spoke into a radio but it seemed it wasn't working, hardly surprising given our location.

Baldy moved, light on his feet, and stood right next to Sam, gun pointed at his head.

The officers raised their semi-automatics again. I couldn't breathe. Time seemed to slow. I heard ticking in my head, an inexorable cosmic chronometer, tapping out my last seconds on Earth. Thoughts of Josh, my dad and my brother fluttered in my brain, but the prospect of their grief was too painful to dwell on. Sam reached out to hold my hand. His fingers were freezing.

The lead officer yelled something that made Bleeker shake his head. He pressed the gun harder against my temple. My whole body began to shake, great tremors that made it hard to stay on my feet. My brain seemed to shut down. I couldn't think clearly. It was terrifying.

I couldn't tell how long we stood there in the netherworld of the old tunnel. It felt like an eon before Bleeker and the officer exchanged words again. This time, Bleeker took the gun away from my head. Baldy lowered his weapon, although he didn't look very happy about it. I took a few deep breaths, trying to calm the shaking and get my brain back to functional. I knew we weren't safe yet. There were still a dozen men with big guns in a small space.

A thought struck me then with the force of a flying bullet. There was another way out. The spiral staircase at the end of the tunnel led up to the wiring closet hidden in the old kitchen. I remembered that Sam had piled shelving in front of the closet door to stop anyone from getting into the house. Still, we stood a chance if we could get that far.

I glanced back over my shoulder, trying not to make it obvious I was looking. A slight curve in the tunnel meant that the staircase wasn't visible, but I knew it was only ten meters beyond where we stood now.

But a look at the gun in Baldy's hand dissolved any hopes of escape. It might as well have been ten miles to the staircase. We'd never make it.

And then the lights went out.

The darkness in the tunnel was absolute. Amidst a tumult of shouted orders, I grabbed Sam's arm and pulled him down to the ground. Seconds later, someone threw a glow stick into the space between the officers and Bleeker's men. It gave off an eerie green light. On both sides, guns were pointed. Baldy had moved closer to Bleeker.

"To the staircase," I whispered to Sam.

We'd only crawled a meter or two when a gunshot boomed. Then another.

My instinct was to get up and run but, with bullets flying around the tunnel, the ground was a better option. Wriggling along the damp floor on our stomachs seemed to take forever. It felt like a war zone, a blur of noise and intense fear. Gunshots and shouting, the thud of boots on the stone floor, the taste of metal in my mouth. I jerked away as a bullet ricocheted off the ground inches from my shoulder, throwing a spray of dust and concrete fragments against my neck.

"Jeez, are you hurt?" Sam whispered.

"No, just scared to death. Keep going."

Another shot. Sam stopped moving. It felt as though my heart stopped, too. "Sam?"

He groaned. "I've been hit," he said. "My leg."

I inched closer. In the faint green light, I saw a small pool of blood spreading on the ground beneath him. "We have to keep moving," I said. "Can you?"

"No choice," he muttered. He pulled himself forward on his elbows and one knee, dragging his injured leg. A few seconds later, we rounded the curve in the tunnel. It was dark here, the light from the glow stick barely reaching us. But the spiral staircase was just a few steps away. I scrambled to my feet and helped Sam to sit on the bottom step. It was hard to think clearly through the fog of raw fear that enveloped me, but I knew we had to get out of the tunnel if we were to have any chance of surviving.

First, I took off my jacket and tied it around his leg. "I'm not sure if that will help, but keep pressure on the wound until I get back. I'm going to see if I can get into the house."

Not waiting for a response, I ran up the staircase and emerged into the corner of the wiring closet. It was so dark I couldn't see a thing. Hands in front of me, I worked my way along the walls until I felt the door. I knew it opened outwards into the old kitchen, so I pushed hard. As I'd feared, Sam's makeshift defense system worked well. The door vibrated but it didn't move.

I pushed again and again, panic urging me on. Frantic, I kicked at the lower panel. It sounded hollow, and I kicked it twice, feeling it give a little. Quickly, I lay on the floor and used the chunky heels of my boots like a battering ram. It worked. The panel gave way and I stood up to peel away enough of the wood to make an opening.

But those damn shelves still blocked our exit. I reached through and took a precious minute to shove aside enough greasy planks to crawl through. Once I was on the other side, I cleared the last of the debris and pulled the door open.

Getting back through the wiring closet and down the spiral stairs seemed to take an eternity, but I was soon with Sam again. He seemed dazed, and I guessed he was going into shock. In the tunnel beyond, there was a lot of yelling but no more shooting. I hooked Sam's arm around my neck and helped him up. "This is going to hurt a bit," I warned.

Half-carrying him, I struggled up the metal stairs. The shouting below continued. I couldn't imagine what was going on down there. I tried not to think about it. All that mattered was getting Sam away from Bleeker and his men.

Finally, we reached the top and crossed into the kitchen with its smell of old grease and smoke. I fumbled in the dark for the light switch, exhaling in relief when the lamps flickered on.

Now that I could see Sam's wound, though, I felt queasy. It was bad, worse than I'd imagined. Blood soaked his trousers. His skin was grey, his eyes half-closed in pain. And his aura was spinning fast. I had to stop the bleeding somehow, but there was nothing in the ancient kitchen that could help, no towels or rugs, not even a dirty old rag. And I was worried Bleeker's men would follow us up the spiral stairs.

"One more push," I said. "We need to get out of here."

I ran though my options. We could go out the front door and hope for help from a passerby, but it was very late. There may not be anyone around at this time of night, and I couldn't leave Sam bleeding on the doorstep while I looked for someone with a mobile phone.

So I made a split-second decision. "We'll go up to the apartment," I told him. "There's a phone line up there. I can call for an ambulance."

I paused long enough in the lobby to turn the key in the lock of the door that led to the old kitchen. It wouldn't hold anyone back for long, but it would slow them down. Then I got Sam into the lift, supporting him as the little cubicle hummed its way upwards. The door slid open on to the landing.

"We're heading to the big sofa," I told him. "You can lie down and rest."

As we struggled towards the archway into the apartment, I heard a noise. Goosebumps prickled my whole body. There was someone in there. Another step, and I saw chaos in the living room. Paintings lay on the carpet, rugs were turned over, drawers of the dressers and tables pulled out.

A man stepped into view. It was Max.

26

"Well, well, you got out of the cellar," Max remarked.

I had no time to think about why he was here. Dragging Sam along, I turned back towards the lift and jabbed at the call button. Max was right behind me. Then his hand was on my shoulder.

"You're not going anywhere," he said.

"Call for an ambulance then. Right now. Sam's hurt."

"I can see that. Put him on the couch."

He watched as I navigated Sam through the debris on the floor to reach the sofa. Alex, standing in the middle of the room, looked stricken. The air over her head still swirled.

"What happened?" Her voice was high and panicked.

"There's a gun battle going on in the cellar. The police and Bleeker." I reached the sofa and lowered Sam on to it. "Sam was hit."

"Bleeker? He's involved in this?"

I thought about that as I lifted Sam's legs and slid cushions underneath them. Had she really not known that Bleeker ran Zeckendorf? It was possible; she'd said it was Max who coached her earlier this week.

I turned to look at him. "Phone for an ambulance. Please."

"Sam is not my priority." He shrugged, a gesture of indifference. "But I will make the call if you agree to cooperate." As he had his gun in his hand, he wasn't exactly giving me a choice.

"Whatever you want. Just get him some help. I need towels and scissors."

"You're not getting them. We have more urgent things to get done here."

I bit back the words that leapt to my lips. If Sam died because Max wouldn't help him, I'd hunt him down and kill him myself.

Alex helped me untie the sleeve of my jacket that I'd used as a temporary tourniquet. I rolled up Sam's blood-soaked trouser leg as high as it would go. The wound, still welling blood, was in his thigh, just above his knee. I couldn't see if the bullet was still in there or not, and I wouldn't know what to do with it anyway. I wadded up the jacket and pressed down, hoping to slow down the bleeding. Sam winced but didn't speak.

"What the hell is going on?" I asked Alex when Max moved away to talk on his mobile. I wanted to snatch the thing from his hand and call emergency services, but he was still holding the gun. "Why is he here?"

"He's looking for something specific, a document," Alex whispered. "He thinks it was in the safety deposit box, but said we had to look here too."

I assumed Max was looking for the list that both Pieter and Bleeker had mentioned. But I didn't care about any of it anymore. I just wanted Sam to be safe. He was looking a little better now that I wasn't dragging him around, but his aura was still spinning violently. The danger was far from over.

"Can you get to the phone?" I whispered to her. "It's in the kitchen."

Her eyes flickered towards Max. It was only then that I noticed a purple bruise on her temple. I looked at her more closely. Her wrist was red and swollen, and she was cradling it against her other arm.

"I'll try." She took a step in the direction of the kitchen, but Max waved the gun at her and shook his head.

"Sorry," she said to me. She sat down heavily on the arm of the sofa.

Max had finished his call and now strode towards the landing. A few seconds later, the doorbell rang. Keeping his gun pointed at us, he lifted the handset to click the front door open. I straightened up, wanting to be ready for whatever came next.

"Alex, take my place. Keep pressure on the wound."

I didn't know if that would be enough. It seemed like hours since Sam had been shot, although my watch confirmed that it had only been fifteen minutes.

There were noises on the stairs and then two people came into the living room. The first was a man I hadn't seen before. Big and muscular, he dwarfed even Max. He was holding Karen by the arm.

I rushed to her. "Are you all right?"

She nodded but her eyes showed her fear and exhaustion.

"How did they find you?"

"I volunteered to meet Max when I got the text from your phone," she said, taking my hand in hers. Her skin was cold, and she was trembling. "I couldn't have lived with myself if anything happened to you or to Sam. So, I told him I'd come with the papers. He sent me an escort, as you can see."

"Oh Karen, I wish you hadn't put yourself in harm's way."

She raised an eyebrow. "I don't have an aura, you said. I trusted I'd be safe."

Her words wrapped a fist around my heart. What if I'd been wrong? What if my aura-sighting capability failed one day? If Karen's trust had been misplaced? I didn't have time to dwell on it though because Max started yelling, first at us to stop talking and then at the big man, who stepped out on to the landing with his gun in his hand. From there, he could keep an eye on us and monitor the stairway at the same time.

Karen let go of me, stood straight and looked around the half-destroyed living room. "So, you're ransacking Eline's home again?" she asked Max.

"I wasn't the one who did it the first time," he said. "If I had, I wouldn't have needed a second attempt. I'm very thorough in my work."

It must have been another of Bleeker's functionaries who turned over the apartment a month ago.

"It's not here," Max continued. "Which means, Karen, that you have it. Did you bring everything?"

She gave a nod and pulled the large white envelope from her tote bag.

"Take the documents out of the envelope and lay them down there." Max pointed to the wall table where the fallen Adam and Eve painting had rested. "Then step back."

Karen did as she was instructed, and we watched while Max leafed through the papers with one hand, keeping the gun pointed in our general direction.

"Everything is here?" he asked Karen again.

"Yes," she confirmed. "Maybe if you told us what you're looking for, I could be of more help."

"The list," he said, as though we were supposed to know what that meant. "The list of current Zeckendorf members. You must have seen it."

Karen and I exchanged looks.

"Why would there be a list of members?" she asked Max. "It would be dangerous if it fell into the wrong hands."

"That's the point, you idiot," he said. "Tomas wrote it up as insurance in case anything ever happened to him. He told Bleeker about it but didn't tell him where he'd hidden it, of course."

"Did Eline know about it?" I asked Karen.

"She didn't," Max confirmed. "I spent several hours trying to convince her to remember."

"You tortured her." Anger welled up, hot coals in my stomach, when I remembered Detective Nouwen telling me that Eline had 'other injuries' apart from the blow that killed her. Karen buried her face in her hands.

"What about Tessa? Did you kill her too?" I asked. "What did you do? Push her down the stairs?"

Max smirked. "Stupid woman. She was like you, always prying."

He carried on flipping sheets of paper. I glanced over at Sam, who was shifting on the sofa, his aura still swirling over him. Alex stroked his hair back from his face. Her aura was circling fast too, which made me very nervous. If Max didn't find what he was looking for, was he going to start shooting?

There was a sudden commotion downstairs, with raised voices and banging on a door. That would be the door from the old kitchen that I'd locked earlier. Was it Bleeker and his men or the police? I dreaded to think what would happen to us if Max and Bleeker joined forces.

Max yelled at his accomplice on the landing and they exchanged urgent words in Dutch before Max gathered up the papers, folded them roughly and put them in an inside pocket of his jacket.

He gestured at Alex and me. "Get over here. We're leaving."

"Then go," I said. "You have what you want. You don't need us."

"You're right." He lifted the gun and aimed it at my head. I heard a click as he released the safety. I'd already thought I was going to die today. The fear of a bullet in the head was just as powerful the second time around. I tried to swallow and couldn't. My legs were threatening to give way.

"We'll come with you," Alex said. "Hostages. To negotiate if the police catch up with you."

She put her hand on my arm to pull me towards Max. The feeling of her hand on my arm helped to ground me.

Max lowered the gun. "Then move fast," he said.

With one last look at Sam, I hurried to Max, Alex beside me. But, always full of nasty surprises, Max turned and pointed the gun at Karen.

"No," I screamed at him. "We're coming with you. Leave her alone."

The banging below grew louder. The big man on the landing yelled something and sprinted off down the stairs. When Max turned to shout at him, I grabbed a vase from the side table and raised it as high as possible before bringing it down on the back of his head. He lurched away from me, dropped the gun and steadied himself against the wall with both hands.

Before I could move, he swung around, his colorless eyes iced with fury. I charged at him, head low, and collided with a block of solid muscle. His hands went around my neck. I couldn't breathe. As my windpipe constricted, I jerked my head up, hard under his chin, and heard his teeth snap together.

The impact was enough to make him stumble backwards. Seizing the opportunity, Alex and Karen both rushed at him, fists flying. But the advantage was soon lost. He threw a punch at Karen, sending her reeling. He scanned the floor, looking for the gun, gave up, and grabbed Alex by the arm. He dragged her towards the staircase.

Clutching her head, Karen dropped into an armchair. After a quick glance to check she was breathing, I retrieved the gun that had skidded under the sofa where Sam lay and took off after Max.

He and Alex were already halfway down the stairs, but Alex was fighting back, twisting and struggling.

Raising the gun, I screamed at Max. "Let her go or I'll shoot you."

Max turned, that smirk of his twisting his lips. "I don't think so." He tightened his grip on Alex's arm and yanked her forward. "Let's go."

He was right. I couldn't shoot him. I had no idea how to use a gun, and anyway the chances were that I would hit Alex, not him. I dropped the weapon and raced after them. Alex, for a second, had managed to grab the banister rail, slowing their descent.

The need to save my friends overwhelmed any rational thought. Yelling a warning at her, I hurled myself at Max like a wild animal. Already moving fast, he lurched forward, lost his footing and began to tumble, still clasping Alex's arm. She flailed around, her hands seeking the banisters and missing them. I managed to grab her shoulder, but Max hung on to her arm. Off-balance, I stumbled forward. Together, the three of us toppled down seven or eight stairs until we came to a bone-crushing stop on the lobby floor.

When I opened my eyes, the vaulted ceiling above me blurred

into bright light rimmed with gold. Cold air chilled my skin. Was I dead?

But no, my ears were buzzing, my knee burned as though it was on fire. The front door was wide open. I raised my head to see that I'd come to rest across Max's legs. Alex lay motionless, face down over his chest. A pool of blood was spreading rapidly on the tiled floor. Was it hers? Panicky, I reached out to put my fingers against her neck. It took a few agonizing seconds to feel a pulse.

The lobby began to spin when I sat up, and I paused to let the dizziness pass. The blood was Max's, I could see that now, coming from a gash on his skull. But he wasn't dead. His eyelids fluttered, and the blood kept flowing.

Pain shot through my knee as I stood up. Everything hurt to some extent, but I hadn't broken anything, as far as I could tell. By the time I was on my feet, Karen had rushed down the stairs and was bending to help Alex as she stirred and sat up.

"Thank God you're okay. When I heard you fall..."

And then there was an explosion of noise as the old kitchen door ruptured, split from its hinges, and crashed to the floor.

I turned my head, terrified I'd see Bleeker standing there. But it was a police officer who stepped through the opening. I let out a quiet cry of pain and joy.

27

A flurry of phone calls followed, and it seemed like less than a minute until I heard sirens screaming towards us. Finally, help was coming for Sam. Karen rushed back up the stairs, telling me as she ran that she was going to check on him.

Still dazed, I put my hand out to support Alex, who was struggling to her feet.

"Get me away from this madman," she said, glaring down at Max, who hadn't moved at all. "I can't bear to be this close to him."

I helped Alex to the bottom stair and crouched down in front of her. She was sheet-white but didn't seem to have any injuries apart from the ones Max had inflicted earlier. "Your aura has gone," I said. "You're safe."

Biting her lip, she struggled not to cry.

The policeman hurried over to us as more officers arrived, crowding through the front door into the lobby. "Don't move until the medics take a look at you," he told Alex.

"Our friend is hurt. He was shot in the leg. He's upstairs," I said. "Can you come?"

"Show me." The officer beckoned a policewoman over. She sat on the step next to Alex and they started talking in Dutch. Leaving Alex in good hands, I hobbled up the stairs with the officer beside me.

Karen was kneeling on the floor next to Sam and she leapt to her feet when she saw us. After a quick exchange that I didn't understand, the officer leaned over to talk to Sam, who was conscious and responded to the officer's questions. But his aura still circled. I perched on the sofa arm, holding his hand tightly, staring at the moving air. Gradually, it slowed and, when a medical team charged up the stairs with emergency supplies and a stretcher, it disappeared completely, the ripples dissolving until the air was still. The pounding of my heart eased, and I released the pressure on Sam's hand, realizing I'd been gripping it so hard it must have hurt. Before I could tell him that his aura had gone, the paramedics asked us all to move away from the sofa. From the middle of the room, we watched them lift Sam onto a stretcher.

"Can I go with him?" I asked as they moved towards the stairs. "I need to tell him something very important."

"No." The policeman held up his hand. "I need to talk to both of you about what happened here."

His radio squawked and he listened for a moment before turning his attention back to us. "Give me a couple of minutes." He eyed Karen's cheek, which was red and swollen where Max had hit her. "You need some medical attention for that. For now, put some ice on it and sit down. I'll be right back. And don't go anywhere."

As if to be sure we wouldn't run away, he left a young officer standing guard at the top of the stairs.

"Want a cup of tea?" I asked Karen.

"Yes, please. That'll do me more good than ice." She didn't move though. "Is Sam going to be all right?"

"Yes, he is."

She smiled even though it must have hurt her swollen cheek. "Good."

As we walked to the kitchen, I noticed the empty white envelope that Max had left on the side table. I picked it up and took it with me.

Sitting down at the kitchen table, I stared at it for a minute. "You said this is Tomas's handwriting?" I asked Karen.

She turned from filling the kettle at the sink. "Yes. He wrote 'Important. Do not throw away.' A reminder to himself perhaps, or to Eline."

I turned the envelope over, checked all the edges and then put my hand inside, running my fingers along the heavy white paper. It felt as though the back was thicker than the front, although the difference was almost imperceptible.

Carefully, I tore the front away as Karen watched with interest. I gave her the piece I'd torn off and peered at the corner of the remaining part of the envelope. There were two layers, glued together along the edges, noticeable only because of a tiny overlap.

My fingers shook as I peeled one layer away from the other. Inside was a sheet of paper, so lightweight it was almost translucent. And on it was a handwritten list of names. About fifty of them. I stifled a gasp and scanned it quickly. Most didn't mean anything to me but, with a jolt of shock, I noticed two I recognized, one the founder of an Italian fashion empire, the other a British energy business mogul, whose high-profile company acquisitions were frequently splashed across the newspapers.

These people were part of Zeckendorf? No wonder Bleeker wanted this list so badly.

"This is it." I showed it to Karen.

"Good lord." She abandoned the teacups she'd been setting out. "Detective Nouwen will be happy to get his hands on this. Let's go find him."

28

"We have Bleeker in custody," Detective Nouwen said as he sat down on a chair next to me.

For the second time in three days, I was sitting with Alex in the hospital waiting room, Karen with us this time. Detective Lange had been here too for a while, taking statements from the three of us, which at least had helped pass the hours as we waited for news on Sam's surgery. I knew he wasn't going to die, but I wanted to hear that the gunshot wound wouldn't leave any lasting damage.

After Lange had gone back to the police station, I'd called Sam's grandmother. It was an emotional call but, always practical, she had quickly taken control of the arrangements for getting her grandson home.

Lost in my thoughts, I realized Nouwen was still talking. "Cornelius Maximillian Tilmans, aka Max, is here in the hospital being treated for a serious head wound and a couple of broken bones," he continued. "He's under permanent guard—not that he'll be leaving his bed anytime soon."

Max had survived his fall down the stairs, unlike poor Tessa.

"And Pieter?" Alex asked.

"He's provided a statement. So far, he's cooperating fully. Says he didn't kill Eline or Tessa."

"Max did," Alex said. "He told us."

Nouwen nodded.

"What happened down in the tunnel?" I asked. "The lights going out, all that shooting?"

The detective's face tensed. "Pieter says he turned the lights off—he set some sort of timer from one of the computers upstairs—to give you a chance to escape. Which you did. But Bleeker's men started shooting. It could have been a bloodbath down there. As it is, Sam and one of my officers were injured. One dead on Bleeker's side."

The sliding glass doors opened, letting in a cold draft. Detective Lange strolled back in, dressed as she'd been before in jeans and a chunky sweater. She obviously hadn't gone home to change.

"Can we go find some coffee?" she asked no one in particular. "I've been working all night."

"Yes, please." Alex pushed herself up gingerly. She had bruises everywhere. Karen, Nouwen and I followed. I was thrilled to leave that plastic chair behind.

We found a fairly clean formica-topped table in a corner of the hospital cafeteria, which was surprisingly busy at seven in the morning. Nouwen brought over a tray of coffees and five sad-looking pastries on a paper napkin.

Lange picked one up and took a big bite. She chewed for a moment, eyes on her notebook, and then looked up at me. "You were brilliant, Kate. Finding that list of names is going to save us months of work."

"You need to thank the others too," I said. "Everyone worked on it, one way or another. But I'm glad it was us who found it and not Max."

"Our research team has been examining the list for the last few hours. It's apparent that many of Zeckendorf's members are senior executives in giant corporations, banks and trading firms. Some work for weapons manufacturers and petro-chemical companies. It's going to take some time to fully understand the scope of their activities, although we already had a good idea of what they did. We just didn't know who any of them were."

Nouwen nodded in agreement with Lange. I remembered his telling me at the cafe that he was aware of Zeckendorf, although he hadn't revealed anything more.

"Zeckendorf is essentially a white-collar crime organization," he said now. "Using sophisticated computer-based tools to manage a wide range of illegal operations. Extortion, money laundering, stock manipulation. And Pieter confirmed that they had a team working on some nasty cyber weapons."

I glanced at Alex. She'd told us about that.

"Bloody hell," she said, which sort of summed up how I felt too.

"We believe that some, maybe all, of the software engineers fled the country last night," Nouwen continued. "But we'll find them."

"Pieter is telling you everything?" Karen asked.

Nouwen and Lange exchanged a look. "He is helping us," Nouwen said finally. "He has his own reasons."

"He was trying to leave Zeckendorf." Alex's face flushed pink as she spoke.

"What?" I asked. "How do you know?"

"He told me when we were looking around the house together. His situation and mine were similar, both of us coerced into working for them because of old family connections."

I glanced over at Nouwen, but he was wearing that neutral expression I'd come to recognize, one that gave nothing away. Last night, Alex had told Nouwen about her role in all of this. It seemed unlikely that she'd be charged with anything. She'd lied to Sam and me, but she hadn't committed any actual crimes.

"Pieter went along with Eline's plan to sell the house, intending to take the money and disappear," Alex continued. "But Bleeker wasn't going to let that happen. He sent Max after Eline and intended to deal with Pieter himself. Then things escalated when you three discovered the vault and the office."

She looked up at Nouwen. "For decades, Zeckendorf had certain police officials on their payroll, who made sure that any attempts at investigating them were blocked."

He nodded. "We know."

There was a long silence between us. I heard the clink of china, the banging of trays, the chatter of the cafeteria staff that I couldn't understand. Alex knew a lot more about Zeckendorf than she'd admitted to us. For a moment, that made me mad, but I realized I couldn't let it bother me. She had risked her life to help us. And I was sure that her feelings for Sam were genuine. Maybe they would both be able to move on from the events of this week. I hoped so.

"And Martin Eyghels?" I asked. "He's not real, is he?"

"He was an associate of Jacob Hals and also worked for the Dutch East India Company," Lange said. "His name was used over the centuries whenever Zeckendorf needed a false name on a document. It became sort of an inside joke."

"None of this is a joke," Nouwen muttered.

"Zeckendorf goes back that far?" Karen asked.

"All the way back to before the house was built. The co-founders were Jacob Hals, and several others who worked with him." Lange grabbed a paper napkin and scrubbed at her fingers. "Hals went on to build the house, and a Zeckendorf member has lived there continuously ever since construction was completed, apart from that period of fifty-plus years starting in the 1960s. The house was an important part of the identity of Zeckendorf."

Poor Eline. She'd had no idea what dangers she would unleash by putting the house on the market.

"Pieter should have warned her somehow, or just refused to put it up for sale." Karen's voice was angry. "But he was only thinking about the money."

"It wasn't really about the money," Alex said. "His desire to escape Zeckendorf clouded his judgment. He should have known they wouldn't let him go that easily. Very few people ever get out." Her blue eyes welled with tears. "If you'll excuse me, I need to phone my mum. I'll be back soon."

"Has anyone spoken to William Moresby?" I asked when she'd gone.

Nouwen shook his head. "Not yet."

Mr. Moresby would wake up to learn that his Amsterdam assignment was over. He'd been so determined to see it through, but there was little chance now that his company would relocate here. My vision of light-filled conference rooms and bustling offices would never come to pass. It had only been four days since I'd arrived, excited about the design challenge ahead of me. But the house had fought back, a hostile and malevolent enemy. Its vast spaces would remain dark and empty for the foreseeable future at least. Nouwen had already told us it would be the center of their investigations for months to come. The crypt in the cellar would be emptied, the remains interred in a proper cemetery. The cabinet room was expected to yield a trove of detailed information about the workings of the organization, and the police had already carried away the damaged computer server. Someone from Zeckendorf had taken the sledgehammer to it in an attempt to cover their tracks, but Nouwen was hoping his tech experts could retrieve some of the data that had been stored on it. Zeckendorf operatives had also removed some of the red boxes we'd seen in the vault, all of which apparently contained diamonds. Maybe they'd managed to haul away some of the gold bars, but not many. Nouwen said the vault had been secured with much of its treasure intact.

I hoped that, one day, the magnificent building would be put to good use. It had plenty of potential. But for myself, I'd be happy to never set foot in the place again.

As if sensing my thoughts, Lange leaned towards me. "I hope you won't go back to London thinking the worst of Holland," she said. "It's a beautiful country and its people are good, most of them at least."

"I know that, and I intend to come back to enjoy it all very soon."

Karen had already invited me to bring Josh over for a weekend.

And then I remembered something.

"Vincent!" I exclaimed. "We can't just leave him there." Seeing the confused expressions on Nouwen's and Lange's faces, I explained about the cat. "Sam loves him," I said. "It would be okay, wouldn't it, for us to find him and adopt him? I can work out how to get him back to England."

Nouwen's features relaxed for a moment. "I can help with that. Give me an hour or two."

Karen smiled at me. "That will be a lovely wake-up present for Sam."

THE END

ACKNOWLEDGMENTS

First of all, special thanks to my multi-talented husband and co-conspirator, James, for reading every single word, providing constructive criticism and making awesome suggestions. This book, as with the others in the series, is so much better for all your help. Here's to many more books and years together.

Thanks and gratitude as always to Diana Corbitt, Maryvonne Fent, Sue Garzon and Gillian Hobbs. We've been doing this for years now. I love your stories and I love how you help with mine. Friendship, fun and moral support. You're the best.

And thank you, of course, to Julie Smith and Mittie Staininger for everything you do.

ALSO BY CARRIE BEDFORD

NOBILISSIMA: A Novel of Imperial Rome

The Kate Benedict Paranormal Mystery Series

THE AURA

DOUBLE BLIND

THE FLORENTINE CYPHER

THE SCOTTISH CONNECTION

ASSIGNMENT IN AMSTERDAM

ABOUT THE AUTHOR

Born and raised in England, Carrie Bedford is the author of the award-winning *Aura* series of mysteries, along with the *Nobilissima* historical novels set in Ancient Rome. After graduating with an Honors degree in English and French, her first job was as translator for a growing technology company. She went on to work in marketing for companies in Silicon Fen (Cambridge, England) and Silicon Valley for the next thirty years. She and her American husband have two wonderful daughters, a yellow Labrador and a calico cat who assists with edit cycles by taking random walks on the keyboard.

Made in the USA
Columbia, SC
30 March 2020